Love Scenes

Love Scenes

♥

Bridget Morrissey

JOVE
NEW YORK

A JOVE BOOK
Published by Berkley
An imprint of Penguin Random House LLC
penguinrandomhouse.com

Library of Congress Cataloging-in-Publication Data

Names: Morrissey, Bridget, author.
Title: Love scenes / Bridget Morrissey.
Description: First edition. | New York : Jove, 2021.
Identifiers: LCCN 2020040875 (print) | LCCN 2020040876 (ebook) |
ISBN 9780593201152 (trade paperback) | ISBN 9780593201169 (ebook)
Subjects: GSAFD: Love stories.
Classification: LCC PS3613.O7769 L68 2021 (print) |
LCC PS3613.O7769 (ebook) | DDC 813/.6—dc23
LC record available at https://lccn.loc.gov/2020040875
LC ebook record available at https://lccn.loc.gov/2020040876

First Edition: June 2021

Printed in the United States of America
1st Printing

Book design by Ashley Tucker

♥

This is a tribute to every homemade
movie we made on a fifty-cent budget
for a living room world premiere.

♥

Week One of Production

Slumped into my sectional with cold pasta in my lap and a glass of water balanced against a pillow, I type my name into the Netflix search bar.

S-L-O-A-N-E.

F-O-R-D.

The first four seasons of my crime scene procedural *The Seeker* come up first. There I am with a dark brunette bob, wearing a lab coat and hustling around, giving everyone coy looks while cracking guarded jokes, making sure my harmless crush on Detective Colfax is only a touch better disguised than my chest, which is always slightly revealed in a V-neck.

The Seeker has filmed almost one hundred episodes. Ninety-two feature me as a clever-but-soft blood spatter analyst named Tess, best known for her ability to coldly analyze a dead body, then turn all fluttery and fumbling around her crush. Not a single one features anything I need to see right now. Getting surprisingly killed off in the third episode of the fifth season of a critically ignored drama? One my own family doesn't even bother to tune in for anymore?

That's punishment enough.

A strange crackle coming from the direction of my kitchen startles me. At 3:43 in the morning, the television is my only source of light, softly glowing onto my tear-swollen face. Otherwise my house is pitch-dark.

For an agonizing stretch I sit frozen, ticking down my options.

1. It's an intruder coming to murder me, and my only weapons are an Apple TV remote, a lethal dose of self-pity, and a fork.

2. It's my younger sister Tyler ending our unspoken standoff and surprising me with a visit, ready to crash in her old bedroom before our first day of shooting tomorrow.

3. It's one of the constant murmurs of this strange old place in the hills of Laurel Canyon, full of crooked nooks and squeaking floorboards. Sloped ceilings and a small stained glass window in the bathroom of all places.

It's obviously number three, I decide with a tentative exhale.

This home was meant for shared gasps at unexplained sounds. For laughter to cover the bristle of shrubbery in the backyard. But Tyler's got her own condo now. A girlfriend to live with and a rescue pup.

I've got leftover bucatini on my lap and a deep-seated fear that I'm not talented enough to ever work in this town again.

Below *The Seeker*, there's one other Sloane Ford property

available to stream. And of course it's *A Little Luck*, because even Netflix is mocking me. The last thing I want to watch is Joseph Donovan's smug grin while I self-soothe with cold pasta and light crying.

A Little Luck was by far the worst filming experience I've ever had. Thinking of that production sends a shiver down my spine, especially considering what I'm facing tomorrow.

Which is exactly why I press play.

The film opens on the lush Irish countryside, cast against searing gray skies. In spite of myself, the sight still makes me suck back a longing breath, gulping like the Killarney breezes are once again lashing my cheeks.

The opener is an overhead tracking shot, following me on a bicycle as I wheel through town. My stunt double shot most of it. It's a seamless transition from her to me. By the time I park my bike next to the market and take off my helmet, only a trained eye would notice that my shoulders aren't quite as defined as hers. My skin a shade paler. The dyed red of my hair a touch more yellow.

The first twenty minutes are pretty stale. My work is fine—I was still doing too much with my face back then, a theater tic I've put a lot of conscious effort toward calming. Mom told me not to start with stage training. She said to do on-camera work and scene study classes outside of college and get a degree in something else. Dad told me he cut his teeth in the theater when he went to California State back in the day, and that all great actors need that kind of foundation.

As usual, I listened to the wrong parent.

A Little Luck drags on until—it pains me to even think it— Joseph Donovan appears. He's the stock boy at the costume store where my character is working. She's an American who has taken a year off school to find herself in Ireland. He's staying in town to save money and earn back his family's farm after they're forced to sell. It doesn't make a lot of sense, but this isn't a movie designed to require an examination of the specifics. It's all about glances. Touches. Wind through hair as lovers kiss atop a cliff.

Off-screen, you hear me say, "Excuse me, it's my first day here. I'm not sure where I'm supposed to go."

Joseph stops lifting boxes, back to the audience. His right hand lingers for a beat. Then he turns toward the camera lens—slowly, methodically—daring us to look away from the chiseled angles of his upsettingly exceptional face.

The director set up the shot so we meet Joseph by gazing up at his six-foot-three frame. His blue eyes pop against the cream of his Aran sweater. A native of Ireland himself, Joseph complained the iconic look was too on the nose. Wardrobe didn't budge. They wanted this moment. The stark contrast of Joseph's boyish features and his brooding edges. His dark blond hair combed into a subtle swish. His ocean-swept eyes touched with hints of sadness. And the brogue. It was all about the brogue melting off those lips.

Good god. It's no wonder I loathe him.

I make it a few more minutes into the movie before deciding there's no way I can watch myself kiss that bastard tonight. Smug asshole. Most unprofessional man I have ever worked with in my entire career. And goddamn brilliant on-screen in spite of it.

His career has skyrocketed since we shot this. And I'm hours away from the start of a made-up producing job handed to me by my famous family to fill the void of my most recent bout of unemployment.

I close my eyes, trying to sleep, needing to wake up in fighting form.

But Joseph Donovan's features are carved into my mind,

etched against the backs of my eyelids like the sun at high noon, burning me.

My mother greets my late arrival with an unbroken stare, arms folded across her chest and aviator sunglasses tipped down past the bridge of her nose, leaned up against the wall of Stage 15. She's wearing a baby-blue crewneck tucked into a pair of tight black jeans. Her long blond locks are in a ponytail pulled through a black ball cap, but she's left the bang pieces out to frame her face, because she hates when she looks too severe.

From this distance, she could easily pass for a twenty-five-year-old. Even up close, actually. She has the skin of someone who has had a professional aesthetician for decades, and the unmistakable glow of a person who cherishes being important to strangers. It's the hard-earned confidence that gives her age away. The no-bullshit facade of a fifty-eight-year-old woman who has seen it all and is no longer impressed by any of it. When the acting world turned on her, she picked herself up and transformed into a producer, intending to make a better life for other women in the business.

Right now she looks ready to turn on me just as effectively.

"Do you really not care about this?" she asks. Years of smoking have left an indelible mark on her voice, a sandpaper grittiness that's as iconic as her beaming smile.

"Hi, Mom. Good to see you too. Yes. Everything is okay. Thank you for worrying." It's hard not to wheeze, having done my best power walking impression to get to her, not a drop of caffeine in my system to offset my lack of sleep.

"You look tired." She pinches my skin, then gives me a

perfunctory cheek kiss. "We've got a lot to cover in not a lot of time. I'm gonna be running around today, so I need you to keep eyes on everyone and make sure we're running a tight ship. You know how crucial the first few days are in establishing a tone. It starts at the top of the chain, Sloane."

"I'd hardly call myself the top of the chain here," I quip. "You made my job up."

The look she gives me makes actual goose bumps form along my arms.

"I'm sorry," I correct. "I turned off my alarm instead of hitting snooze. It was an accident that will never happen again."

"Oh, Sloaney, please don't act like you're new to this. Not now. Always set at least three backup alarms. I can't have everyone on set thinking you can get away with whatever you want just because you're my kid." She says all of this without breaking pace, dragging me along like we're doing our own Aaron Sorkin walk and talk. "At least you're dressed well."

The only helpful decision I made last night was to set this morning's outfit out on my dresser, feeling that strange kind of restless dread that made me both overplan and underprepare. Naturally I've ended up in nearly the same look as Mom, only in a different color scheme, with my shirt a muted yellow, my jeans a vivid blue, and my unplanned ball cap a heather gray. The best thing about having a long bob is being able to plant a hat on my head and have my whole style look intentionally casual, when the truth is I barely had time to brush my teeth, much less my hair.

"Twins." I gesture to our complementary ensembles, hoping to lighten the mood.

"Don't be generous," she scoffs. "I haven't been allowed to play a thirty-year-old since I was twenty-five."

This version of my mother—Kitty Porter: *boss lady*—is utterly incorrigible. I never thought I'd say it, but I miss her usual wandering 6:00 a.m. phone calls to me, talking about her cats and her yoga mat and her favorite Brené Brown quotes.

She once spent twenty full minutes detailing the way the sunlight in her office was streaming onto a picture of Tyler; our younger brother, Powell; and me. It's a black-and-white portrait shot by Annie Leibovitz, and we're all piled onto one another like puppies. Tyler was eleven and had recently chopped off all her hair but hadn't yet solved how to style it. It was a scrappy brunette mess, dangerously close to bowl cut territory. Powell was nine and cute as ever. As far as I'm concerned, he still looks the same. Like a soft butter roll just out of the oven, with his hair that same iconic blond as Mom's. And then there was fourteen-year-old me rocking the classic braces-and-bangs combo, my hair a greasy brown and ironed straight as a pin. Even the bangs.

"I won't screw up again." The tremble in my voice surprises me. She hasn't made me this nervous since I bravely admitted to her that despite her sage advice, I was going to study acting in college after all.

"Good." She does the eagle-eyed hand gesture she picked up from Robert De Niro in *Meet the Parents*. "Keep eyes on everything. And make sure Tyler's calm."

"I'm on it."

The problem is, I haven't looked at the call sheet. I don't know who the first AD or the second AD is. Or what we're shooting today.

Knowing too much hurts too much. It amplifies the ugly voice in the back of my head that reminds me that once upon a time, the leading role in this production was supposed to be mine.

I do know that the movie has a working title of *Horizons*. It's a romantic World War II drama. My stepdad wrote it. My sister's directing it alongside him. My mom's going to be acting in it for the first time in almost twenty years. She's playing a supporting role, a widow named Vera who battles an illness while also having a secret love affair with the Black woman who lives down the hall. That role will be played by my dad's other ex-wife, Melanie Davidson, mother of my youngest sister, Sarai, who just turned eleven and surprisingly does not have a part in this project. *Yet*.

It's a good old-fashioned nepotistic family circus over here.

And in another world, I would be the center of it all. The face on the poster. The top of the call sheet. The main character, a schoolteacher named Elise whose life gets upended when her old neighbor returns home from the war right as her mother's illness is progressing.

Instead I'm here as a consulting producer, and no one—not even me—has any idea what that job really entails.

When I was growing up, summertime meant moviemaking time. Tyler would take one of our parents' fancy video cameras into the backyard of whichever house we were staying at for the week, and she'd direct Powell and me through one of our many terrible homemade remakes. Who isn't a fan of two siblings playing love interests that refuse to even hug? Makes for a stunning re-creation of *Titanic*.

In spite of Powell and me begging Tyler to turn every remake into an action film where we kill each other, there was a magic to our backyard passion projects. A desire among all three of us siblings to find a way to capture a good story. We could transform the pool at Mom's Calabasas mansion into the Atlantic in 1912. We could turn the gate in front of Dad's Beverly Hills estate into the prison cell from *Chicago*.

I started visiting my parents on set when I was old enough

to walk. I've watched directors yell in my mother's face for no reason. Sat in my dad's trailer while he argued with important people about call times and script changes and hairpieces. Witnessed my parents' marriage to each other dissolve before my eyes, all over on-set jealousies, box office numbers, and critical praise favoring one of them over the other. I know how terrible and toxic show business really is. I've always known.

But there's a part of me that's always wished for it to feel like it did in the backyard with my siblings. Pure and spontaneous and fun, fueled solely by the desire to create something memorable together.

We almost have that here.

Almost.

Most of the soundstage has been transformed into the entire fourth floor of a 1940s apartment building, with cameras around the apartment that Elise shares with Vera. Their living room is done up in muted reds and soft lavenders. There's just the right amount of clutter. Stacks of papers probably meant to be Elise's writings. Sewing and knitting tools strewn about. A coffee mug resting on a faded newspaper. A small window for daylight to spill through.

I wander into this half shell of a home, feeling truly awake for the first time this morning, running my finger across the coffee table as if expecting to collect dust. That's how lived-in and real this world feels, with the magical, curated quality only a good film set can bring.

Life, but bigger somehow. Safer.

The kitchen is off to the side, as narrow as a tunnel with faded checkerboard tiles on the floor. This is where the leads will have part of their big love scene. A flame of jealousy flares up inside me. It takes a village to get a great performance out of an actor. I know if I were Haven Church, I'd be really excited by all the work my family has done to help her bring Elise to life.

But I'm not Haven Church. I don't have twenty-three million followers on Instagram or an entire generation of young people who grew up watching me on my own multi-cam sitcom. I am thirty years old, my career hanging on by a fraying thread, only here because of a very embarrassing opening in my schedule that's allowed me to be completely free for the next five weeks.

"Looks magnificent, no?"

To my left stands the writer and codirector of this movie, and Mom's new husband, Guy Cicero. *New* is the wrong word, because they've been married for fifteen years, but any person after Dad will always be new. As is anyone after Mom on his side. Unspoken rules of divorce.

"It's really good," I tell him as he pulls me into a tight, sincere hug. "Thanks for letting me be a part of it after all. I'm sorry I'm late."

"Please! Of course! You know I always wanted you here with us." Guy makes a broad gesture, his arm circling the whole sound-stage, stopping once he's swept past me. "It is *almost* as I pictured it all," he says, leaving me to interpret that as I please.

"It's perfect," I assure him.

"No. But it's a place for an adventure to begin." He pauses with his typical flourish. "Your sister was looking for you, by the way."

He proceeds to follow me until we find Tyler huddled in a dark corner behind the bathroom set, poring over the shot bible. Her hair is shorter, only a few centimeters past a buzz cut, and she's got on her signature slouchy black clothes, draping off all her sharper angles. She's always been so much longer and leaner than me you'd think we had one different parent between us. But she got Mom's flawless skin and Dad's angled jawline, and I got Mom's button nose and Dad's thick brows. Powell got almost nothing from Dad at all. He's Mom 2.0: blond hair, forest-green eyes, and a smile that lights up like a Christmas tree.

Tyler's the coolest of the three of us, catching the best genetics and the most interesting personality traits. Secretly soft inside with a fascinatingly serene exterior. A wicked sense of humor that appears in hushed tones, only heard if you're paying close attention. And a silly side that's even more private, coming out in moments of sheer hysteria, like when the two of us stayed up for an entire night doing impressions of our dad, making each other laugh so hard that my stomach was sore for three days afterward.

She and I haven't seen each other in person since Dad was in the hospital. Our last communication of any kind was via professional email regarding my role on set. Truthfully, the haunting memory of her signing off from that interaction by typing out *Warmly, Tyler* was the only thing with enough power to wake me up today.

We both know my taking this producing job came solely from the emotional toll of Dad's heart attack. Reality hits harder under hospital lights. You forgive before you're ready. You agree to responsibilities you don't actually want because it means being around people you love, even when they make you so upset you could scream.

I tap her on the shoulder.

"You made it," she says when she realizes it's me, letting out an audible sigh.

"Of course. Couldn't miss your directorial debut." It comes out sarcastic when I actually meant it to be earnest.

The words sit in the air, stale.

"Remind me what we're shooting today?" I ask.

"You shithead. You didn't even look at the schedule, did you?"

Admitting incompetence has always been the fastest way to even the playing field between us.

"We're doing all of Calvin and Elise's first kiss," she continues. "And the beginning of their second kissing scene."

"I always say to start with the tough stuff," Guy chimes in. "That way you're sure that what you have is going to work. *Throw the actors to the wolves.*"

He's wearing a backward newsboy cap and thin glasses with light yellow frames. A timelessly Guy Cicero ensemble. The happiest-looking half-Cuban, half-Italian man to ever wear a corduroy blazer with patches on the elbows. It's as if I can see him delivering this exact line on the set of every movie he's ever made, the actors standing before him ever changing and him staying almost exactly the same, the passage of time only evident through the creasing around his eyes.

"He wanted our first day to be the full sex scene. I was like, 'Guy, these people just met,'" Tyler adds. "We don't do movies like that anymore."

Guy throws his hands up. "I know, I know. But in a movie like this, if the sex scene doesn't work, the whole thing is a bust!"

I give him the laugh he's looking for. We can't let this be awkward. We have to be professionals here.

Except we're also family. Hard to set boundaries with each other when we've never had them before.

To pivot, I shake hands with him, and then with Tyler, who looks confused until I say, "As your resident consulting producer, thank you *so much* for this consultation. I look forward to many more."

"You're the worst," she tells me. Then she goes serious so fast it gives me emotional whiplash. "Thank you for doing this, Bub. I know this won't be easy for you. I really appreciate it."

"Of course," I say quickly, not looking to dwell. "I'm gonna go get some coffee."

It's a quiet scene by craft services. Crew members move around in all directions like ants on a hill, finalizing small details until it's time for action. My entire drive here, I told myself not to care. That no good would come from wishing things had been different.

No matter how it came about, taking this producing job was ultimately my choice. And I will commit to it like I commit to everything else in my life: headfirst while silently panicking.

"Would ya look at who it is?"

The voice stops me in my tracks, my hand midway toward reaching for a banana. I cover for the pause as best I can, desperate not to reveal even the slightest trace of nerves.

"Is that not Sloane Ford I see? Staring at the fruit bowl like it's tea leaves telling her a fortune?"

I turn around, and there he stands in a taupe button-down, sleeves rolled up to midbicep, suspenders holding up loose brown slacks. He has on circular wire-rim glasses, and his hair is combed back to show us every pore of his deceivingly cherubic face.

My hand squeezes the banana so tight that the insides start to push out of the skin.

Joseph fucking Donovan.

"Can I help you?" I ask, keeping my tone even.

He has the nerve to laugh. A piece of his newly darkened hair dares to fall across his forehead like he's an Irish James Dean. He's trying to charm away all the bad feelings between us, using his brogue like it's got some sort of mystical power over American women.

"Funny way to greet a war hero such as myself."

I take it all in. The prosthetic burns on the tops of his hands. The trace of a fake scar above his left eyebrow. The calculated swoop of his hair. He looks every bit the part of the romantic hero. Unfortunately, no amount of costuming can cover up his incompetence.

"It wasn't meant to be a greeting." I look past him as if I can see in the distance some task that requires my immediate attention.

He follows my eye, seeing nothing, then whips around again. Smirking. "I was surprised to hear you turned down Elise."

"As if I was going to take the role with you as Calvin. Now if you'll excuse me, I have some stuff to do." I leave my squished banana inside the basket, quietly cursing myself for not pouring a cup of coffee first.

"Wait a second."

Joseph jogs up to meet me. He rests his hand on my shoulder to stop my momentum. When I turn to face him, he looks puzzled.

"I want this shoot to go well," he says.

I suppress an eye roll. "I'm sure you do."

"I'm catering lunch today," he explains, like it's meant to impress me. It *is* a nice gesture, one that always helps to establish a good tone on set, but it doesn't need to be announced.

"Okay." He cannot possibly expect me to give him credit. Not after what we've been through.

"It's coming from a small spot over on Magnolia in the Valley. They do a proper spread."

"Nice."

"It's the least I could do," he says.

"Most definitely."

"I hope you know I'm really grateful for this job."

I can't help but stare at him. Silent. Processing.

Stewing.

"Sloane, I know this'll sound like a joke, but I'm not who I used to be," he says finally. His eyes cut into me so deep I almost believe him.

Then I remember what an incredible actor he is. Emmy nominated just last year.

Nothing good comes from believing a man like Joseph Donovan.

I stumble away from him, nearly knocking over a set wall in the process.

"You forgot your banana," he calls out.

"No I didn't," I call back.

This is exactly why I should've trusted my instincts when I first said I didn't want any part in making this movie. Because here I am. Headfirst. And silently panicking.

2

Mom waves off the green-apple cloud of poison she's blown into the air. "I know, I know," she says, surprised to have been discovered behind the actor trailers. "At least it isn't a cigarette."

"We need to talk about Joseph." After hours of waiting for a chance to corner one of my family members alone, the moment is finally here. "He's going to ruin this movie."

Mom swallows a laugh. Takes her vape pen back out, this time luxuriating in her pull. "You've mentioned that once or twice before." She holds her exhale. "Has he done something today?"

She releases a puff of sweet-smelling smoke slowly, like hissing out a kiss of death. She's always been a force of nature in a work setting. It's impossible for anyone to trip her up. Her power lies in her disorientation tactics, like being this brazen with the habit she supposedly gave up years ago.

The difference is, she's never been like this *with me*. And the change is so startling it's got me forgetting how to stand up straight.

In a stroke of genius, I decide to disorient her right back. "When you asked me to play Elise, you knew that I had a major conflict with my show schedule then," I say, shifting gears without warning.

"There was literally no way I could have made both *The Seeker* and this movie work."

"Obviously we would have moved production for you," she dares to argue back.

"That's not what you told me then."

She shrugs her shoulders. "And you told me you'd never do a period piece."

She'd pitched the project to me over the phone, running late to a laser hair removal session and unable to answer a single question I had. Thirty minutes later there was a Deadline article up announcing Joseph Donovan as the male lead of the new Guy Cicero romantic war drama.

Until that very moment, I'd figured if my family was going to write a role for me opposite the guy who almost made me quit the business, someone might have mentioned it in the group chat once or twice.

And when it comes to me and period pieces, she knows full well that conversation is delicate.

Her attention shifts to my upper thigh. "Hold on. There's a stain on your pants." She licks her finger and hunches over to try to remove the crimson-colored blob on my jeans.

Avoiding another encounter with Joseph at craft services, pointedly ignoring his catered spread, I Postmated myself an anti-inflammatory smoothie filled with beets and strawberries and whatever else is supposed to keep me anti-inflamed. Now I'm wearing part of it, and of course this stain looks like blood spatter to me.

I was network television's leading blood spatter analyst, after all.

Four spraying droplets around a large undisturbed pool. Fatal gunshot wound. Entered from behind. Very close range.

It's definitely not accurate, but it's what they would have had me say on the show, each beat underscored by the swelling electronic symphony of my character's theme music.

Only now it's me who's been bled dry, and there's no one left to solve the case besides my mother.

"Please stop," I say.

Mom gives me a cutting look. "Why aren't you working?"

It's a perfect, undefeatable response. Stunning in how preposterous it is. "Probably because I don't actually have anything to do here," I say. "We both know I shouldn't have agreed—"

One of our production assistants appears, gently tapping on Mom's shoulder, cutting off my impromptu resignation. "Ms. Porter. You're being requested on set."

"Please. Call me Kitty," Mom tells the girl. "Is there some kind of problem?"

"Um." The PA shifts from foot to foot. "Kind of? Joseph is having trouble with his dialogue."

It takes every ounce of restraint possible not to give my mom a smug glare. I opt for a knowing look into the middle distance instead, like there's an audience somewhere that's seeing all of this unfold, knowing I was right all along.

"Do you know why they need me? There are two directors. Can neither direct him?" Mom asks.

The PA looks like she would walk straight into the ocean if given the choice between having this conversation and disappearing forever. "I'm not sure. Guy told me to find you."

"Let's go learn why my husband has requested me."

We can't enter until the red light in front of the soundstage turns off, so we stand in various states of distress. Mom sighs every few seconds like she doesn't have the time for this inconvenience. The PA bites her lower lip while watching clouds pass overhead.

Once we have the clear to enter, Mom darts across the sound-stage to the heart of the action. The script supervisor is feeding Joseph the correct lines, putting a strange affectation on her voice, quasi mimicking what must be Joseph's generalized American accent. *"Elise. Whatever it is that has you avoiding my eye, you can tell me. I can handle it."*

Joseph attempts to parrot the line back, somehow fumbling it. "I will handle it. No. I *can* handle it. I can handle it. *I can handle it.*"

"Take a breath, Joe." Guy fails to follow his own advice. His face is ruddy from pent-up frustration. "All will be good, my friend."

"Can I read it myself?"

"Of course," Guy assures, handing Joseph a copy of the script.

As Joseph quietly scans the page, the whole crew collectively inhales, willing him to commit the dialogue to memory. After a solid minute, he looks around the soundstage, smiling at everyone, trying to make eye contact with each person along the way. He finds me and I look off, pretending not to have seen him at all.

"Got it," he says to everyone. "Sorry for the trouble."

The exhale is palpable.

They start the scene again. Joseph misses his mark when crossing the apartment. He almost knocks over a lamp.

"Christ," he says, catching it. "I'm sorry. Keep rolling." He takes a few steps back and starts from the top. *"Elise, I know that when I left, I was . . .* shit. What was I?"

"We're farther down," the script supervisor tells him.

"Right. Right." He turns. *"Elise, whatever it is that has you looking past my eye, you can't tell me. I mean you can. You can tell me. I will handle it."*

The whole moment plays like something that would make it onto a blooper reel if the tone were different.

This?

This looks like a meltdown.

"Cut." Tyler pinches the skin between her eyes.

Guy takes off his pageboy cap to rest his hands on his bald head.

It's fascinating seeing every crew member do their best not to give one another too many judgmental glances. Mom goes and fixes herself a cup of coffee, taking more time than needed, methodically ripping sugar packets and stacking them into a neat pile. She double taps the wooden stick she's used to stir in her cream and sugar, then goes over to an emergency conference with Guy by the video monitor.

"I heard you guys are killing it in here," I say to Tyler. I want to continue being smug, but I can't deny that deep down, seeing her this tense has me worried.

"Joseph is . . . having a hard time," she admits. "He made it through maybe three lines of dialogue this morning before seeming to black out and forget everything he's ever known."

"Classic," I can't help but mutter.

"We've already been adjusting coverage to get him out of frame for some of it. Guy keeps trying to change the dialogue. It's a mess. He's the one who wanted everyone to show up and *be collaborative* and *create together*. It's looking like a rehearsal or two should've been included in the *creation*. This isn't the kind of thing that can be fixed in post."

I can almost taste blood I'm biting my tongue so hard. "What does Guy think Mom can do about it?"

"Put the fear of God in Joseph? I don't know. I told him not to find her. He didn't listen."

We look over to Mom and Guy. Mom has her hands turned backward on her hips with her head cocked to the side, making a face that could best be described as profound confusion colliding with deep dissatisfaction. She points to Joseph and beckons him over with one little hook gesture from her pointer finger.

"First-day jitters are not uncommon," Mom starts. "But we need to know you're committed to this project."

"I'm committed. I swear," Joseph says.

"Good. Then listen closely." Her voice drops to a whisper I can't hear.

Joseph is sweating, I notice. Pools are building in the fabric beneath his armpits as he nods furiously at whatever my mom tells him. Wardrobe clocks this too, and two assistants approach the mini–meeting of the minds to change Joseph from one shirt into another identical one. For a moment he stands there in only a white undershirt with his arms extended, like a mannequin waiting to be dressed, listening to Guy wax poetic about the art of filmmaking while Mom explains the timeline of the shoot.

"If we aren't done on time, it will be expensive," Mom says, loud enough for everyone on the soundstage to hear. "I'm funding a lot of this project myself. You can understand why I wouldn't want that."

"I should insert myself into this conversation. Yeah?" Tyler asks me.

She already knows the answer, but she still waits for my nod of validation before making a move. She picks a bad entry spot into their little circle, and she has to keep dodging flailing arms and frantic shuffle steps.

All the while, the camera crew takes it back to one.

Haven Church, the lead actress, wanders to her starting position. They've played to her every strength. Hair dyed platinum blonde and done up in perfect pin curls. Doe eyes winged and wide. Dangerous red lips. A powder-blue shirtwaist dress with a belt that cinches tight around her frame. But she wears an alarmingly vacant expression that I hope is a by-product of the Joseph meltdown.

When Mom releases him from their talk, Joseph moves to his mark. He repeats his lines to himself, avoiding eye contact with every person around him, Haven included.

I've never seen him like this. On screen or off. Usually when the camera rolls he's riveting to watch, even while screwing up. There were so many takes of *A Little Luck* he saved through sheer charm alone, managing to muster up a loose outline of the intended dialogue and doing it with so much likability that the writers accepted most of his on-the-spot improvisations.

Not that they had much choice. We never would've finished the movie otherwise.

They run the scene again. Joseph makes it to the "I can handle it" line, says it with one mistake, takes it back a few lines, then gets it all out correctly. His acting is flat and strangely self-conscious, like the work of a college freshman on their first day in a scene study class.

Mom claps to herself. Our first AD, Tammy, pumps her fist.

This is so wrong. We shouldn't be celebrating adequacy. Not on day *one*. That's for the last week of filming, when everyone is exhausted and the finish line is in sight. Leave it to Joseph Donovan to set the bar this low. Because of him, no one is addressing the fact that Haven is as interesting to watch on camera as a piece of blank paper.

To her credit, it's hard to be lively when you're working with someone who hasn't even bothered to learn the dialogue. Eventually, you figure out that most of your scene partners are never going to give you enough when it's time for your camera coverage.

That you have to use your imagination to transform the Joseph Donovans of the world into someone better.

In this business, you have to be your own hero.

No one else will do it for you.

Watching Haven make choices I'd never make is hard to stomach. I'm not above admitting that much, even when this setup is my personal hell.

I swallow back my rude thoughts and tell myself to help her out instead. "Hey," I say, walking up to where she waits for the next take, making sure Joseph can't hear us.

"Oh. Hi!" She's so surprised to hear from me she's blushing, her eyes widening with every step I take closer to her. It's very clear she's heard more than once that her part was actually written with me in mind.

"I come in peace, I promise."

This makes her smile. Several sentences seem to die on her tongue before she says, "Okay. That's good."

"I'm here about this . . ." I make a sweeping motion with my arm, trusting that she can fill in the blanks.

She lets out an uncertain, uncomfortable laugh, clearly interpreting the blanks differently than me.

I offer her an easy laugh in response to let her know my intentions are good. "I worked with Joseph five years ago, and he almost ruined my career." I'm so blunt she gasps. "I want to make sure that doesn't happen to you."

She stares on in shock. "Okay . . ."

"I'm serious. The only way I got through it was to throw out everything I'd been taught about acting."

"What do you mean?"

"You can't make your choices based on what he gives you in

the scene, because right now he's not giving you anything. Right?" We exchange a look of great knowing. "Have you ever done any CGI work?"

"Yeah," she says tentatively.

"Perfect. Treat working with him like you're actually looking at a tennis ball on a stick." This makes the both of us laugh. It's that bonded, I-see-you-and-you-see-me kind of laugh. "You're gonna be great."

Actual tears form in her eyes. Which makes sense. She must be the kind of actor who is very good at accessing emotions but not as good at actually speaking dialogue in a truthful way. Two very different skill sets that most people don't recognize as separate.

"Thank you," she says with a surprising amount of gratitude. "I really appreciate it."

"I hope I'm not overstepping. I just know how hard it can be."

"It really is," she says with candid panic.

"You're gonna be great," I remind her again.

Right before action, she flashes me a big smile.

Then she goes on to do exactly the same thing she did in the previous take.

It's fine.

It's not like my entire family has put their money and reputations on the line for this project.

By the time we're supposed to release the talent, Joseph and Haven still haven't finished the whole scene. Mom, Guy, and Tyler make an executive decision to wrap as planned and tack the last bits of coverage onto another day.

It's a risk.

So was casting Joseph Donovan in the first place.

Not that anyone asked me.

Mom comes up behind me on my way out and puts an arm around my neck. I think it's meant to be sentimental. I don't tell her it's basically a choke hold.

"Sloaney," she whispers in my ear, the both of us overlooking the apartment while a crew member rearranges misplaced props. "I know you don't think you have anything to do here, but that's not true. You're very important. We need you."

My face goes hot, the power of being needed by my mother hitting my system like a fast-acting drug.

"*You have to help him,*" she whispers.

I twist out of her hold. "What do you mean?"

"Joseph. I need you to get him to learn his lines."

"Mom. That is *not* my job."

"Your job, which I so graciously created to help you through a tough time, is to make this production run smoothly. You agreed to be a part of this team, and right now, this is what the team needs from you."

"It's hard for me to feel bad when it turns out he's just as terrible as I told you he was five years ago!"

"Honey, casting Joe was Guy's decision," Mom says, flicking her wrist.

"It was a bad one."

"Cut him some slack. Guy has known Joe his entire life. Joe's dad starred in Guy's first movie."

"I know," I say bitterly, even though I didn't.

"Then you can understand why Guy wants Joe to do this. It's all family here. From top to bottom. If you won't do this for me, at least do it for your sister."

This is, of course, the right thing to say. As angry as I am, I don't want Tyler to fail. "Fine. But I expect a pay raise. And a bigger credit. *Executive* producer."

"Baby girl, that's not how you negotiate."

"Don't 'baby girl' me. I'm almost thirty-one. And I'm saving your ass right now."

"You'll always be my baby." She kisses me on my forehead.

Joseph walks by with a bag slung over his shoulder. "G'night, Ms. Kitty. Thanks for the talk. I need a good arse kicking every so often." He hesitates. "G'night, Sloane."

"One second, Joe," Mom says. "I want to run something by you."

Joseph comes and stands beside me.

"Would it be okay if I sent Sloane to your trailer in the mornings to help you with your lines?" Mom asks. "She might not remember this, but she used to do that with me when she was little." She pinches my cheek, doing everything she can to soften this blow. "She's quite a good scene partner."

Joseph turns to me. For the first time all day, there is a flicker of liveliness in his eyes. A white-hot spark of the troublemaker I met five years ago. "That's all right. I think I've got it," he says, his brogue maxing out like speakers on full blast.

His refusal makes my blood boil. "Someone has to make sure you don't ruin this entire production."

It comes out harsh enough that he winces. It doesn't matter that every person here knows it's true, we're supposed to speak of his failings in hushed tones, all the while coddling him like an infant.

Not me.

Not this time.

"That was hardly my plan," he challenges.

"Are you sure? We're already behind schedule because of you, and it's"—I check an imaginary watch on my wrist—"day one."

It's incredible how quickly I decide to fully commit once Joseph dares to be this nonchalant. This is not a game. This project is employing a hell of a lot of people, and I'll set fire to him myself before he's allowed to be the one to burn it all down.

"It was just an idea," Mom says. "Now go home and get some sleep. I want you rested and ready for tomorrow." She's softer with him now than she was with me this morning, when all I did was arrive late.

Joseph tips his head and keeps walking, another small wave before he's out the door.

"Are you kidding me?" I say to Mom. "You're gonna let him refuse like that?"

"I thought you didn't want this job?"

"I—I don't," I say weakly.

"Come to set an hour before call time. He'll be here." She leans in again. "I told you."

"Told me what?"

"You were important."

3

Joseph opens his trailer door holding a cup of breakfast tea and wearing an expression of complete shock.

He's got music on in the background. "Sister Golden Hair" by . . . America, I think. My dad would be disappointed in me for not being confident in this. When I was growing up, every song we ever heard became a pop quiz on music history when Dad was around. Now whenever something he considers classic plays, I try to tick as many boxes as possible before looking up what's on: song title and artist, minimum. Album and year of release if I know the song a little better.

Dad is supposedly fine now. "Better than ever!" as he says whenever I try to ask about it, using his patented Alexander Ford jovial tone, the subtext all but screaming not to press any further. Still, I can't help but find small ways to keep him with me, as if constantly preparing for the day he's really gone. And sometimes it feels like if I can't name a song title, artist, and album, I will manage to forget him altogether. Even though he's still here.

I'm aware it doesn't make sense. I wish that made it less true.

"Yes?" Joseph says in greeting, leaning against the side of the doorframe.

"Good morning. Nice to see you too." I wave my copy of the script at him. "It's time to rehearse."

"Pardon?"

"Is this America?" I ask.

He follows my eyeline to the space behind him. "I don't think it's that messy in here. Maybe the Irish have different standards?"

I almost laugh before remembering he isn't allowed to be funny. "I meant the music you have on."

"Oh. I don't know. It's a playlist." He shakes his head. "Are you really here to rehearse? Didn't I tell you yesterday that I didn't need it?"

"And I told you that you couldn't ruin this movie. So here I am. Are you going to let me inside?" My hands are shaking so hard my script is wavering. I've also got an iced coffee with me, so I force out a small shiver, hoping it seems like I'm somehow cold from holding it.

"I suppose I don't have a choice." He angles himself to allow me to pass, my arm brushing his torso.

He's right. His trailer is as beige and sparse as expected at the beginning of a production. There are a few personal touches already scattered about, though. A blue-and-green-plaid blanket on the crinkling leather couch. Two boxes of tea beside an electric kettle. A very expensive bottle of whiskey that appears to be unopened. And a framed four-by-six photo of a young woman standing alone in front of a field, smiling.

I set my belongings on the coffee table, then pick up the photo to examine. "Your girlfriend?" I ask, trying for some reason beyond my own comprehension to create a sense of normality here. Take the energy between us down a notch or two.

"My mam." He takes the frame from my hands.

The photo has a weathered effect to it I assumed was a stylistic choice. "Oh. Sorry."

"Don't be. She'd be flattered, I'm sure."

There's an awkward pause, neither of us knowing how this should go. "Will she be visiting—" I start, right as he's saying, "What have you been—" We both say sorry at the exact same time.

Joseph clears his throat. "You go."

"I was asking if your mom would be visiting set."

"Ah. Don't think that'll quite be possible." He looks at his phone on the speaker dock. "You were right. This is America."

"Oh god. I forgot. I'm sorry."

"It's all right. Everyone has to die eventually."

"Dark."

He gestures to the couch. "Enough about my dead mam. Since you've forced your way into my morning routine, please take a seat. Would you like some tea?"

I jiggle my cup of iced coffee on the table in front of me. The sun has barely come up, and caffeine has already dialed me to eleven. My pulse will not settle.

My day started with learning that my ex-boyfriend dropped an entire album about me overnight.

Now I've made Joseph talk about his dead mother.

It only gets worse when he sits on the couch, crossing his foot over his other leg, so close to me that our knees almost touch.

"You know, I wasn't lying when I said I'm not the same guy I used to be," he tells me.

"Really? Because I sat through some textbook Joseph Donovan shit yesterday."

"Can I be honest?"

"Can you?"

He rubs his chin, fighting off a laugh or a scowl. "I didn't give a shit about *A Little Luck*."

"No kidding."

"I thought the script was terrible, and I shouldn't have agreed to do it so soon after my mam died. But everyone said it was good to keep busy."

"Everyone lied to you."

"They do that a lot." He readjusts his legs. "I didn't care about anything back then. This is different. I think I care about this too much."

I roll my eyes. "Come on, man. If your excuse for ruining an entire day of production is *caring too much*, it's time to workshop a better story."

"Probably." He smiles at me. A cutting, devilish grin they'll plaster across the eventual *Entertainment Weekly* spread they do on this movie, where Joseph will pretend to dance for the camera, forever frozen in a little Gene Kelly skip, hamming it up for a giggling Haven Church.

I know better than to be duped by a man this charming. This is *exactly* how I got an entire album written about my shortcomings. I listened to a handsome creative type talk about his problems, and I did everything I could to help him feel better instead of telling him the truth.

That resulted in Kearns Adam, indie folk star, rasping his way through a chorus about me that features the lyrics *Solemn girl in blinding light. Never looked me in the eyes. Always took me by surprise. When she kissed me in the dark.*

I will not make the same mistake twice.

Joseph takes the script from my hands and starts flipping through the pages. "If you want to leave, I can tell your family you came and worked with me."

"Absolutely not. If you go out there and suck again, it's now *my* fault."

He pauses to study me. It would be too much to look away, so I take it, steely eyes glaring right back, daring him to make any sort of visible assessment. "You really don't have a single bit of faith in me," he says, almost like this is a revelation to him.

"You've never once shown me why I should."

"Have you given me a proper chance to?"

My cheeks are getting hot. "Was two months in Ireland together not enough time? Or our entire press junket afterward? Or twelve hours on set yesterday? I forgot you deserved a minimum of ten chances at redemption. My bad."

He turns his head to look through the open blinds over the couch. He's close enough for me to see facial hair that's started to grow back after a recent shave. In profile, the clench of his jaw is evident, creating something like a dimple.

I already hate myself for agreeing to this. "We're going to start at the beginning of yesterday's scene, even though we already shot some of it."

"Sure," he says, distant.

"Look, let me level with you for a moment." There's a touch of pleading in my tone, which I have to correct. He does not get to do this to me. Not *again*. "Clearly no one's ever told you the truth before in your life. I don't want this to be any more awkward than it already is, and I really don't want you to go on set today and do whatever it was you were doing yesterday. So let's agree to wipe out our past bad feelings for the moment and start fresh. Okay?"

"Sure," he repeats with the exact same inflection.

"Oh my god. This is your *job*. One that will be making you lots of money. You're not being held against your will to be here."

"Christ," he cries out, awakened from whatever spell had him staring out the window. "I know you don't believe it, but what happened yesterday hasn't happened in years. And while I'm not being held against my will, you damn well might be."

There are millions of dollars on the line. Plus the professional reputation of almost everyone in my entire family. Oh, and my personal relationship to every one of them too.

"Well, you're basically refusing my help," I counter.

"As I *said*, you don't even want to give it. So no, quite honestly, I'm not too keen on taking it."

For as much as he claims he's changed, he still seems as impossible as ever.

"Here I am anyways." I emphasize it with a half bow from my seat.

"Yeah. About that I read somewhere that you left your show," he dares to mention. Salt to the wound.

"*Mm*. Thanks for bringing it up."

He looks up at me through his eyelashes, taking a small sip of his tea. "It's a shame. You're the only good thing about it," he says with his lips pressed to the mug.

"Oh for fuck's sake. Do not sit here and act like you watch *The Seeker*."

He breaks into a little shit-eating grin, full of mischief. "Tess Doyle. Works in the lab. She's in love with Colfax but she keeps her distance. She knows he has it in for Detective Rodrigo, and in the end, Tess loves her work more. She had a blue streak in her hair for the first two seasons, but they got rid of it by season three. Gave you the little short brunette clip you've got now."

"Okay. Thank you to Google for giving you that information."

"There was an episode last season about a killer clown, and you had this brilliant moment where you're looking at the crime scene photo and you say, 'Reminds me of my aunt.' Not a single person acknowledges it, and you don't explain." He pauses to chuckle. "God. I laughed for ages at that."

This is past unexpected and into downright bizarre. What do I need to do to make sense of the Joseph Donovan sitting across from me? He's right in that he's not the boisterous, belligerent asshole from our time in Ireland. This version of him is mercurial and impossible to parse, shifting in a matter of minutes from fussy to nonresponsive to cheeky *Seeker* fan.

"Let's set some ground rules." I have to pivot into something easier to understand. "You are not to be late. Ever. There is no being rude to a single person on this set, even if your costume itches or the lights are in your eyes. You will respect everyone like they are important and worthy of your time. You will know your lines. You will say them like they matter. We do not leave this trailer until you are ready to give a great performance. Got it?"

Everything I've asked for is everything he did wrong on the set of A *Little Luck*. And yet I was considered the high-maintenance one for asking for better working conditions, developing a whispered reputation that I've never been able to escape, no matter how forgiving I am of behavior that shouldn't be forgiven.

After a long stretch of silence, Joseph whispers, "Got it." We're about to start the work when he adds, "Can I expect the same from you?"

The audacity of the question makes my jaw drop. From his expression, arms folded and brows raised, it's clear he's serious.

"Yes," I say through squinted eyes, my subtext screaming, *Obviously*. My heart pounds against my chest.

He nods, satisfied as ever.

I grab my script and turn to the Elise-Calvin reunion scene. "Let's start. We don't have a lot of time."

Our first few attempts at reading together, he trips over most of his lines. All this talk of having changed and here he is, messing up for an audience of one. It's not productive to be aggressive when I need him to be better than this, but I can't help but put down my script and ask, "Why are you doing this?"

"I told you I didn't want any help," he says, petulant.

"Oh my god. Are you literally trying to prove to me that you don't need this? My sister Sarai wouldn't even do that, and she's eleven."

"I'm not. I just . . . Look, I don't do well when I'm uncomfortable."

"We're actors. Our entire job is getting comfortable with being uncomfortable. This is no different than the dozens of other jobs you've done, where—*according to you*—you haven't been like this. What makes this so unique?"

He bites his lip, looking everywhere but at me. "Sorry."

"There's no need to say sorry." I ease myself into my softest tone, remembering that it really will be my ass on the line if he screws up again today. "You can't fix it by apologizing anyways. You fix it by being better."

He says nothing.

"Seriously, you have to let go of whatever is making you act like this, and start again. That's the beauty of making movies, isn't it? There is always another take."

If he has an argument, it dies on his tongue, another storm cloud passing over.

Slowly, read by read, unbearably patient coaching from me and far too many exasperated grunts from him, the magnetism that's made him such a success returns, like he's overcome some kind of twenty-four-hour flu that stunted his ability to perform. He starts to resemble the man I last saw in that prestige miniseries that got him his Emmy nomination. Vibrant. Affable. Loading his dialogue with surprising depth.

If he fails me on set today, he's doing it on purpose.

Together, we exit his trailer. The warmth of the sun catches the golden-blond undertones in his dyed brown hair. There's a kiss of color along his neckline and the faint trace of a tattoo soon to be covered up, just the black ink top of what I think is an arrow.

We part without a goodbye.

I find Tyler sitting in front of our soundstage, dressed in black from head to toe. She's got her phone on the ground and her arms on her knees, slouched over herself to look at the device.

"Everything okay?"

"Oh." She takes out an AirPod. "Hey."

"Ready for day two?"

"You'll have to check with Guy. Or Mom. You saw how yesterday went. I'm not important enough to consider."

It seems no one is immune to the Mom effect around here.

"Look," I say, settling into the only role that's ever gotten me any respect: big sister. "You gotta show them you're in charge too. Maybe try throwing up a middle finger and screaming?"

"I'm just not the type of person that's going to yell over someone to be heard." Tyler's so deep in her own head she's treating my joke as a serious suggestion. "And Guy talks a lot. I had no idea a person could have that much to say about how he wants people to breathe."

"I could kidnap him and keep him in my trunk, if you want? I've got granola bars and water bottles back there. I could hold him safely for a few hours. As for Mom . . . you're out of luck there."

Tyler stands up and brushes off her legs. Low-slung harem pants tucked into black Converse, and a slouchy black tank. "I need to be more like you," she says, ignoring my second (generous) attempt at lightening her mood. "Say what I need to say and not feel bad about it."

"Do I really do that?"

Her eyes, keen and secretive, narrow at me. "Ask Joseph Donovan."

"Wow." I'm impressed she's dared to mention his name to me. She's clearly out of sorts. "You know, I'd *love* to, but I was too busy spending the last hour of my life making sure he doesn't ruin your movie."

"See? You just did it."

"Cute."

Tyler looks around, her gaze landing on the wall of our soundstage, beige concrete that stretches up nearly forty feet high. "Tell me this will all be worthwhile," she says in a rare moment of vulnerability, managing to tug on my heartstrings once again.

"Of course it will," I assure her.

I only wince when she looks down at her phone.

"Oh, by the way, have you listened to Kearns's album?" She takes out her other AirPod. "It came out last night."

"No," I lie. "But I'm sure it's trash."

Back at home under my covers, drafting emails about my fast-approaching annual foundation gala, my phone buzzes with a text from Tyler that says, You were right.

She let me leave a little early. I entertain the thought that Joseph managed to set it all on fire afterward, which hurts more than I expect. Our rehearsal was awkward, and he was guarded and difficult and all-around weird with me, but he was ready.

Then Tyler follows up with Kearns's album is trash.

Everything I draft in response gets deleted before I press send. Have you listened to it yet? she asks a few minutes later.

I respond immediately. Still no, I type as the album blares from the Bluetooth speaker on my dresser. My bedroom is flooded with the sound of Kearns singing. It's nothing like his speaking voice, which is flat and low, a hint of Carolina twang remaining after a decade spent in Los Angeles. He sings with a searing lilt, every word coated in the kind of soft-spoken intensity that makes you turn up the volume. He's warbling and sometimes off-key. Mesmerizing all the same. This is the very guy that used to croon me to sleep in the early days of our relationship, stroking my hair and making up a lullaby just for me.

I don't really care, I send.

Kearns got his start as a classic white-guy-with-a-guitar musician. This record has him experimenting with different rhythm sections and unusual woodwind instruments. It frustrates me that there's a lingering pride crashing up against my anger. We used to spend hours in this very bed talking about how he wanted his sound to evolve into something like this. I'd talk about my hopes for my career, and he'd share his, detailing all the ways he wanted his music to grow while I shared all my dreams of being able to define myself as someone other than the daughter of two famous people.

The centerpiece of his album, "Smoke in the Mirror," sheds most of this expanded backup, the intro only an unnerving drum line battling against Kearns's angry guitar licks. Then the singing kicks in, and there's no need to crank the volume to catch Kearns's intensity. This is the only track that's sung directly to me, and I feel it in my marrow, how deep his resentment lies. The incessant drum section hammers along at the exact beat of my heart.

What was I to you?
Always just a fool?
The hit man on your star-filled marquee
Beneath the family rule

What did you expect?
Beyond obedience
Drinking champagne, saying nothing
Your favorite accident

You're just smoke in the mirror
So afraid to live the truth
Light a match and burn me down
Before you'll face the proof

If we're talking mirrors, listening to this over and over has been like looking into a fun house one. The viewpoint is so distorted that it's comical. But every so often I catch an angle of myself I didn't know existed. Even if it's not accurate, it still terrifies me to know someone else sees me this way.

What's worse is that he knew how wary I was of letting people in. After a lifetime of seeing my every dalliance summarized in two sentences underneath a picture of me outside a fro-yo shop, mouth wrapped around a plastic spoon, someone in my circle leaking to the press what "really" happened with my "disastrous" love life, always relating it to my parents' divorce.

I told him how hard it was for me to show someone the truth. I made myself be brave enough to expose to him all my less-than-flattering angles. For the first time ever, I was myself with someone other than my family.

And he used it all against me.

"Hey."

I turn my head to find Tyler standing over my bed, staring at me with a mix of pity and shock.

"Holy shit." I fumble with my comforter, covering myself up as if I'm somehow indecent, even though I'm in full-coverage pajamas and she's the sister I used to take baths with as a child. "What the hell are you doing here?"

"I listened to most of the album on my ride home. I wanted to make sure you were okay."

"I'm excellent." After all the times I've walked past her old bedroom wishing to see her, she finally comes over and lets herself in for the exact thing I want to handle alone.

"It was this song that made me come to you," she tells me.

We go quiet, intently listening to the second verse.

How good did it feel?
To have me at your heel?
You walked atop me
Never stopping
Showtime sex appeal

Shining daisy girl
Give them all a twirl
Lips in crimson
Pressed atop mine
Promising the world

You're just smoke in the mirror
So afraid to clear the air
Hold my heart then break it clean
Telling me that all is fair

Tyler kicks off her boots and gets underneath my covers with me.

We lean back against a stack of pillows, angled enough to see ourselves in the mirror above my dresser. This is how we spent so many nights post-divorce, side by side in my bed sharing a comfortable silence. We're much older now, and my bedroom's more sophisticated these days, done up in tasteful neutrals with pops of green instead of that lavender-and-zebra-print theme I insisted on as a kid. But the feeling is almost the same, a heaviness between us that we aren't ready to discuss. We just know we can't face it alone.

Back then, all the words we couldn't say aloud were never about each other.

The song fades out with Kearns singing, *"Light a match, burn the proof,"* over and over, like a hex to keep me away.

It's astonishing how easily he can lie. Because he's the one who broke up with me. Who told me he was tired of the monotony of our life. You'd never know it, listening to this. You'd think I tossed him to the curb and laughed while I drove over his belongings.

I wish I had. Maybe then I'd feel better.

"For the rest of my life, I will be *this* person to a million strangers I've never met, no matter what I say," I admit to Tyler, too tired to hold it inside.

It would hurt less if I thought she was someone I could actually be, but she's yet another role in which I've been miscast, and it's all I can do not to be buried under the weight of the persona.

"It's very clear that Kearns is being petty," Tyler assures me. "No one's listening to this thinking it's true."

"I know." But I don't believe it. Not even a little.

My head is heavy with small memories. Kearns's hand brushing his long brown hair out of his eyes. The feel of his palm on the small of my back as we'd walk out of a restaurant. All the times I came home to find him sitting beside Tyler, the two of them watching TV together.

Who was the fucking liar between us?

His name isn't even Kearns Adam. It's Adam Kearns. He flipped it, and suddenly he became the next Ben Gibbard. He flipped our relationship. And he's coming out the hero for that too.

"I'm sorry I didn't talk to you about the movie before Mom offered you the part," Tyler whispers, barely audible over the blaring music.

"Fear of the Canyon," the album's title track, has started.

I live in fear of the canyon
As dark and deep as lovely woods
With a daisy girl who never could
Wipe the shadows from her eyes

There it is again. Daisy girl. His old nickname for me. A calling card he's scattered throughout, in case all the references to celebrity and having a famous family somehow got by me. Or anyone else with even a cursory knowledge of the past three years of his life.

Tyler's watching me expectantly. It takes a second to step out of the shadow of my memories and into what she's said about *Horizons*. Maybe she brought it up to distract me, but the timing still feels wrong. Way too late and not enough.

"I thought you of all people would've known how much that would hurt me," I challenge, turning down the music with a remote. "And to cast *him . . .*"

"I know." Her voice is so soft it's almost inaudible. After a long beat, she says, "You're so good at what you do. Don't let Kearns make you think any different."

Her whole life, she's never been able to fight me.

Kearns's music definitely hasn't made me contemplate my abilities as an actor. More like my ability to be a human worthy of unconditional love. But that's a topic for my therapist, so I say, "Thanks," and leave it at that.

Just when I'm about to open my mouth and start a real conversation—ask her why she bothered to come over when she won't actually *say* anything to me—she leans over and gives me a quick, awkward squeeze.

"I wish I could stay longer, but I have to get back. Mara isn't home tonight. There's no one to let out Opal. She hasn't gone potty in hours," she says.

It stings. More than it should. In the past, she never would've left me like this, after seeing concrete proof that I'm not handling everything as well as I want everyone to believe. This would've been easier if she hadn't shown up in the first place.

She tried, but only halfway.

"I get it. I haven't gone potty yet either," I joke.

"I hate you," she says, our signature send-off.

"Hate you too. See you tomorrow morning."

"Fuck Kearns Adam. You are so much more than his shit music," she tells me as she lets herself out.

As soon as I hear the click of the front door's bolt lock, I turn the music back up and put on "Smoke in the Mirror" again.

Light a match.
Burn the proof.

4

Our third day of production begins like the one before: Joseph at his trailer door with a cup of tea in hand and classic rock in the background.

"Again?" he asks.

I've got my iced coffee in hand and my copy of the script, marked up with all the notes and ideas I came up with after Tyler left me alone to wallow. It was the best way to pass the time, having sent so many late-night emails about my upcoming foundation gala that the event coordinator called me to ask if everything was all right.

"Making sure you know your lines is the only real task I've been given," I explain. "So until further notice, you'll see me here every morning."

Across from where I sit on the couch, Joseph's bottle of whiskey remains unopened, and the photo of his mom has been moved to its original place, on a shelf above the stovetop. Everything is basically the same as it was the day before, except there's conveniently an extra coaster set out on the coffee table. Joseph makes no mention of it, and neither do I.

I do, however, put my drink atop it.

Joseph brings over his cup of tea, setting it on the other coaster, then sits beside me again. "I have a question."

This makes me bristle, a hot flash of vulnerability hitting me out of nowhere. There's nothing he could ask that would embarrass me, and I'm still nervous. Can he sense a vibe between me and Tyler? Does he know about how I told Haven to treat him? Is he going to ask if my dad is okay? Is he going to press the issue of why I really turned down the part of Elise?

"What?" I try to sound flippant.

"Are you really done with acting?" he asks.

My practiced PR line floats off my tongue before I can reconsider. "I'm taking each day as it comes," I tell him, knowing full well it sounds hollow and false. He hasn't earned the truth.

Joseph scrunches his lips. There's a furrow between his brows that deepens as he nods at me.

"What? What's the face for?"

"Nothing." He taps his fingers on his jeans. "Seems like a load of shit is all."

My jaw drops. "Are you kidding me?"

"If you asked me about my career and I told you I'm *taking each day as it comes*, you'd never let me live that down."

He's right. And I hate him even more for knowing that. So I double down. "Well it's true."

"All right then, what is each day bringing you, Sloane?"

"You can judge me all you like, but I'm not actually here to impress you."

"Hmm. You're deflecting."

"And you're being annoying."

"That sounds like an upgrade from yesterday." He leans back, arms folded across his chest. "Whatever is really going on, I hope you're not done with acting forever."

I roll my eyes at him. "Please stop paying me empty compliments."

The smirk falls off his face, and we plunge into a silence so strained I search for something unaffected to say and find a surprising amount of remorse bubbling under the surface instead. The problem is, I really can't tell if he's serious. And it's hurtful for him to keep pretending that he is.

"You think I go around telling everyone in town they're actually good at their job?" he asks finally.

"Yes."

He waits before he speaks, observing me. Thinking. *Calculating.*

"Well, I don't," he says, daring me to ask for elaboration.

Another stretch of quiet threatens to consume us. "We need to rehearse," I remind him.

He checks the time on his phone. "Can't we be friendly with each other for a little longer?"

I wish it wouldn't get me into trouble to gut punch him. "I don't need to be your friend."

"Okay. Perhaps I could be something less than your mortal enemy then? For at least another minute or two."

"Please. I don't have enough time in the day to waste on making you my *mortal enemy.* What are we? Medieval knights?"

He laughs, like I was trying to be funny. Which maybe I was. Maybe it does amuse me a little, to spar with him. Just the tiniest amount. "C'mon Sloane. You hate me. It's clear as day."

"Actually, Joseph, I choose kindness. Thank you very much."

He laughs harder. Which was potentially my intention.

"Can we get back to work now?" I ask, fighting off a smirk.

"Fine. I lay down my sword. Your wish is my command," he says with a hand pressed to his heart.

♥

On the soundstage, the cameras are set up around Calvin's apartment. His place is across the hall from Elise's. Since their second kissing scene, the one that leads up to their big love scene, takes place at dusk, our lighting crew works to create a hazy purple-hued glow coming in through Calvin's living room window.

Tyler sits ramrod straight in her director's chair as Mom looms over her, tapping her foot on the base of one of the camera stands. Mom's arms are tightly crossed, and her head bobs along with every word. She's wearing wedge sandals with socks today, a look I was confident we'd banished from her wardrobe years before. If she didn't have a stylist, she'd probably wear this on a red carpet. For all her strengths, fashion has never been one of them.

When I get close enough to hear their conversation, I catch Mom saying, "So I can't stay?" in her most accusatory tone. I attempt a one-eighty, staying uninvolved, but Mom sees me. "Is Sloane allowed to stay?"

"Mom. It's not personal," Tyler whispers. A life of mouthing words to each other in the quiet of my bedroom has made me an expert at deciphering her softest tones, and this is one notch above soundless.

"Guy doesn't mind," Mom counters.

"And if this were only Guy's movie, that would be great. But he asked me to direct with him. I'm allowed to make at least one decision here. And I want a closed set. Our intimacy coordinator agrees. The less people around, the better for the actors."

"I'm not some predatory man," Mom protests, so thoroughly missing the point that I step up behind Tyler to provide backup.

"Tyler's right. We should have the bare minimum here. Joseph gets weird when he's too uncomfortable. Trust me, I've seen it firsthand. And it's not about whether or not you're a predator, Mom. It's about what's best for the actors' comfort levels. You don't deserve access to this scene just because you're someone important on set."

Mom takes a moment to look me up and down, a full-body evaluation that makes me shudder. "Don't you dare do it," she says to me. "Not now."

"Do what?"

"Sleep with him. That's the last thing we need."

It's such a stunning moment, as quick and unexpected as a slap to the face. I can't do anything but gape at my own mother, who for all her faults has never been *this* casually cruel to me.

"Mom. What the fuck?" Tyler says, loud and clear.

"Oh, c'mon," Mom continues. "I wasn't born yesterday."

I am acutely aware of all the surrounding crew members shifting their attention to us. One of the guys on the lighting crew almost tips an entire light post onto the floor. Tammy the AD does the same shuffle pivot of avoidance I tried a moment ago. Two PAs huddle back by craft services in full gossip mode. This is so wildly inappropriate and unprofessional of my mother, in every way possible. No one on this set should be subjected to this, and yet here we are.

I open my mouth to stop things from escalating, but Tyler cuts me off.

"You forced Sloane to become his on-set acting coach, and then when she tells you what will be best for his acting, you go after her like she's ready to spread her legs and take Joseph on the kitchen counter midscene?" It's very difficult to get Tyler this angry. When someone succeeds, it's like hitting a fire hydrant. Almost impossible to contain.

This is getting very ugly very fast.

"This isn't my first movie, Tyler," Mom chides. "But it *is* yours." She walks all the way off the soundstage in her goddamn socks and sandals, not even glancing back at us.

"Nice, Mom! Really mature," Tyler spits out after her. Her shoulders are up to her ears, and she's stalking around in small circles. "What the actual fuck?" she mutters to herself. "You're doing your job. The one *she* made you do." At once, tears fill her eyes. "This whole movie is *cursed*."

"Don't say that. It's not," I assure her, even though I can't deny how fast things have already crumbled around here, for no reason. "Mom must be worried about having to act again. I don't know." I'm trying—and failing—to find reasoning that has any substance behind it.

Tyler shakes her head. "Everyone's worried about something. It's no excuse."

I rub my hand on her back in soothing circles. It's a lot easier to comfort her than it is to examine my own feelings, which at the moment seem too massive to even acknowledge.

"I don't understand how she still thinks your thing with Joseph is some kind of sexual tension issue," Tyler continues.

"Does she now?" I manage to say, keeping up the rhythmic circles on her back, needing her to elaborate before she realizes what a bad idea it is to tell me this much.

"She has it in her head that you exaggerated all the stuff that happened in Ireland."

I pull my hand back. It's not all Tyler's fault, but she's revealed herself to not be blameless either. Maybe the curse *is* real, because there's a venomous feeling snaking up through me.

"We all saw what happened here. It probably doesn't scratch the surface of what he was like in Ireland," she whispers, making sure the crew can no longer hear us. "It's fucked she made you be the one to help him, after all that. *Fucked*, I tell you. And then she has the nerve to say that to you afterward."

I muster up a nod, squeezing my lips so tight they must be turning white.

"We spent so much time during casting talking about how much he must've changed, because he was so great every time he came in for us. I was the one who said we had to do all of that. Mom wanted to offer him the job without even seeing him read for it." Tyler sighs. "You were right, he really is good at what he does. He had me fooled, and you know it takes a lot for me to root for a presumably straight white guy."

I hiss out a breath that makes Tyler stop cold. She looks at me, recognition dawning on her face.

"So I'm clear," I start, my pitch low and dangerous. "All of you decided it was no problem to cast Joseph Donovan in this movie because Mom thought I was mad I missed my chance to sleep with him?"

"Sloane, no." She reaches for me as I pull farther back.

My voice gets even quieter. And deadlier. "You all thought that not getting to ride Joseph Donovan's dick had me so pissed I almost quit the business altogether? That the prospect of his lucky fucking charms was so intoxicating to me I cried every single day? In fact I even went so far as to make up a whole narrative that he was a bitter drunk who showed up to set half in the bag and barely aware of the plot, but there was nothing to be done about it because he was the top of the call sheet and they'd written the movie basically for him? I whipped all of that up in my sex-crazed mind, incapable of doing my job when I knew that the gift of what was in Joseph's pants wouldn't get to be inside of me? And the least my beloved family could do was cast us in a romantic war drama together and capitalize on the white-hot heat of our sexy, sexy rivalry? Then I turned the role down, and suddenly having hot chemistry with our hot lead became a distraction instead of a benefit. Am I right?"

Tyler's gone pale and her face is slick with a fresh layer of sweat. "Sloane."

"No? What did I miss?"

Tyler leans in even closer. "It sounds really bad. And I see now how wrong it was. I should have told you."

"Yeah. You should have told me a lot of things. But at least now I know how much my family values my feelings." I stalk off to craft services to eat an apple I don't want. I won't be like my mother and leave. I committed to this job, and I will complete it. Headfirst and silently panicking.

This will not break me.

By the time the actors are ready, I feel like a freshly sharpened knife, waiting for a chance to cut someone clean through.

Mom does not return.

There's only the bare minimum crew as requested. Of the people currently on set, only Tammy the AD witnessed my mother's blowup in person. Word has traveled, though. It's in the eagerness to appease Tyler. The quiet, gentle way everyone addresses me, like they know I'm wounded. All the glances. It's impossible for me to miss them.

Of course Joseph saunters onto the soundstage oblivious to it all. He's always been impervious to on-set drama. There's no other explanation for how he could've endured our entire shoot in Ireland. There was a point when we were having cast and crew meetings about his behavior almost every single morning, and he'd still waltz onto location with a shit-eating grin, asking who catered lunch and what time we were having it.

Right now he's in a white undershirt with suspenders clipped onto forest-green slacks. A tendril hangs down on his forehead. They've touched up the brown rinse in his hair, liking the contrast of the darkness against Haven's bright blond. She wears nothing but a peach-colored slip.

"Hey," he says, putting a hand on my shoulder. "Thanks for helping me earlier. I think today's gonna go pretty well."

His palm stays pressed onto the open skin beside my tank top strap. I can actually feel the crew making note of it, as if the action is somehow bolded for emphasis.

"No problem," I say quickly, brushing him off and walking toward a shadowy corner to sit down.

Before he can react, the intimacy coordinator brings him into a discussion with Haven over what they're about to shoot.

Right before the scene, Elise has been through hell, and she's realized that she's pushed Calvin away for the wrong reasons. He's just fought for her honor against a date gone wrong, and she's worked up the courage to come clean about her true feelings, the ones she hedged around during the first, lighter kiss scene we shot earlier. This second moment between them is very sweeping and most certainly over the top. It will only work if both actors fully commit. If there's even a hint of reservation or a wink at the absurdity of it all, the whole sequence will crumble into unbearable cheesiness.

I take a deep breath and lean back, enveloped by darkness. Ever since I was a young kid, I've preferred to watch from the floor. It feels more interesting somehow, to see the actors work from this angle instead of spending the whole day staring at a small-screen monitor version of the action. Watching here is like being a front-row voyeur to a stranger's most intimate moments, while knowing you have their permission to watch. And in today's case, it keeps me out of most everyone's eyeline, which is about the only victory I'm going to get.

My script sits in my lap, open to the second kiss, all my high-lights and markings like codes I try to imprint onto Joseph's mind through willpower alone.

Mom's accusation echoes in my head as I watch him go through the blocking with Haven, our intimacy coordinator discussing their boundaries.

With Joseph, I've been stern to the point of rudeness, not accepting compliments or allowing our conversations to veer toward the truly personal. I have not had a single thought about sleeping with him. In fact I've held myself like my mother does with almost every single person on this set, and she's the one who attacks me for it.

My gaze traces the set from left to right, stopping when Joseph locks eyes with me. He smiles, warm and friendly, another of his countless attempts to wipe the slate clean between us.

I smile back, because I can smile at him. It doesn't have to mean anything.

Then, unbelievably, he winks.

Before I can scrape together a cohesive thought, I pull myself off the floor and gather my things. Hurry to Tyler's side. "It's better if I'm not here." The adrenaline pulses so hard through me that my hands start to shake.

Does everyone assume I'm going to end up sleeping with Joseph Donovan, *including* Joseph Donovan?

"What? Why?" Tyler's energy juggles between frantic and angry. We haven't had a blowup like this in years, and we're obviously lacking practice in how it should all go down. "I know you're mad, and you have every right to be, but I really need you here."

"If Joseph doesn't know this scene by now, it's his fault. I don't want to make everything worse by being on a closed set when I don't need to be," I explain, knowing it doesn't make much sense, but there's not enough time to craft an excuse with more sound logic behind it.

As I stalk off set, I swear I hear Joseph call my name.

I don't take the time to glance behind me to be sure.

5

The silence from my phone is more unbearable than the quiet in my house, where I've shut myself inside, driving straight from set yesterday and not looking back. I have now officially missed an entire day and a half of production.

There's a persistent ache in my chest I've come to know well. Anxiety, my most unwelcome friend. It usually comes with no obvious explanation, a powerful trickster who likes to surprise me right when life seems good, staying as long as it pleases, leaving without fanfare but with the lingering promise that it will return when I least expect it. This time, it's different. The correlation is obvious.

This goddamn movie.

Tyler hasn't called. Mom hasn't apologized. Powell hasn't texted to say Mom hates me.

Mom's words cut deep, even when I rationalize it all as some strange manifestation of her own anxieties. She's developed a reputation for being a producer who is as blunt as she is heartfelt. Except this is different. I can't understand what she hoped to gain by throwing out an accusation like that. Or for doubting my truth in the first place.

Still, not knowing if Joseph was able to get his lines right has me crawling out of my skin. My job isn't trivial anymore. And thanks to my mother, I fled the set over a wink from Joseph Donovan, which is probably about as commonplace as a wave from a pageant contestant on a parade float.

It's second nature for him to give off an effortless charm. Hell, it's curated. Probably encouraged by an entire team of industry people coming together to build the Joseph Donovan Brand. Boozy Irish boy full of sly winks and quick cracks and tight-fitting tees.

I know this.

I have always known this.

I even know what it's like to have everyone push a brand onto you. There was a time when my team cycled me through a handful of Sloane Ford iterations. First they wanted to capitalize on my childhood spent in martial arts training and market me as the kind of ingenue who could meet your parents at seven and kick the bad guy's ass at eight. When that fell flat, it was because they thought I made more sense as the smart girl not next door, but in a house on a high hill, always in view but forever out of reach.

"Fitting for a child of Hollywood," a director once told me.

When *that* didn't work, it was obviously because my charms were better served in indie roles. Lean into the idea that people might find it fascinating to see me—a born-and-raised Southern Californian who came out of the womb into a birthing pool in the middle of my parents' old Bel Air estate—as a down-on-her-luck waitress living in a small town.

When *that* didn't work, they wanted me to do period pieces. Be the next Keira Knightley. She can't make them all, they told me. And if I'm playing someone of a completely different era, my own life story may be a little less "distracting."

That's when I learned to refuse. I'd always hated trying to

corner any kind of market. Even more than that, I hated the idea that every part I took had to be something that worked in harmony with the narrative of my personal life. The story of Sloane Ford would always run counter to the story of whatever person I inhabited on-screen. So I ended up hung to dry on a TV show that no one in Hollywood bothers to watch, aside from apparently Joseph Donovan. That's gone too, and I'm asking myself why any of it mattered in the first place. It was work. It was acting. It was a hell of a lot more than I'm doing now.

How did I end up nothing more than an ungrateful product of nepotism, biting every hand that ever fed me?

My phone starts vibrating, the screen lit up with a number I don't recognize. Curiosity gets the better of me, and I answer. "Hello?"

"Sloane? It's me, Joe."

A shot of adrenaline zaps through my every limb. I'm off my couch and into my kitchen, hands reaching for the refrigerator door, phone sandwiched between my shoulder and ear.

"I got your number from your sister. I wanted to make sure everything was all right," he says.

There's a bell pepper, a pitcher of water, butter, and hot sauce in my fridge. Ice and frozen broccoli in my freezer. And half a bag of frozen strawberries. "Ah. Yeah."

"You didn't show up to my trailer this morning."

Would a smoothie made of only strawberries and water taste good? It would be loud, at least. A decent excuse to hang up. "It's a long story."

"I've got time, if you wouldn't mind sharing it."

"I'm starving, and I'm actually about to eat, so . . ."

"Would you get some food with me then? I know you live in the canyon somewhere. I can pick you up."

"How do you know that?"

"'Fear of the Canyon' sort of gives it away."

Oh great. Even Joseph is playing Kearns's new record. "Please stop listening to that music."

"I'm not. I think he's a bastard. But I've heard about it."

If it were anyone else, I'd ask where or how, but with Joseph, I truly don't want to know. Getting a late-night meal with him already sounds ripped from the pages of the narrative my mom has crafted for me. Talking about my ex-boyfriend feels like even more dangerous territory.

"This seems like a bad idea," I admit, realizing too late that saying it out loud makes it even worse.

"Why?" There's genuine curiosity in his tone. It's entirely possible he never heard the story of what happened yesterday. If I am lucky, he will go his whole life never hearing it.

I give him my address instead of explaining myself, then hang up before I can reconsider.

Screw my mother's accusation. I know the truth.

Determined to care as little about this meal as possible, I don't change out of my yoga pants and sleep shirt. It's a highlighter-pink Disneyland tee that belonged to my dad, straight from the midnineties. I stole it from him during the divorce and never gave it back.

When Joseph pulls into my driveway, I expect a call or text that he's here. Maybe a honk. Instead there are three short knocks and a "Sloane. You in there?"

I open the door. Joseph's got on a slate-gray fitted tee, his hair damp from what must have been a post-filming shower, dripping onto his shoulders. He has one hand on the doorframe and the other in the back pocket of his jeans.

"Where else would I be?" I ask.

"Halfway to Vegas, maybe. Or living in a different house than the address you gave me."

"Good point." I throw on shoes and follow him to his car.

He drives an old orange Camaro, because of course he does. The interior is neat and smells crisp, some high-end essential oil thing clipped to the air vents. There's only a water bottle in one cup holder and a packet of gum in the other. Classic rock pumps in from an upgraded sound system. This time it's "Reelin' in the Years" by Steely Dan.

"*Can't Buy a Thrill,*" I say as I turn it up. "Nineteen seventy-four. No, wait. Nineteen seventy-two."

"Excuse me?"

"It's the name of the album and the year it came out."

"Good to know, in case I'm ever held at gunpoint and asked about . . . the year this band's album came out."

"This band? It's Steely Dan! Why would you be listening to Steely Dan if you don't even know Steely Dan? No one stumbles into listening to white dad rock like Steely Dan."

"Why do you need to say Steely Dan four times? And why don't you tell me why you left set yesterday and didn't show up today."

"That is none of your business."

"I've now missed a rehearsal with my acting coach. It has officially become my business." His fingers tap along the steering wheel to the beat of the music.

I turn the song up louder. "Sorry! I can't hear you over all the Steely Dan!"

Joseph puts a hand atop mine to stop me from continuing to turn the dial. I pull mine back and tuck it underneath my thigh.

"My mother said something really rude to me, and I got in my head," I admit.

"What was it?"

"I don't want to repeat it."

He takes a sharp breath.

"That's not negotiable," I add.

He must pick up on the genuine hurt in my tone, because for the rest of the drive, he does nothing but put music on shuffle and quiz me on the albums and release years.

We end up at Mel's Drive-In. It's a seat-yourself place, and thanks to my family, it's become a habit for me to pick a spot with my back to a wall. That way I can see everyone else in the restaurant and whether or not they're going to approach our table. It mostly happens with my parents and occasionally with Powell, actually, who has quite a cult following from his side career as a drag queen. Only when I'm out of state does it happen to me.

Ever since the miniseries and the Emmy nomination, Joseph has moved into an echelon with the others. The kind of famous face that makes eyes light up in public, even in Los Angeles. He's someone people want to say they ran into at a diner. Whose picture they would go to awkward lengths to grab, cherishing a shot of him with his mouth half-wrapped around a Reuben. It doesn't help that he's the kind of handsome that strains your eyes if you look at him too long. It seems impossible, his face.

I walk ahead, leading us to a corner spot along the front side of the restaurant. It's pure fifties Americana in here, jukeboxes and glossy red vinyl booths and pictures of Hollywood stars of all eras scattered about. There's even a shot of my parents near the back, the two of them holding hands while walking the red carpet. It's from the Golden Globes right after Powell was born. Mom's in a gold slip dress and Dad's in a classic penguin tux. Mom's hair looks the same, always perfectly layered and blown out, the shiny, beach blond people bring in to color appointments for reference.

She's smiling like a present waiting to be unwrapped, looking at Dad while he has a hand lifted up into a wave, eyes on the crowd out of frame. *His* hair is what gives away the midnineties of it all. Practically shoulder length and casually slicked back, some of it waving near the bottom and lighter brown than the rest. He kept it long until after their divorce, when he pulled the ever-classic breakup haircut move and buzzed his head.

Joseph slides into the booth across from me. I realize we've never sat face-to-face like this in real life. Only when we worked on *A Little Luck* did we have to do any kind of eye-to-eye gazing. Instinctively I grab for my menu, paying extra attention to my food options.

The table starts shaking. It's Joseph's leg, jittering.

My role as perpetual nuisance is the safest version of myself to be, so that's where I start. "Did you remember all of your lines without me?"

"Most of them."

I drop my menu down to stare at him. "Really?"

"I'm kidding."

"Hilarious."

"I'm known for my humor," he deadpans. "No, I wasn't the problem. Not exactly."

This piques my interest. "Was it Guy and Tyler?" I gulp. "Or my mom?"

"Your mom is a force of good. Guy could talk a little less, but he's great. Tyler has a real eye. I like when she gives me direction. Dead-on kind of woman."

"What was the problem then?"

"I thought I was imagining it at first, but—"

A wonderfully jovial waiter appears for our drink order. We both get coffees. Joseph adds on a strawberry milkshake. All the while his unfinished sentence hangs in the air between us, a cloud that could either pass or bring rain. He waits for the waiter to get farther away, craning his neck to track his distance from us.

Then he turns back, and there doesn't seem to be any Joseph Donovan Brand here. He is open. Maybe even nervous. For a fleeting moment I entertain the idea that he's about to admit he also thinks we have unresolved sexual tension between us.

Great. I've managed to create more problems in three days than most film sets have over the entirety of their shoot.

The exit isn't very far from here, and it's a straight walk. I can call a Lyft on the way. Would he follow me? That would be mortifying.

I could also stay and hear him out. It would be validating to know that I'm more than some solemn girl in blinding light who never kisses people in the dark. Then again it would prove something to my mom that isn't even true in the first place.

God. I need to order a drink.

"—she is very nice and all. There's just nothing between us," Joseph says, continuing a thought I haven't been following.

"What?"

"On-screen, I mean."

"Wait. Who are you talking about?"

He gives a strange look. "Haven," he says, clearly repeating it. "She's a bit—"

"Wooden," I finish before I can stop it from coming out of my mouth. I promised myself I wouldn't say that to anyone. And here I am blurting it out to Joseph Donovan in a twenty-four-hour diner while the *Grease* soundtrack plays in the background.

"God. Yes. I thought I was the only one." Joseph lights up, excited to have me engage in this conversation. "When I touch her in a scene, she stiffens up. And that's after I've made sure it's okay in the first place. We're acting. What can I do? I try chatting with her between takes. Making her feel comfortable. She seems like she is. She's quite funny in real life. I think she may be a bit—I don't want to sound like an asshole saying this—I think she's in over her head?"

"You do sound like an asshole saying that." I start massaging my temples. There was a flicker of time where I was considering letting him tell me he has feelings for me. Now I've admitted I think Haven isn't a very good actor.

This was a bad idea indeed.

Joseph taps his fingers along the table in some kind of mental piano arpeggio. "Today was worse than yesterday. Tyler had to call for at least three more breaks than we needed. And they weren't for me, if you can believe it. Guy started running the scene with us between takes, playing each part for us. God's truth, he and I had more chemistry than me and Haven."

"I see," I say carefully. "It takes some actors a little time to settle in. Look at you," I dig. "And also, you apparently watched the first season of *The Seeker*. Hardly anything to go on my highlight reel in there."

"That's not true. That scene with you and Colfax when he asks you to explain to him the spatter pattern from his brother's death, and you have to tell him it was suicide."

"You need to watch better television."

He comes back with "You'd think you'd be grateful to have a fan."

There he is. The asshole.

"A fan? Fuck you. I have fans. Plural. And they're wonderful. A lot of them even go out of their way to support my foundation, which means a lot to me."

"What's your foundation?" he asks.

"It helps underfunded schools gain better access to music and the arts."

"Glorious. I'll support it."

"You're not serious."

"I am." He takes out his phone and starts typing. Manages to pull up my foundation website. Shows me the screen, then starts scrolling on his own. "Would ya look at this. A gala coming up. Can I go?"

"No."

"But I'm about to donate ten thousand dollars. Surely that's enough for an invite. It says there's going to be a celebrity jam band led by Daniel Traverson, star of *The Seeker*." He gives me a pleading look. "Sloane, I cannot live my life having never seen Detective Anthony Colfax lay down a guitar lick."

The waiter brings our coffees and Joseph's milkshake, light pink with whipped cream and a cherry on top. He asks if we're ready to order, but my slack-jawed shock at Joseph's pledge is enough to make him back away, muttering something about how he'll give us another minute to look over the menu. Joseph takes the maraschino cherry off the top of the whipped cream and bites down, pulling until only the stem remains between his fingers.

"I really can't tell if you're joking," I say. "It doesn't mean anything to you, but that kind of money would make a real difference."

"Watch this. I'm putting a little message into my phone to tell my accountant to move some funds around." He swirls his milkshake with a straw, then takes a long sip. "This is good. Would ya like some?"

"Um, no."

He takes another big slurp. Finishes typing his reminder, then leans back, arms sprawled out across the length of the booth.

"These scenes with Haven and me are the biggest ones in the movie. And they're shit. I know they are. Guy knows they are. Tyler. The PAs. Our costume designer. It's very clear everyone knows what we're shooting is utter shit. I can't believe I did this, but I asked to go into overtime today so we could finish. They wouldn't allow it."

This movie really might be cursed. Joseph Donovan just pledged $10,000 to my foundation. I've ordered a coffee when I really need a shot of tequila. What the hell is happening?

"I know it's my fault too," Joseph continues. "I'm too in my head. It's hard now, being sober. There are a lot of thoughts up here and not enough ways to quiet them."

Now that he's brought up sobriety, I can't order a drink. Who knows if they even serve? The waiter returns, finding me once again in a place of utter shock.

"I'm good with only coffee," I tell him.

"You said you were hungry," Joseph challenges. "*Starving* was the word you used."

"I . . . am . . ."

"What do you want to eat?"

"I don't know."

"She'll have a grilled cheese," he says.

If eyes could truly pop out of heads, mine would slingshot clear across the room. "Oh my god. Never again in your life try to *order for me*."

Joseph smiles at the waiter. "Give us a bit more time, would ya?" The man nods and slinks back behind the counter.

For the first time since we sat down, I take survey of the other people in the diner, knowing if I look at Joseph right now it's possible I may crawl across the table to wring his neck.

There are three younger people in a booth along the adjacent wall. They look to be in their late teens or early twenties. My eyes lock with one of them for only a moment before she pretends to be looking out the window. Her friend nudges her shoulder and whispers in her ear. Then shows something on her phone, looking from the screen to me to the screen in a matter of seconds.

"Do you really hate me so much that you don't want to break bread with me?" Joseph asks.

"It's complicated," I say quickly, trying to figure out if any of them are going to approach us. The one who was first staring seems the likeliest candidate, her fingers flying over the keyboard on her phone, typing furiously. "You were really fucking hard to be around when I first met you."

They're definitely going to come over here.

"I . . . I'm really sorry."

The way he says this gets my attention. It's candid, unexpectedly raw, and suspiciously void of snark or any attempt to reroute. There's a pained look on his face, laboring almost. He's rubbing his hand across his mouth, looking up into the hanging light fixture above us.

"The truth is, I don't remember much from then," he tells me. "I remember the press junket a year later. And how you wouldn't speak to me between interviews. But I can only come up with a few memories from the shoot, and we were there for what? Two months? I called my manager this afternoon and asked him about it. He said you were trying to get me fired the whole time, but the team wouldn't do it because I was a bigger name than you."

The memory bottoms me out. How useless I felt. Nothing more than a dolled-up prop, expected to work fifteen-hour days with someone who wanted to be absolutely anywhere else. Tears well in my eyes.

"That about sums it up," I say.

"Would you tell me what I was like?" It's as if he's hiding behind a wall as he asks it, peeking around the corner, afraid of what may be on the other side if he exposes himself too much. But even this small glimpse, this sign of a true heartbeat from him, of remorse instead of dismissal, is enough to spur on my real truth.

"Insufferable," I admit. "You told me on more than one occasion to stick to my day job. Which, that *was* my day job, so it was definitely a confusing sentiment. You once yelled at a grip for breathing too loud. You made up more than half of your dialogue on the spot. And every time we kissed, your breath smelled like sour whiskey."

"Christ. You should've forced me to have a breath mint."

"I actually tried. You sucked on it for two seconds, then spit it into a napkin and said it was messing with your process."

Joseph buries his head in his hands. "Shit. I am unbelievably sorry, Sloane. I know it's not enough to just say it, but I want to be clear." He spends a moment running his fingers back and forth through his hair, eyes squeezed shut. "I want to do something to make it right. What if I put all the money I made from that movie towards—"

"I'm sorry to interrupt." The whispering girl from the other booth has approached our table.

Joseph startles upright, and I let out an exasperated hello.

"Hi," the girl says back. "Could I have a picture?"

Joseph nods, and I start sliding out of the booth. "I can take it for you," I tell the girl.

She giggles nervously. "Oh, I was actually hoping it would be with the both of you."

Surprised, I focus on my dad's mantra when it comes to fans. Be ten times more gracious than you think. A hundred times nicer than you feel. It's not the healthiest way to set boundaries, but we are an industry of people pleasers, and from the countless times I've met actors I've loved that turned out to be assholes, I know how much it stings when we're less than kind. So I paste on a winning smile, hoping my eyes don't look too glossy.

"I just watched A *Little Luck*," she adds as explanation.

Joseph nudges my leg under the table. "Funny you should mention it. We were just having a chat about that shoot." He picks up his chin and narrows his eyes to a smolder. His brogue thickens, dancing off his smirking mouth. The Brand is back in full force.

His transformation stuns me. Because it confirms what I felt earlier: He really had let his guard down.

The girl turns back toward the table where both of her friends are watching expectantly. "It *is* them. I told you," she stage-whispers.

Her friends stand up and march over, sheepish.

"Nice to meet you all," I say. "I'm Sloane. This is Joseph."

We stand up while the girl grabs our waiter to come over. I think he assumed Joseph and I were some indecisive, bickering couple out for a late-night meal. Now three people are making a small scene and asking for our picture. Despite his bewilderment, the waiter is ultimately a good sport. He leans back into the counter, holding the phone horizontally as he snaps several pictures of us, smiling wide to remind us to do the same.

The three fans give us quick hugs, their leader lingering just to say, "You guys are really good in that movie. It's on Netflix if you want to watch it." She starts off, then circles back. "That was a random thing to say. You lived it. Okay wow, I'm gonna disappear now!"

"I actually rewatched some of it recently," I tell her, helping to soften the awkwardness she's clearly feeling.

"Really?" Joseph and the girl ask in unison. "Isn't it good?" the girl tacks on.

"Sure." If I wasn't in it, and I hadn't lived the hell of that shoot, it's exactly the kind of movie I would have watched on Netflix as a teenager and absolutely loved. Which warms my heart.

I'd never thought of it that way before.

The girl smiles. "Thanks for the picture." She's brimming with earnest excitement. As she walks away, she yells out, "I hope you guys are dating!" which makes her friends topple over into hysterics upon her triumphant return to their table.

This shifts the mood between Joseph and me. Our waiter makes another attempt at getting our food order. It's Joseph this time who tells him we won't be getting anything more. He throws two twenties on the table, and we exit.

Joseph waves at the group as we walk past, and I call out a goodbye.

They break out into hysterical laughter once again.

As soon as we're in the car, Joseph wastes no time picking up where we left off before the interruption. "The way I behaved on that set was clearly a much bigger thing than anyone let me believe. I really am sorry, Sloane." He reflects for a moment. "You said something the other day when we were rehearsing. I'll butcher your words, but it was something about how saying sorry doesn't fix it. Changing does."

"Yeah."

"That's what I was thinking about when the girls came up to us. I want to put the money I made from that shoot towards something else. A charity or organization of some sort. Is that appropriate? And I'm not talking about your foundation. I do plan to donate to that too, by the way. I could look into names of the crew members who worked on that shoot with us. See if I can send them something? I don't know what I'm saying really. Just that more should be done and that seems a good place to start."

"That's a good idea," I say. Truthfully, it is. But it's also entirely too much, processing his desire to do real, tangible things to make amends for his past behavior. I lean my head against the window, watching storefronts pass by in a neon blur. "I left set yesterday because my mom accused me of wanting to sleep with you."

The car takes an unexpected swerve to the right.

Joseph's hand presses across my chest as if he could somehow hold me back from harm. "Shit. I'm sorry. Thought I saw a squirrel. Your mother said *what?*"

"That I missed my chance to sleep with you in Ireland," I elaborate. "And since I'm not playing Elise, I must stop my quest to bed you so that this well-oiled production machine isn't ruined by our hot-and-heavy affair. And because of that I learned that no one in my family believed me when I said you were terrible to work with. So there you have it. That's why I didn't show up today."

"Wow."

"Yeah."

I turn up the volume on the music, filling the quiet with Crosby, Stills, and Nash, paying close attention to my cuticles. Headfirst and silently panicking.

"That's fucked," Joseph says after a while.

"Indeed."

We spend the rest of the ride in silence.

When Joseph parks in my driveway, he almost leans over to hug me but thinks better of it and stops. "You've got about every right to never come back to set again. I understand if you don't. But if it matters, I haven't had an acting coach I liked until you.

And I've been a foolish bastard. Never realized that I've only had good scene partners up to now too."

He's trying, but it's late, and I'm tired. "It's a blessing you can't understand until you've worked with someone who sucks." I get out of the car and put a hand up in goodbye, ready to crawl back into my corner of the canyon, needing solitude and darkness to make sense of what's just happened.

I spent an evening with Joseph Donovan, and he wasn't insufferable.

6

On my return to set, day five of production, I opt for a slow approach through the soundstage, detouring solely to see how I'm greeted. Tyler catches sight of me first, waving from a distance then making a hard pivot in the other direction, busying herself with anything but me.

My mother sees me next. She says nothing at all.

My stepdad throws out a jovial "Hello, Sloane!" with a big gap-toothed grin, and it is scraps to a starving dog.

I subsist on it all the way to Joseph's trailer, reminding myself that I am back because I've found a way to be truly valuable to a production, and for the first time in my life, it's not only because I'm the daughter of famous people.

Fanfare is simultaneously the lifeblood of my craft and the bane of my existence, because praise is a drug that must be given in exact doses. Too much and you're left embarrassed and vulnerable. Too little and you crave it.

Then there's the worst-case scenario: expecting it and receiving nothing at all.

Joseph is ready for my arrival this time, opening the door

before my fist can knock. "You came," he says, eyes wide and smile grateful.

"Who knows what would have happened if you were left to your own devices too long."

"Chaos," he assures me. Despite my firmly rooted desire to never be impressed by him, he manages to hit the exact sweet spot I'm missing. "See your mam yet?"

"I did. She looked at me and kept walking."

Joseph sits down in his spot on the couch. "That's pure shit."

It's not that I thought he'd forget what I told him—it's pretty memorable—it's that I'm surprised he cares how it affects me. "It is what it is."

"You're not bothered by it?"

"No." I make my voice casual, unaffected. "Isn't that amazing? I'm just your classic *strong woman*. What's crying? Never heard of it."

"That's not what I meant." He leans back, grinning. "You know, you're very good at showing me when I'm not good at things."

It's probably meant to be a compliment, one that I'd normally take pride in, but it flashes me back to Tyler's comment from the other day, about how I say what I mean and don't feel bad about it. Kearns's music gets louder in the radio of my mind. *Grab my hand and make me jump, then leave without a glance.*

"So I've been told," I say softly.

Joseph makes a small sound, somewhere between a gasp and a sigh. "Shit. I wasn't trying to be an ass. I swear."

This makes me go tight-lipped, unsure how to play it. The more time I spend with Joseph, the less anger remains over everything that's happened between us. Then my mother's accusation rears its ugly head, making me second-guess my reaction to every single thing Joseph does. What does it mean to let him in, even a little? How will that look to her?

And then there's the whole admission of his sobriety last night and the knowledge that he has an unopened whiskey bottle sitting in his trailer at all hours, waiting for him like a threat. I'm starting to feel responsible for him in more ways than one.

"It's all good. Let's get going."

There's a loaded energy in the room. We attempt to rehearse our way through it, but Joseph's left foot won't stop shaking. Every few lines, he gets up to pace.

"I can't remember," he mutters when he fumbles the same line again, our fifth or sixth run-through. It's a simple one. *Of course you can* is all he's supposed to say.

I've read it enough that even I know it by heart. I know the entire scene, actually, so he's telling the truth.

"This really hasn't happened to you on your other jobs?" My question comes out more curious than accusatory this time.

Joseph gives it great consideration, his eyes roaming every corner of his trailer like an answer will pop out behind his tea collection. "Of all the movies my dad's done, my mam's favorite was *Twilight on Clarke Street*," he offers up. He waits for my nonexistent recognition. "That's the one he shot with Guy."

"I've never seen it," I admit. "I've heard it's good."

"It is. We didn't really talk much about Dad's stuff growing up. Mam wanted us to be normal. That's why we stayed in Ireland while Dad went all over the world. But that was the one movie of his she let us watch."

My parents never let me miss a movie of theirs. Ratings were not guidelines that mattered in our household. I was eight when I saw a sex scene with my dad in it, which wasn't anywhere near as shocking and confusing as my mother's death scene in a very intense thriller I watched at age six.

"Not to bore you with my process here," Joseph continues. "But I usually take projects because I like the idea of the experience more than I care about the final product. I'll sign on if it's a different character than anything I've done before. Or it's a chance to live in Prague for two months. Or my team thinks I should do more action. Or I want to work with the director or something. And I *do* want to work with Guy and Tyler," he makes sure to clarify, holding up a hand as if to silence my objection. "But really, I took this job because it would mean something to my mam."

The dead mother card is a strong one, and it's not one he seems to be playing for effect. In fact, there is no effect here at all. He's as open as he was last night, free from the flourish he puts on for most people.

He pauses to look at the photo on the counter. "She'd be signing the cross if she knew what I was doing in the love scenes, but you know, of the few flicks of mine she saw, she always preferred my more sensitive ones. And she'd like knowing that Guy's here with me. She thought most Hollywood people were snakes. But she always liked him."

"Guy's a good egg," I confirm.

"This is the first time since she died I've let myself try to do something she'd appreciate. Really try. You know what I mean? Not phone it in for a paycheck or make it count because I know there could be award buzz. So of course I'm total shit."

"I can understand that. But you're being so hard on yourself right now that you're forgetting what makes you great at acting in the first place," I tell him.

"You think I'm great at acting?"

A small cough escapes me. "I think you need to relax. Take it line by line and not place so many expectations on yourself all at once." I hesitate, knowing now I have to bring up what I should've asked first. "What's different about right now? Why are you missing your lines again?"

The air gets tight once more.

"I dunno," Joseph lies. "Just lost myself for a bit."

All of this tension, I realize with surprise, is over *me*.

He wants to get things right between us, and every time he's so much as tried, I've been there with my arms crossed and one eyebrow raised, daring him to fail.

I haven't been wrong to do that. I know I haven't. He deserves to be held accountable. But I haven't been giving him room to change either. He's shown me he deserves that too.

"Joseph," I blurt out when we're out of his trailer and he's well on his way to prosthetics. "You're not gonna fuck this up today. All right? You're ready. And you're *good*."

He turns around. Even with enough space between us for a school bus to safely park, I can see the way a smile sneaks up on him. He melts into it, slow and serene, the quiet reveal of gratitude on his face piercing straight through me.

"Nice thing is, if I do fuck up, I can blame you, right?" he calls back. "Thank Christ you're a *strong woman*."

Guy is one of those people who can't help but mouth along to whatever someone else is saying. Ever since I privately talked to him today about giving Tyler space to do her thing, he's doubled down on his silent mimicry, the ghost of Tyler's every sentence on his lips.

She's asking Haven to be softer. To sit in the space longer and let her conversation with Joseph be more patient. It's meant to be a slow-burn romance. Right now, it's feeling rushed.

Joseph waits at his mark. He has an elbow leaning on the couch, and he's looking around, tapping his foot to a beat only he can hear. Our eyes meet. I'm about to look away when he points to something behind me.

My father has come to set.

A small crowd is already forming around him, as it always does when Dad enters a room. Someone asks how he's doing, and he fakes at grabbing his chest, then does a throwaway gesture, rolling his eyes, as if to say, *Heart attacks! So hilarious!*

One by one, the remaining crew shifts their attention to his arrival. Tyler stops midsentence, noticing Haven's gaping.

"Alexander!" Guy billows. "What a lovely surprise!"

A shadow of annoyance crosses Dad's face. "Hey, Guy. Good to see you!" He moves from his small crowd to accept Guy's warm embrace.

In all the years Guy has been married to my mom, I've never heard him say anything but glowing things about my dad. He seems to genuinely like him. What he doesn't know is that my dad cannot stand him. It's the first thing Dad mentions after every function where they're forced to interact. For a man well known for his easygoing persona, Alexander Ford is deeply rattled by someone even more easygoing than him.

Side by side they make a funny pair. Powell once pointed out that they look like Arnold Schwarzenegger and Danny DeVito in the movie *Twins*. It's all I can ever think about when I see them together. One time Powell even photoshopped Dad's and Guy's heads onto the movie poster and sent it to Tyler and me in a group text. What I wouldn't give to see them dress alike in real life.

"Let's go ahead and take a five," Tyler says, defeated.

Why waste time getting garbage footage when every person needs to get the Alexander Ford excitement out of their system? Free from responsibility, most swarm him like bees to a hive.

It's only when the crowd redistributes that I see my little sister Sarai is here too. Somehow she's even taller than she was the last time I saw her, which was only two weeks ago. Built like Tyler, shooting straight up with nothing adding on elsewhere, with jet-black curly hair and brown skin like her mom's.

She makes her way over to me.

"My mom told me you guys are behind schedule already," she says, so perfectly on the cusp of childlike sweetness and preteen edge that everything she does manages to make me self-conscious, even when it's not meant for me.

"Basically. But we're doing better now. Although Dad dropping in unannounced probably won't help," I tell her.

"I told him we shouldn't come yet. Do you want me to make him leave? Because I will." Her arms fold across her chest as she looks up at me, waiting for the go-ahead. She reminds me so much of myself as a kid when she gets like this. Desperate for respect. Eager to prove she can hang.

"Let's wait a little bit before we go kicking Dad out. Let him have his fanfare."

She rolls her eyes. "He needs it."

Her ability to cut right to the heart of the matter is a large part of how I ended up here after all. When we were all huddled together at Cedars-Sinai, waiting to hear how Dad was doing after the heart attack, I looked around the room and realized that I'd turned down a part in this movie for no reason other than my own pride. I'd first refused the project based on some perceived notion that doing period pieces would make me stuck in the genre forever.

Then it became about casting Joseph Donovan.

Then it was about how mad I was at all of them for not considering my show schedule.

But I'd just been killed off *The Seeker*, and Dad was on the verge of death, and taking the movie meant spending time with the people I loved most in the world, and it seemed like the silliest, pettiest thing I'd ever done, not accepting a part that had been written for me to play.

I blurted, "What if I told you I could do it?" right as Tyler told Powell, "Haven Church is playing Elise."

Tyler halted. "Wait, what did you say?"

I avoided her eyes. "Nothing. Shouldn't the doctor be updating us soon?"

"No. You said you could do the movie."

"It was a random hypothetical," I lied.

"No it wasn't."

"It absolutely was."

Sarai overheard us bickering. "They killed her off of her show," she announced to the entire room, a secret I'd revealed to my dad that she'd overheard.

My entire family stopped what they were doing and looked at me, downright mortified. It takes a lot of work for a crime show to randomly murder you off when you're a lead, and every single one of them knew it. Mom, Guy, Tyler, Powell, Melanie. Dad's girlfriend, Daya. Even Melanie's new husband Terrence understood that, and he's a tax accountant.

For a person who chose a life in the spotlight, there has yet to be a glare quite as harsh as my entire family casting judgment upon me all at once. They all had this despairing look, like they'd just been told their childhood dog had bitten someone and needed to be put down.

"*Sweetie*," Mom whispered.

"She told Dad because he's the only one who wouldn't freak out," Sarai informed everyone, once again correct, and excellent at riling up a crowd.

I wanted to be mad. If it were Powell, I'd have been pulling his hair. But it was Sarai. Sweet baby Sarai. My sister young enough to be my daughter, with the megawatt smile and the eager hope for approval. The baby whose birth healed more rifts than could even be listed, uniting our sprawling clan. She was the one who made us into the big, strange, unconventional blended family we are.

I was powerless.

"Your timing couldn't be worse," Mom had said, as if that could ever possibly make me feel better. "We've already finalized things with Haven. It's a done deal."

Powell was almost choking on his own laughter. I slapped his arm for good measure.

"We might be able to bring you on as a producer or something though," Mom pitched. She was already pulling her phone out of her pocket and typing. "That's not out of reach with shooting starting this soon. As long as we can have you on set every day. We could use the extra eyes. And I—"

Then the doctor came in to tell us that Dad was recovering nicely, and the rest was history, all set in motion by the eleven-year-old standing in front of me, missing the first top molar on either side of her mouth, making her grin look infinite.

When the hysteria fades to a low roar, Dad actually leaves a crowd he's entertaining to come find me.

He looks good, but his face is wearier than I've ever seen it. Still, there is a magnetism about him that's hard to qualify. I've only felt it around a handful of other public figures. President Obama. George Clooney. Tom Hanks. No matter what he's wearing or how exhausted he looks, you can sense he is someone you should know. Mom used to call it an aura. Whatever it is, it's palpable even when he's dressed down in a navy-blue quarter-zip pullover and old boat shoes.

He wraps his arms around me and squeezes.

"You feeling good?" I dare to ask.

"Heard you're holding the whole thing together around here," he says, blatantly ignoring my question.

"Who told you that?"

He tips his head in Joseph's direction, who is most definitely looking our way.

"Don't we hate him?" One of my favorite things about my dad is that he loves to gossip, and he loves to declare a secret enemy. At least *he* believed me when I told him I hated Joseph back in the day.

"He almost made me quit acting, yeah," I say, hedging.

"Right. And then your mother cast him without telling you. I remember now." Dad takes a beat. "He's Michael Donovan's son, right?"

"Yes. And his illustrious family legacy has once again landed him a role he does not deserve." My disdain sounds so false it's almost cartoonish.

It lands wrong even for my father, who furrows his brow. "I do like his dad."

"And I like Kearns's sister. Bad people can have good family, Dad."

At this point I'm playing a character instead of speaking the truth, because I can't remember how to talk about Joseph anymore.

Mom appears beside us with her arms crossed and one eyebrow raised. "Would you look what the cat dragged in." She kisses Dad on both cheeks, then takes another scan of him from tip to toe. "Color's coming back to your face. That's good." Her attention shifts from Dad to me. "Is he the reason we're on break before noon?"

These are her first words since our fight. It's bone-chilling in a way, how easily she slides into using me to start a little snip with Dad. So comfortable I almost accept it in lieu of an apology, because it's the most familiar she's been all week.

"Tyler wanted Haven to clear her head a little more before we kept shooting." I'm fumbling, not wanting to be involved. It's not necessarily a lie. More like a flexible version of the truth.

Mom shakes her head. "I take *one* meeting off set, and the rope goes slack." She narrows her eyes at Dad. "I'm sure you swinging by unannounced hasn't helped much."

"I thought you told me I could stop by whenever I wanted?" he asks.

"Didn't Melanie tell you we're already behind schedule?"

"Is ten minutes really going to derail the whole shoot?"

"Don't act like you don't know the value of ten minutes, Alex."

They are in their groove now, tossing quips like they're playing a lazy game of catch, daring the other to drop the ball.

"I'm here to watch, Kitty," he says, as if he isn't aware of the effect he has on a crowd. As if production didn't come to a complete halt at the mere sight of him. "And to get a family dinner on the books for this weekend. It's been too long."

"We're busy."

"Not on Sunday night you're not. Sarai knows the schedule through Melanie." Dad smiles, knowing he's caught her. "I'd like everyone to come to my place around six. We'll finish up early."

Mom takes a step back and looks out at the crew, pointedly ignoring Dad's request. "Does everyone here want to make a movie, or are we all still gaping at my ex-husband?"

There's polite laughter from most crew members and then a lot of hustling, each person hurrying to their appropriate place on the set.

Joseph makes a pit stop to where I'm standing. Under his breath, he says, "I can see where you get it from." He pats me on the shoulder before returning to his mark.

Mom takes an extra glance at the space where I can still feel the warmth of his hand, her face caught between a grin and a scowl.

7

Week Two of Production

Two skyscraping white columns frame the front door of Dad's estate. The older I get, the more I recognize this entire aesthetic as excessive. It's very Dad. He loves things that look important. His collection of antique pianos. His Tesla. The family Christmas cards where we all wear black turtlenecks.

Some of it is done in a tasteful way. That's thanks to the long list of powerful women who have loved him enough to rein in his vision over the years. The latest is a twenty-eight-year-old comedian named Daya Suvarna, who stands between the columns, waving as I drive up.

Daya is the freshest voice to enter the comedy game in a long while. Way too funny for Dad, and obviously too young, but his resurgence as a genuinely hilarious sitcom star has placed him into a whole different dating pool. Daya cast him on the sitcom she writes and stars in: *Lucky Strike*. It's about the daughter of two Indian immigrants forming a bowling team with her parents and some of the locals in town. Dad plays the owner of the bowling alley.

Never in my life would I have thought he'd agree to play such a lovable, airheaded doofus on camera, but he's brilliant on it. The closest he's ever come to playing someone like the real him, the one that exists when there's no one around with a press badge or a camera.

"Sloane!" Daya cheers when I get out. "You're right on time." She has her long black hair up in a chic topknot, and she's wearing a cream mock-neck tank under a black flare-leg jumpsuit, bright red lipstick perfectly popping against her brown skin. She looks so effortlessly casual and cool I can't help but feel a bit ridiculous about the fact that I'm running five minutes late because the jeans I really wanted to wear still had that smoothie stain on them.

"Is everyone else here already?" I ask.

"You want me to tell you no, but the truth is, most of them were an hour early." She leans in closer. "Your mother got here at three, just to prove a point."

"Welcome to life with my parents."

I thought it would be impossible not to focus on the fact that Daya is two years younger than me and dating my father, but she's so confidently herself that she won me over almost instantly. The rest of my family was a tougher sell. She convinced them to like her in the hospital room after Dad's heart attack, when she filled up a bout of tentative silence by saying, "Guess my poison finally got him." It was a statement that should have crashed and burned, but her delivery was dry and full of so much sarcastic conviction we all cracked up. If there's one thing my family respects, it's guts.

And levity. That was the first time we'd smiled since we got the news.

"Your family is really hard to know," Kearns once said. "I feel like they all hate me."

I never told him that they did. Now that he's singing songs about me on every late-night talk show that will have him, I wish I had.

Daya ushers me through empty, spacious rooms, chasing the sound of chatter in the formal dining space. It's where we spend most holidays together, a backyard extension with a gigantic zebrawood table that seats ten.

Every seat is already filled except for one. Dad at the head. A seat open for Daya. Sarai to the left. Melanie and Terrence beside her. Powell sitting at the other head. Tyler beside him. Mom and Guy.

And Joseph fucking Donovan.

As if things aren't awkward enough, here he is laughing with Guy, sipping on a glass of water, cheese board remnants on his side plate. They've already set out the main course buffet-style on a long table against the sidewall. Waiting for me, I guess. A thousand questions on the hows and whys sit poised on the tip of my tongue, ahead of all my greetings for my family.

"There she is! My Sloanius!" Dad declares, getting up to hug me. "We were worried you weren't going to make it."

It's truly only seven minutes past the hour. "So you gave away my seat?"

He takes inventory of the room. "Well, shit!" he says, cheery as ever. "Lemme go in the kitchen and grab one of the stools."

Dad's exit catches Joseph's attention. "Have I taken your spot?"

Everyone's casual talk fades to nothing, waiting for my response as if I am the queen of this particular chair, about to give an official ruling. "Hi everybody!" I deflect, forcing a small wave. "Sorry for being a few minutes behind."

"You're always late," Sarai states. This garners more snickers than I care to hear.

Joseph is already up and improvising. "I can lean against the wall."

"Don't be silly, Joe," Mom chastises. "Alex is getting you a chair."

Daya follows Dad out of the room, saying something about the stools being the wrong height and needing one from the other dining table instead.

Tyler's girlfriend isn't even here, and she lives with her. Why in the hell has Joseph Donovan made the cut? And why is it affecting me this much?

"Please sit," Joseph insists.

"It's fine."

Naturally, Joseph gets up to wait beside me, neither of us wanting to sit in the coveted chair until another one is available.

"You don't have to do this," I whisper to him.

"Yes I do," he whispers back.

Dad and Daya finally return with an extra chair. After much rearranging, it's decided Joseph will squeeze between Guy and me. It's so tight we are truly elbow to elbow.

"Lucky for you, I'm left-handed," I tell him.

"I know," he says.

Our dinner begins with each of us getting up to fill our plates. The spread is classic Dad, his grandmother's spaghetti recipe, baskets full of freshly baked rolls, and several different salads. We haven't had one of these family dinners since Sarai's birthday. It's such a comfort, even in the chaos of this production. To smell the garlic and tomatoes. To hear the Steely Dan spinning on his record player. To see everyone in one place. Dad's two ex-wives. All of my siblings. Everyone's new spouses.

And Joseph Donovan.

Dad kicks off the meal with a secular prayer for the continued health of our whole family. Listening to his speech, it's impossible to think that this almost disappeared. That we almost lost him.

It's so overwhelmingly sad I push the thought away and dive into my food, hoping there comes a time when I don't tumble toward despair during every visit with my father.

It doesn't take long for the group conversation to move toward *Horizons*. Mom and Melanie start shooting their scenes together this week.

"You two are playing lovers, right?" Daya asks, pointing at the two of them.

"Right," Melanie says. "So Kitty's the mother, and she's got Parkinson's. I'm the nice lady down the hall who's been coming over to keep her company when her daughter isn't home." She wiggles her eyebrows at Mom, who shimmies her shoulders back.

They each have a new husband in the room, so it's hilarious how Dad is the one most uncomfortable with all of this, practically itching as Mom and Melanie fake flirt across the table. They love it, of course, amping it up to piss him off. Melanie has on a long blue shawl, which she lets slip off her shoulder just so, revealing the matching tank top she wears underneath. She's done boxing and Pilates for decades, in such good shape I'm positive she could lift up this table and bench it if she wanted. Her hair is up in a colorful protective wrap that accentuates her neck.

Daya, good sport that she is, starts clapping. "I truly cannot wait to see this."

"It's going to look magnificent!" Guy chimes in. "Tyler has a plan for it that will entrance the audience! She doesn't need this old man at all!" He sneaks in a wink to me.

Right when Dad is about to choke on a piece of the garlic bread he made, Mom and Melanie pull back, laughing.

Powell, brat that he is, has to add a punch-up anyways. "My score is going to be *sensual*," he assures, teasing.

He makes no mention of the fact that he's been on set every day since the blowup between Mom and me. No other composer needs to visit daily to understand what kind of music the movie requires. Powell is there to keep the peace, because he's always been the Mom whisperer, her last-born child but her number one lackey.

"It'll be *something*, that's for sure." I take the dig solely to watch Powell's cheeks redden in indignation.

He was born with an excellent ear. Barely a day passed that Mom and Dad didn't discuss it, even post-divorce. It was the one thing they agreed upon: Powell's otherworldly gift for music.

"Fuck off, Sloane," he curses.

"Fuck yourself, Powell," I curse back.

"That's enough of that," Dad says, stern. "Sarai is here."

"You say fuck all the time," Sarai adds.

Her timing is so hilarious that Tyler and I die laughing. We lock eyes from down the table, this whole sequence uniting us so fast we've forgotten all that's transpired in the last few days. The realization dawns on both of us at the same time, and we sit back in perfect unison.

"Hey now," Melanie warns. "I don't care what your father says in private, we don't speak like that at the dinner table."

"Sorry," Sarai mumbles. Her watering eyes remind me she's only eleven, and she can't yet see how funny this will one day be to her.

"No, no. I'm sorry. I started it," I say.

Mom shakes her head in disappointment. Suddenly I'm right there in the trenches with Sarai, feeling embarrassed for no real reason, fighting not to show it on my face.

Our meal continues with the usual industry talk. Mom plays coy on whether she'll act again after this. Sarai complains about not being asked to be in the movie. We make it all the way around the table, ending on Powell explaining what he's planning for his upcoming drag show.

No one asks what's next for me.

Pretending not to notice, I lean into Joseph. "Who invited you to this?"

"Daya," he tells me. It's the most random answer of all, made stranger by the fact that he follows up with "And I have no idea why." He takes a bite of spaghetti. "Nice company, though."

I assumed it was Guy. Or maybe even some cruel test from my mother. Daya is a plot twist. Why would she want Joseph here? I try to recall the whole meal, remembering the few times she attempted to pull Joseph into the conversation at large, each effort stifled by someone else shifting the talk in a new direction. She'll learn eventually that anything you want to say in the family has to get out in under five seconds or it's lost forever.

When Dad and Daya leave the room to bring out dessert, the conversation turns to Joseph.

"Ready for tomorrow's sex scene?" Guy asks him with a mischievous laugh. It's cruel timing made even crueler by the fact that this is a land mine of a talking point.

Tomorrow will be another closed set.

"Sure." Joseph's leg presses into mine ever so slightly, some sign of solidarity that I think I'm making up until he turns to me and makes quick but meaningful eye contact, reminding me he's very aware of the entire dynamic between my mother, him, and me.

Dad and Daya interrupt the moment by bursting into the room carrying a huge sheet cake with an active sparkler atop it, fireworking upward in an explosion of golden light. The spectacle is *almost* as bright and shiny as the gigantic diamond now on Daya's left hand.

"We're engaged!" Dad and Daya announce in unison.

8

My mother calls me on my drive to the studio, at 6:04 in the morning. My hair is in the same half bun I slept in. Without looking down to check, I'm almost positive I have on two different shoes. I am running so behind I didn't even stop for coffee. So there is no room in my morning schedule for an argument over today's closed set, or Dad's new engagement, or Joseph daring to look at me, or whatever it may be.

Mom calls again. And again.

The repetition makes me panic. Maybe everyone's slightly awkward, hasty departure after the engagement announcement triggered another heart attack from Dad. It sounds preposterous at first, but after call number four, I'm convinced I'm correct, picking up the phone with tears in my eyes.

"Finally," Mom says before I even greet her. "Haven won't go nude."

"Huh?"

"Haven is refusing to go nude. We negotiated all of this in her contract. It's only the side of her left breast. In a medium shot. She gets to choose which take she likes best. And we hired that woman specifically to manage all of this stuff. Make sure it's all done *correctly*." I can practically hear the air quotes in her voice as she talks about our intimacy coordinator, as if she's angry that we've made progress toward making actors feel safe at work when she never got the luxury. "Now Haven's saying she doesn't want to do it at all." This is one hell of a way to finally open the line of communication between us. She reads my stunned silence as permission to keep talking. "Of course that's all we're shooting today. She couldn't tell us this two days ago? No. She had to let me know last night after I got home. Via text."

"Maybe she's changed her mind. Let's get to the lot and find out before we panic." As the words leave my lips, I realize my error.

"If you'll recall, I'm not allowed today," Mom reminds me. "She's already called me this morning to say she won't do it. Since you're the only producer there, I need you to handle it."

Now my made-up job is important to her again. "I'm not forcing her to get naked. No one has died from a lack of side-boob in a movie, Mom."

"Sloane, I have to get to yoga. I start shooting tomorrow, and I *will* be doing my nude scene. Make sure today's taken care of." She hangs up on me without a goodbye.

She doesn't even have a nude scene.

When I arrive on the lot, Joseph is sitting outside his trailer holding an iced coffee.

"I thought you were a tea drinker," I say.

"This is for you, actually." He hands me the coffee, then stands up to let me inside. His teakettle is whistling. "Consider it a peace offering."

"For what?" The iced coffee looks delicious but I don't take a sip. Instead I set it down on the coaster he keeps out for me and my love of drinks with condensation.

"Am I wrong to say things have been a bit strange between us?"

"Define strange," I bait. "Attending my dad's engagement dinner at the request of his next wife strange?"

He hesitates. "Before that, actually. Didn't I break one of your rules when we went to the diner? You asked me not to run my mouth about anyone on this set. I went and did it anyways, talking about Haven."

"Oh. Yeah."

His eyes don't meet mine. We both know the weirder part is what my mom said, but neither of us needs to mention it.

"Is that Joseph Donovan I see? Staring into his mug like his tea leaves are telling him a fortune?" I ask in my most exaggerated impression of him, every word coated with his lilting, lyrical way of speaking.

The callback makes him grin. "I promise you, from now on, these lips are sealed." He makes a zip gesture and tosses away an imaginary key.

"Hold on a second. There may need to be an addendum to the rules." I explain to him what's going on with Haven and how my mother expects me to handle it.

"Christ alive. Tell Haven *I'll* get naked. If your sister and Guy want a tight shot of my ass, they can have it. Free of charge."

I have to laugh.

"All this time, all I've had to do is agree to nudity to get you to laugh at me?" He sits beside me on the couch. "I dunno how much she will listen to me, but I can talk to Haven. I did convince my mam to let me get a tattoo when I turned eighteen. This can't be any harder. Of course I convinced my mother after it was already done."

"Maybe." I finally sip my coffee. It's a cold brew with a splash of cream, exactly the way I like it. "Thank you for this, by the way. I was running so late I didn't have time to pick one up for myself."

"Don't mention it. I figured you could always use another. I'm just glad you came."

I'm glad too, I think to myself.

We try to go about our usual rehearsal process, but neither of us can focus. Haven's trailer is right next to Joseph's, and every time we hear someone walk by, both of us flick the blinds to see if it's her. Eventually I suggest we relocate to the steps of his trailer to watch for Haven's arrival.

There's not enough room for us to sit side by side, so Joseph ends up on the ground in front of me, my knees pressed into his back. It feels easy to have him rest against me. Nice, even.

I shudder, but I don't move.

Our stakeout in plain sight goes on for a long while. Joseph entertains me with a song his dad made up when he was a kid, set to a tune I know but can't place. His version lists the names of all his siblings.

"Dad came up with it so he wouldn't forget everyone when they'd ask about us in interviews. I swear it," Joseph tells me.

Donald, Lizzie, Patty, and Joseph too.
Declan, Caleb, with Rose the last one through.
A family of seven babies, all from one wee lady.
She's cute and she's sweet, a rare little treat.
My angel Margaret girl.

There's a tenderness to his singing voice that reminds me of Kearns. Something truthful about where he sings from, but smokier than Kearns's voice. More unfiltered.

When Kearns used to sing for me, I remember thinking it was like seeing the inside of his heart somehow. Like the sound of his voice came from someplace deep within him, a private chamber of truth he bravely showed to the world. Now I know what it's like to be on the other side of that. To be the darkness someone sings about. The target of their growling, angry heartbreak.

I think I'd like it better if Kearns's voice sounded like a lie.

"Six siblings? I have a hard enough time with three," I say to Joseph.

"And there's twenty-three years between Donald and Rose. With me smack-dab in the middle." He looks at the time on his watch, knowing he should be on his way to prosthetics by now. "She'll come," he assures.

"It's funny. You don't have middle-child energy."

"What does that mean?"

"Like Tyler, she's a middle child. Now there are four of us, but growing up, she was the one between Powell and me. And she's always had this peace about her. It's not even like she's quiet or forgotten or whatever they say about middle kids. It's this ability to complement all kinds of energies. She can hang with a group of, I don't know, gamers in the same way she can hang with a group of kindergarteners. And she's the exact same with both groups, and they both leave loving her. She got away with absolutely everything as a kid, because if she was left out of something, you'd end up missing her too much."

It hurts to say it. To miss her this much myself while seeing her every day.

Joseph folds his arms across his chest and leans away from me. "Are you saying that a group of gamers wouldn't accept me into their fold? I haven't been given a chance to try. It'd be harder without throwing back a few pints, but I think I could find a way in.

When I really want something, I'm pretty damn good at figuring out how to get it." He pauses. "And kids love me, I'll have you know."

"Easy. I get it. You are beloved by all who know you. Trust me. I'm clear on that."

He half laughs. "Hardly. I'd say I'm dead last in my family in terms of favoritism."

"Really? Why? Don't you wiggle your eyebrows at them and do your usual 'I'm a wee jammy bloke who can get away with it all' thing?"

He turns back to look me in the eye, startled recognition all over his face. "You are the only one besides my family to call me on that. They all make fun of me whenever I'm home. My older brother Donald refuses to watch any interview I do on American television. He says I sound like a leprechaun."

"If you know you're doing it, why do you keep it up?"

"When I started leaning into being Irish, I started to book jobs in the states," he explains.

It's quite a candid thing to admit. I've sat across from countless industry people with visibly different noses or jawlines and listened to them tell me they've never had work done on their face. I don't even judge them for it. Everyone has a right to their secrets.

Hearing the truth is refreshing nonetheless.

"Plus it makes my dad gloriously angry," he adds. "His brogue has faded from so much time here in America. He doesn't appreciate me sounding like more of a countryman than him."

We're so wrapped up in conversation that we don't see Guy and Tyler approach us. From the breezy mood radiating off them, they must not know about the nudity issue yet.

"Why are you sitting outside?" Tyler asks. "Not that I mind," she quickly adds on. "It's good. Just curious."

"This is a grounding technique I begged Sloane to try with

me. What I need to find my character," Joseph tells her, so dry it reads as truthful.

"That's the spirit!" Guy pats Joseph on the back. "Nothing like the smell of fresh air to get you out of your own way! I always start my mornings with my bare feet on grass, no matter the season or the place." He gives Joseph a kiss on the forehead. "Good work."

"Thanks for doing that with him," Tyler says to me mid-Guy-forehead-kiss.

"It's no problem." I'd be lying if I said it wasn't at least a little satisfying, to see her cool demeanor peeled back for me.

"See ya soon," she says with a weird wave.

"To another great day!" Guy adds. They continue on toward set, leaving Joseph and me alone once more.

"Why didn't you tell them about Haven?" I ask.

Joseph leans his elbows on the step behind him. His muscles pull against his shirt, the barest hint of his lower torso exposed. "I was liking this conversation. Wasn't ready for it to end yet."

It warms me. Against my better judgment. Against everything I've told myself for weeks.

Years, really.

But I can't commit to forgiving Joseph all the way, because that feels like a betrayal to the younger me, the one who promised herself never to let a guy like him charm his way out of consequences.

She didn't know what I do now. That she really was meeting him at a bad time. That doesn't cancel out what he did, though. And it makes me worry that at the slightest sign of trouble, he's going to become that person again. It doesn't help that in the back of my mind, there is the memory of how Kearns warped my vulnerabilities into villainy and made me out to be a fool.

I hate to be a fool.

"Why didn't *you* tell them?" Joseph challenges, right as Tyler reappears. Her pace is quick and scattered, her head whipping in every direction. Joseph takes a resigned breath before getting up and opening his trailer door. "I'll try calling Haven."

I hear the ringing on the other end. And the click to voicemail. Over and over.

"I don't suppose we can shoot B-roll of my ass for the next twelve hours?" Joseph jokes.

Somehow Tyler, Guy, Joseph, and I end up in a production van on the way to Haven's apartment. Our driver battles weekday freeway traffic to the best of his ability, which is to say that we spend a lot of time sitting, waiting. Not even Guy Cicero is speaking.

"This feels like that scene at the end of *Notting Hill*, when they're trying to get to Julia Roberts's press conference," I offer up, hoping to lighten the mood.

Joseph nods in appreciation. "Great flick."

These are the last words spoken in this giant black van, aside from our driver letting us know we've arrived. We unpack one by one, no game plan discussed beyond Guy whisking us away saying we have to "go get our girl."

There's no open parking where Haven lives, so the driver drops us in front of her high-end beachside apartment complex. It smells like salt water, the ocean right across from where we are. Palm trees and impossible blue skies, gentle waves rushing in, this whole setting would look fitting on a postcard. Too bad not one of us cares to preserve this particular moment.

If Haven's not answering calls, do we really think she'll answer her door? I wonder to myself but don't dare ask aloud. Pointing this out may bring everyone to tears.

Joseph saunters up to the lobby attendant. Folds his arms and leans his elbows on the counter, giving the kind of eye contact designed to make knees buckle. "Hello there." He looks down for a second to read the attendant's name tag. "Darren. Hello, Darren. Could we be let up to Haven Church's place, please?"

The obvious, appropriate answer is no, but the young man clearly recognizes Joseph. He swipes his card to give us access to the elevator and directs us to room 1153.

"I hate that that worked," I tell him as we click upward floor by floor.

Joseph runs a hand through his hair. "Better than standing in the lobby though, isn't it?"

"I don't know. You queer-baited the attendant to get us here."

"Who says it was bait?"

My phone vibrates within seconds. It's a text from Tyler. I knew I'd never root this hard for a man that was completely straight.

Aren't you always saying no one in this town is completely straight anyways, I answer.

Because they aren't, she responds.

There's no answer when we ring Haven's doorbell. Guy takes to rhythmically knocking, pasting on his wide, gap-toothed grin and singing out Haven's name. Tyler chimes in with gentle taps on the door. "Haven, please. If you're in there, come out. We've got a whole crew waiting for you and nothing else to shoot today. We don't need the nudity. Please. Just come to the door."

The dead bolt clicks.

Haven appears, wedging herself into a small space between the door and the frame. She's wearing a matching lavender pajama set, her bright blond hair is piled into a bun atop her head, and her eyes are red from crying. Without all the makeup, she looks younger than twenty-three. And terrified. "Why did your mom say I had to go naked then?"

Tyler gives me a quick, panicked look. Our mother's refusal to step out of her antiquated mindset is truly going to tank this movie. "Because she's a contract woman. She was going by what you signed off on. But she forgot to run it by me beforehand. I don't think we need it. If you'd like, you can leave your slip on altogether."

Joseph's hand flicks into my side. I make eye contact with him, and he gestures toward Guy, who has backed away from the door to have some sort of existential crisis. He's mouthing Tyler's words while furiously shaking his head as if trying to exorcise a demon from his body.

"The beautiful thing about this movie is that the connection between Elise and Calvin is so well established that a hug between the two of them would be electric," Tyler continues. "We could sell the whole moment with a look, if we wanted."

Guy might pull a muscle in his neck he's so dismayed.

My phone goes off. It's my mother calling. Surely Tammy the AD has told her by now that her directors and her lead have fled to the coast to attempt a rescue mission.

I show the screen to Joseph. "This isn't good," I whisper into his ear.

"Hasn't been since Guy stole a production van and drove us to the beach," he whispers back, his breath brushing against the baby hairs on the side of my face.

"Haven," he says louder, sauntering toward the door. "I've been in this position a few times before. The person everyone's waiting on. I know you've got your reasons, and they're a thousand times better than any shit excuse I ever had. But I promise, you'll feel much better if you come to work. We all will. I think every person here would be glad to do this scene whatever way ya like best. Contracts be damned."

Haven takes an apprehensive step forward, still in her pajamas. Joseph coaxes her on with the same gentle hand an animal welfare person would use to rescue a frightened stray.

To the relief of us all, she keeps moving.

We take the stairs instead of the elevator, a silent, eager processional, as if constant motion will keep her from being upset. Maybe she's more like a newborn baby? Whatever's going on, Tyler and I keep a moderate distance, with Guy at the back, muttering to himself. Apparently nudity clauses mean a lot to him.

All the while my phone vibrates on and on, Mom persistent in her efforts to reach me. There's no way I'm answering. Not until Haven is in full costume—be it a slip or her birthday suit—and we're setting up the first take.

But Kitty Porter is a smart woman. When we're one floor above the lobby, it's no longer my phone going off. It's Guy's.

"Hello, sweetheart," he answers.

"What the hell is going on?" Mom asks, the phone volume turned up so loud she might as well be inside the stairwell with us.

Tyler grabs my arm in a panic. Joseph looks at me with wide eyes. Now it feels like we're covert ops on a mission that's seconds from failing.

"Sweet sunshine," Guy says, soft and calm. He must think we can't hear the other side of this conversation. "Everything is perfect."

"Then why are there no actors or directors on this set? Thank god I was able to come in, even though I'm not *allowed* to be here. As much as I'd love a chance to drive to the beach and build sandcastles, I guess I'm the only person on this entire team who was hoping to work today."

"My sweet, all is well. We should be back soon."

"I expect this kind of shit from my children, but you? You have to take the reins or—"

"Yes, dear. We'll take care to be safe. I love you too." He hangs up. "Sorry. Just my beautiful wife calling."

We reach the end of the stairs. Haven comes to such an immediate halt that I almost fall into her. Joseph opens the door from the stairwell to the lobby, and he's waving her through. But she's not moving.

"Everyone hates me." There's a waver in her voice, the last little sonic blip before a tidal wave of tears.

"No, no, no," we all assure, a desperate chorus.

"I know everyone thinks I suck. Now I'm putting us behind, and you're all getting in trouble for coming to get me. And it's all over my boobs."

"Boobs," Guy echoes, for no apparent reason.

After an awkward beat, Tyler goes, "Just so unnecessarily sexualized."

I shake my head at her.

"This is a *big deal*," Haven continues, thankfully oblivious. "This whole thing. I started on Nickelodeon, you know? I thought I wanted to do something more mature like this. But I'm not ready." She sits cross-legged on the floor, firmly on the stairwell side of things. "I can't do it."

"Haven dear, when you're old like me, you'll wish you showed a breast or two," Guy tries. Even Joseph knows this isn't the way, and he shakes his head as furiously as Tyler and I do.

"Don't listen to him," Joseph says.

Haven starts crying into her hands. I take a seat on the floor beside her. Wrap an arm around her and let her cry.

"I booked my first movie a few months after I graduated

college," I start, unsure if this is the right time for this story. Better to try than never know. "It was this horror film called *Because You Said No*. And funny enough, because my mom said no to me getting naked, I agreed to go fully nude for it. Both boobs. Butt. Even crotch. Oh, and covered in blood."

Haven looks up at me, shocked. "Really?"

"Mm-hmm. And I thought I didn't care at all. That morning, sitting in the makeup trailer in just a robe, I was totally calm. A body is a body, right? I get to set, and I take off the robe. I'm fully butt naked in front of a small crew of mostly men. And someone comes in with the blood bucket. That's when I start to feel my breaths turning shorter and shorter, almost hiccups. I'm getting teary and panicky. A stress rash breaks out across my chest. The director notices it and goes, 'It's gonna be covered in blood. It's fine.' And the blood bucket guy is like, 'Can I dump this on you?'"

I take a beat, remembering the cold shock of that moment. The reality that no one cared that I was scared. They cared that production would continue. It was go big or go home, and I didn't want to go home.

"I didn't think I had a choice," I tell Haven. "So I shot the scene as I agreed to it. Which at the time I thought was brave. Now I know it was bullshit. They didn't end up using the full-body shot in the final cut, but you do see my boobs and the top half of my butt. That's not even the point. The point is that you *do* have a choice here. You really do. I'll make sure of it. And any person on this set that dares try to make you feel bad for being nervous will have to answer to me first. You're a human being. You're allowed to be scared. But I've got you."

At least thirty seconds of echoing silence pass, everyone fixated on the girl sobbing beneath my arm. Suddenly, she stops. Stands up and wipes her cheeks with the back of her palm. Straightens out her pajama set and readjusts the lopsided bun on the top of her head.

"Let's go," she tells us, completely anew.

No one moves.

"Hurry, before I change my mind!"

We scurry toward the door, tripping over our own feet. We're out of the apartment complex and nearly sprinting toward our production van. Haven isn't even wearing shoes. I finally remember to look at mine, and they are in fact two different sneakers: one black, one gray.

Before I climb into the van, Tyler grabs me by the arm. "You always say you loved doing that scene."

"That's because it makes Mom mad. And at the end of the day, I don't mind anymore that I did it. But they were assholes about it on set, without a doubt."

"I'm sorry that happened to you."

I tilt my head toward Haven. "Best thing we can do now is make sure it doesn't happen to her."

Haven's mood seems to lighten with every passing mile. She sits beside me in the first back row, with Tyler, Joseph, and Guy in the far back.

The entire ride, I can feel Joseph's eyes on me.

Unfortunately, no one bothers to tell my mother about my motivational speech, because as soon as we walk onto set, she pulls Haven into a meeting.

And she fires her.

9

I used to tell people the longest week of my life was right after my mom filed for divorce but my dad didn't want to leave until he had a new place, so he moved all of his stuff into the living room. For seven whole days we lived in some kind of Alexander Ford pop-up store, walking through stacks of old scripts and piles of my dad's clothes to get to the kitchen. Sitting atop a mountain of blankets and pillows whenever we wanted to watch TV, careful not to knock Dad's gigantic mobile phone off the coffee table.

It was the first time I realized how awkward life could be. How hurt people do irrational things because they can't process their own pain.

And honestly, how petty actors are.

That week doesn't hold a candle to the last four days since Mom fired Haven. My phone causes me so much stress that my stomach starts churning at the idea of another phone call. If it's not someone on our production team, it's one of our lawyers trying to reach Mom. All the while she's been deep in the world of her character, shooting her scenes with Melanie. I have to marvel at her ability to shut everything out and do her work. It's almost eerie.

Joseph hasn't been here. There's not much Calvin without Elise in this movie. My job as acting coach is sidelined. I've taken on most of Mom's responsibilities instead. Turns out my fake producer gig is not so fake anymore.

In between takes, Guy and Tyler watch videos the casting director sends them. They're circling back to a few names they'd been entertaining before they hired Haven.

All the while, I keep thinking of that final day of Dad in the living room. How when I woke up that morning he was packing up the last of his belongings. He looked me in the eye and said, "Sloane. Listen to me. Don't ever let your pride get in the way of your happiness."

I was eight. I had no idea what he meant. What stuck with me was the way he said it, like I was his equal. It made me feel important in the exact way I'd always wanted to be. I pressed my hands onto his cheeks and told him I'd never forget.

Every morning on my drive to set, I ask myself if this is the day I pack up the boxes, so to speak. Put pride aside and go for my own happiness. Then my phone goes off and I'm disabling another delicate land mine over the Haven firing, telling PR people how to handle the press. Ignoring the questions over whether any of this will be addressed at my annual foundation gala, which is getting closer and closer.

I've also been working to figure out how to rearrange our shooting schedule to accommodate a recasting without tacking extra days onto production, which is actually impossible, and we're definitely going to need an extra week, but we're trying anyways, because that's like seventy percent of what Mom's job is. Pulling off impossible things for the sake of saving money.

The solution to a lot of this is obvious. It's downright glaring. But no one has offered it up, and I can't bring myself to say it.

Was this how it felt on day five or six for my dad, trying to read scripts on the couch while Mom made us peanut butter and jelly sandwiches in the kitchen? How many times did she ignore his presence before he realized she'd done her part, and she wasn't going to give him any attention until he did his? I hated my mom then, for deciding that we were all better apart than together.

I understand her now. How she held her ground while her entire world crumbled. She kept her chin up and kept moving. And I understand Dad too, refusing to give up. The both of them stubborn as mules.

No wonder I am the way I am.

When we break for lunch, Tyler sits beside me, tossing me a bag of salt and vinegar chips while she eats a veggie burrito.

"Dude. Mom is really good," she says, whispering through her chews. "Everyone always talks about Dad. But if this ever actually gets released, they're going to be talking about her."

"Hopefully it's not just to say that she should have let the part go to an actually queer actor." I can't help but dig. For all the extra work I've taken on, Mom has barely uttered more than a cursory thank-you to me.

Tyler hasn't said anything at all, moving out of her awkward stage and into treating all of this like it's completely normal. Like *we're* normal, she and I, instead of near strangers to each other.

"You do know that Mom is bi," she says casually.

"Stop it."

Powell plops down on the other side of me with the same burrito Tyler has. "She dated that French actress," he tells me. "Pauline Carteaux. Before she met Guy."

"I think I'd know if that were true." I shove a chip into my mouth. The vinegar is so tart my eyes water. "Pauline was her best friend."

"That she brought to Christmas and took on a Hawaiian

vacation?" Powell flips up the lip of his water bottle and hands it to me. "Trust me. I'm her favorite. I know all."

"Oh stop. She doesn't have favorites," Tyler says. "Just children that she likes better."

She types something into her phone and then shows me the screen. A flood of photos of Mom and Pauline Carteaux from the early 2000s pop up. Pauline is tall and slender, the kind of long-fingered French ingenue that used to make cigarette smoking look chic. The pictures show Mom and Pauline holding hands while walking out of a restaurant. One is a shot of Mom whispering in Pauline's ear, her hand holding Pauline's neck just so.

My childhood memories of Pauline begin to take new shapes. The delicate gold-and-sapphire necklace Pauline got me that Christmas, far too sophisticated for a ten-year-old, which made it a perfect gift for me. I wore it for years. Even had the chain fixed more than once. That Christmas morning, when I opened the box and squealed in delight at what was inside, Mom had squeezed Pauline's leg. They shared this private look I always assumed was about me. But it wasn't.

It was about them.

"I really thought Pauline was just her best friend," I repeat.

Pauline was around so much and suddenly disappeared. I never gave it a second thought. In grade school, I brought a different friend along for our family vacations every year. By about the eighth grade, I realized that my only real friends were my family anyways, so I stopped trying to squeeze someone else into the equation. The same seemed to be true for everyone else.

Year by year, the family social circle grew smaller and smaller until only blood or marriage remained. After a life of people making assumptions about us, it became easier to only be around the people who'd lived it all beside us.

"Well, Mara is my best friend *and* my girlfriend. People can be both," Tyler says.

"*Second*-best friend," I correct, taking a bite of her burrito. "After me." It sounds so hollow. If Tyler dared to push back, even a little, the statement would collapse.

She doesn't. She keeps chewing, staring at her burrito like she can't miss a single bite, ignoring the fact that I've already stolen one.

Powell dabs at the corners of his mouth. "Have you never googled Mom before? It's pretty common knowledge. And also part of the reason people got so pissed at her after the divorce. They thought she was gay and the marriage to Dad was a sham, and since it was the nineties, he was a hero for getting out of it. And because Mom wouldn't publicly deny it, the projects she had lined up all magically *went in a different direction.*"

White-hot rage washes over me. For Dad in the living room. For Mom's career. For Mom shaming me for supposedly wanting to sleep with Joseph. For her firing Haven without considering how hypocritical she is for doing it.

For me wearing that necklace long after Mom and Pauline had split, no one clueing me in that it might be upsetting to her to see a daily reminder of a failed relationship proudly worn by her oblivious child.

"That's such bullshit," I say.

"Yeah, dude," Tyler says. "I thought we talked about this before?"

"Somewhere along the line we forgot to have the 'Mom is bi-sexual and the patriarchal media let that ruin her career and she still hasn't unpacked all of that and instead harms others along the way' conversation."

Tyler's eyes widen. "She said she'll talk about all of that when we do press for the movie," she skirts. "So no worries on the straights stealing queer parts. And like I always tell you—"

"*No one in this town is really straight anyways,*" I finish. "Yeah, yeah. I didn't realize you were talking about our parents."

"As far as I'm concerned, Dad has spent his whole life pining for Harrison Ford. But that's a personal conspiracy theory," Powell offers up.

Suddenly, it's clear to me what metaphorical boxes I have to pack. They aren't the ones I thought.

Mom doesn't have a free moment until late into the night. She's in her costume: a dark blue cardigan and a wool shift dress in gray, loose but still flattering. Her hair rests on her neck in a casual low bun. There are a few tendrils out to frame her face. She looks perpetually exasperated and elated, sighing out after every take like she's gotten off a roller coaster. I find her sitting in her chair paging through her script.

"Can we talk?" I ask.

"Don't tell me. Haven's agent is threatening to blacklist me? Let him try. I can't help that she didn't honor the terms of her contract. Business is ugly sometimes. No one is famous enough to stop an entire day of production over the side of a boob."

"Her agent *did* call, but that's not what I wanted to talk about."

I'm about to give up when I think better of it. Nothing will change if I don't try.

"You didn't fight for her. Don't you wish someone would have fought for you back in the day?"

It's a cheap shot, but it's true.

"Sloane, look me in the eyes and be honest. Was she any good in the first place?" Mom asks.

"That's not the point." Two seconds into this conversation and we're already falling farther away from each other.

"Of course it is," she counters. "It might ruffle some feathers, and I am more than willing to take the brunt of the trouble, but at the end of the day, I did what was best for this movie."

The hypocrisy continues to astound me. Firing Joseph was a non-option, yet she pounced on the first chance to let Haven go. "I can't believe I was actually coming over here to say sorry to you," I hiss out.

Mom almost laughs. She holds the script still, her finger resting on a highlighted line of dialogue. "For what?"

My throat wants to close up around the words. "For how I treated you after you and Dad got divorced."

She squints her eyes for so long there must be some glaring typo that no one's caught. "Please." There's a manufactured lightness in her voice. "That's all water under the bridge. You were a kid. Far from the worst thing any of you have ever done to me."

It's such an obvious dismissal. The kind of thing you say when you're still very hurt but you're not expecting it to be acknowledged. If I ever want to be better than she is, to actually learn from her mistakes, it requires owning up to my wrongs while still keeping space for the hurt that's happened since.

"I know. But I've been thinking about it. And I'm sorry," I say firmly.

Mom sets her script down on the chair. Stands up and takes a step toward me. Places one hand on either shoulder. Stares deep and long, far longer than I'd normally allow, but curiosity has me willing to see where this is all going. "Don't dwell on the past so long that you forget how to live in the present."

It's been a while since I've heard one of her inspirational adages. They are her biggest defense mechanism, I realize. Well-curated sayings that sound so nice and simple that people want to nod in agreement. But she doesn't actually follow them. That's the thing. Her entire career as a producer is built upon dwelling on the past.

"Do you think you actually do that?" I'm fighting to keep the wind in my sails and continue on my apology mission. "And sometimes people do things in the past that they should be held accountable for," I add, thinking of her but also of Joseph.

She looks off to where Melanie is sitting. "Mel," she calls out. "Come here for a second."

Melanie readjusts her boots before standing up. It's a classic actor sight. She's in a chin-length, pin-curled black wig, white blouse, and long blue striped skirt, same color as the earrings she wears, all perfectly 1940s chic, and then gigantic, fluffy boots on her feet.

"Don't drag me into a fight," she warns.

"How did we get over the both of us being married to Alex?" Mom asks her.

"Oh good lord, Kitty. Why are we trying to have this conversation at eleven o'clock on a Friday night? It's not going to be that long before the shot's set up."

"Sloane here asked me if I think I dwell on the past or if I move on, and I thought that there was no one better to talk about that with than you."

Melanie's left eyebrow arches. "I see."

She thinks for a long while, crossing one leg over the other. "You have to remember that in the beginning, Kitty and I were holding so tight to our own pettiness that we couldn't even be in the same room. The PR spin was that we were all friends though, so they seated Alex and me at the same table as her for the Golden Globes one year. Kitty and I got so drunk we were ready to throw punches during commercial breaks. And then I got pregnant with Sarai, and the one thing everyone could agree on was that we wanted her to know her siblings. So Kitty and I met for lunch to come up with a game plan. Now that another kid was about to be in the picture, we had to figure out how the hell we were gonna deal with each other. I sit down, and before I can say a word, Kitty goes, 'I don't like you because you got everything I wanted but couldn't have.'"

I look to Mom then, finding her nodding. She breaks into a small smile. "I went into that meeting saying, 'Screw it, I'm going to tell her the complete truth. If all the cards are on the table, we can figure it out.'"

"When she said that, I leaned back and told her to keep going. And she said that Alex could never handle when her success seemed to be bigger than his. And he sort of supported her, but he never encouraged her. That when she got that Oscar nom, he didn't smile right away. And when he got his the year following, he gave himself a little fist pump. Did it again when he won. Small things that don't seem like much, but when you're married to someone, they're huge. I knew the two of them didn't split because of cheating, and I knew that they could be competitive, but I'd never heard her side of it. She started explaining things to me about Alex. Things I didn't like hearing, if I'm being honest. When she was done, I said, 'Okay. I hear you. Now I'm going to tell you my side.' And I said I didn't like how she seemed to still feel entitled to Alex because she'd had his kids."

"It got heated," Mom adds.

"Oh. We were yelling. Whispering, but yelling. Our waiter stopped coming over. Neither of us touched our food."

"I definitely left that meeting thinking I'd made things worse, not better," Mom says.

"Same for me. But when Kitty and I saw each other again, it felt like, 'All right, I know what you're about.' When she'd try to nose her way into Alex's schedule or act like she knew things about him that I hadn't learned yet, she'd look at me and get correct. And when Alex would hype me up in front of her, talking about projects studios were developing for me, I'd tell him to keep his mouth shut for a minute."

Mom puts a hand on Melanie's shoulder. "We grew this quiet respect for each other."

"Sarai came, and Kitty was one of the only people outside of my own family to start checking on me. Not checking on Sarai and me, but *me*. Making sure Alex was letting me get enough sleep. Asking if I had enough time to get out of the house and get some air. Offering to watch Sarai anytime I needed to catch my breath. It was annoying at first, I'm not gonna lie, but then I realized that she was doing it not to prove she knew more about Alex than I did, but because she wanted to make sure I got what she didn't. She ended up being the first person I called when I was thinking about leaving him. I knew she'd understand. Your dad is a good person and a good father, but after a while, loving him is like trying to hold on to a live wire. Kitty didn't try to talk me into it or out of it. She listened to me. And when I ultimately decided that your dad wasn't the man I wanted to be with for the rest of my life, it was Kitty who came with me to get the papers from the court." Melanie laughs. "So yeah, I'd say she can move on. Past that damn lunch, we didn't owe each other anything, and she kept showing up anyways."

"You were stuck with me," Mom says, pulling her into a side hug.

Melanie squeezes back hard. "We make a good team. Used to drive your dad up a wall, until one day I said to him, 'Is there a reason you want all the women in your life to hate one another?'"

"That one cut him deep. He called every woman he knew. His aunt. His sister. One of our old nannies," Mom tells me. "You know your father doesn't like when people hold a mirror up to him. But he learned. He can be a little stubborn, but if you prove him wrong enough times, he does try."

Mom and Melanie share a big laugh over that, proud members of the Alexander Ford Ex-Wives Club.

How can she not see the hypocrisy? It's because she doesn't like the mirror either. Here I am holding it, and she's using it to show me something else entirely. To distract me.

Cruelly, I think of Kearns's song. *You're just smoke in the mirror, so afraid to see the truth. Light a match and burn me down before you'll face the proof.*

It's time for the actors to take their places. Melanie excuses herself to swap out her boots for kitten heels, leaving Mom and me standing face-to-face.

"I'm guessing you were really looking for me to tell you I never should've said what I did about you and Joe," Mom says.

My lips stay squeezed shut.

"You're right," she adds. "I'm sorry."

It surprises me that she folds. At this point, I expected it to happen somewhere near my fiftieth birthday. Or maybe never at all.

"Yeah. That sucked." All the comebacks I'd planned to give her fade into nothing.

She leans closer. "No relationship is ever worth sacrificing your talent."

Somehow this apology morphed into another veiled insult. It all feels impossible. Right when we make headway in one direction, we backpedal somewhere else. "I agree," I say through gritted teeth. "If you haven't heard, I'm kind of the subject of a very popular album right now. Can't imagine I'll make that mistake twice."

Abruptly, Mom pulls me into a hug. It's stiff at first. Tense. But determined, her arms gripping hard around my torso. "I told you never to get that house in the canyon with him and Tyler. All those fruit flies. My god."

It doesn't make sense, but I hold her tighter. What she did continues to sting. There are so many ways I want her to love me better. Yet the beat of her heart pattering against my chest still fills me with relief.

I want to acknowledge progress. I also don't want to get hurt.

It feels like I can never win.

Mom breaks from me, dusting off the place where my head rested on her shoulder. She straightens her dress and takes a cleansing breath. "How do I look?"

"Perfect."

She turns on her heel to walk to her mark. "Oh, and when do you start?" she asks, her back to me.

"Start what?" I call back.

A makeup artist comes to do quick touch-ups on her face, freshening the soft mauve color on her lips. Mom rubs them together, then blots on a napkin. "You've been trying to get someone to ask you this all week. And your sister, love her though I do, is afraid you will leave, so she won't do it."

Tyler, who had been sitting in her director's chair talking something over with Guy and our DP, perks up. "What's going on?"

"Is everything all right, sunshine?" Guy asks Mom.

"Since none of you will do what's necessary, I'm offering Sloane the part myself."

One by one, every person on set turns in my direction.

"She's spent two weeks running scenes with Joe, so she knows the script. She's practically the same size as Haven. She'll fit into all the costumes. Her hair is too short and too dark, but we still have a few more of my scenes with Melanie to get through. Plenty of time to figure out an appropriate style. And she's already shown a great level of commitment to this project. I have no doubt she'd be ready to go as soon as needed."

I'm reminded of the moment in the waiting room after Dad's heart attack, when my family found out I'd been fired from *The Seeker*. The spotlight once again shining on me without warning.

"Plus there are no worries about whether or not she will go nude, as evidenced by the fact that at the age of twenty-two my beautiful baby girl turned over not just her breasts, but her entire body to a no-name director for a horror flick that only grossed eight million dollars domestically." Mom wags a finger at me. "Lucky for her, this is directed by the best in the business. And there is no better name to go at the top of the marquee than the one we all wanted in the first place: Sloane Ford."

My eyes well up to the midline.

Without the unnecessary shame around nudity, if she'd said all of that to me that day on the phone, I probably would have taken the part.

Yet she didn't.

And these circumstances are far from perfect, but for once, she's giving me something not because I am her daughter, but because I've worked for it.

Tyler gets out of her director's chair and comes over to me. "I kept thinking you'd bring it up if you wanted to do it," she tells me meekly. "And it's okay if you don't. I get it. I just want you to be *here*."

"I tried to pull you aside the very day we fired Haven!" Guy informs me. "Alas, these wise women said this was a sensitive topic that required time. I hope we've given you enough."

"You have," I say.

"And?" Tyler urges.

It's been months since I've wanted a part. Years, really. All this time I thought I was done. Inching toward a retirement at the ripe old age of thirty. Feeling this right now, I know I was waiting. I had to crawl my way back to this work.

To love it again.

"I'll do it," I say. "I'll play Elise."

The whole soundstage erupts in applause.

10

Week Three of Production

I can't believe my prayers have finally been answered!" my manager, Glori, hollers, loud enough that other patrons look over at us. "Sloane Ford is doing a period piece."

We're on the covered patio of a popular breakfast spot, the trellised wall behind me decorated with various succulents. There's a nice summer breeze coming in, cooling the nervous heat that's settled into the core of me. Our server places a votive candle on our table and tops off our water glasses.

"No. Sloane Ford is making a movie. That's all."

"Yeah, yeah. Whatever helps you sleep at night. Can I just be glad to take you out to a celebratory lunch for landing a huge part?"

Glori is Gloria Shields, a sixty-three-year-old white woman from New Jersey who proudly buys most of her clothes at Marshalls, then happily tells anyone who will listen about the $3,000 full-body laser treatment she just got done. She is a walking paradox and a gut punch of a woman, and there's no one I'd rather have as my manager.

Even when she pisses me off.

"A part I landed because my mom fired the person who came before me," I remind her.

Glori gives me a warning look. "It does not matter if you're the best actor in the entire world. People will still say you got where you are because of your parents. And they're not wrong. Your parents did give you this life. But you're the one who controls where it goes. And you tried to throw away a perfect opportunity because you were afraid of being boxed in. Now the opportunity's come back around, and I say it's time for you to stop worrying about what other people are going to think of you. Go and do your job. Show them why it had to be you. Regardless of how it happened."

"Yeah." It's a sad world when the only person left for me to celebrate with is also someone responsible for my career. "Wanna hear something weird that only you will find interesting?" I pivot.

"Of course I do."

"I got a ton of texts when the announcement went out yesterday. Certainly a lot of people coming out of the woodwork for this. But *The Seeker*'s very own Daniel Traverson *called me*. Three times. I didn't answer."

Glori takes a long swig of coffee. Her lipstick, a sleek magenta that matches her nails, transfers onto the rim. "That's so strange. Must've really wanted to congratulate you," she says. "Oh, by the way, tell me how it's going with Joseph Donovan after all."

I narrow my eyes at her. "What do you know?"

"Why do you think I know something?"

"Because you love to talk about Daniel Traverson. You once

told me you watched *The Seeker* for him, not for me. You begged me to try to date him. Now I tell you he called me three times, and you're changing the subject."

"Eh. The past is past. I'm more interested in the roguishly handsome Irishman who nearly ended your career before we even got it started."

"No you're not," I challenge.

There are few people in my life as predictable as Gloria Shields. I've never seen her nails painted a different color. I can order for her at every restaurant we've ever been to together. When she finds something she likes, she holds on forever. She used to be Dad's manager too back when he was still married to my mom. Mom loves to joke that it was hard to say who was more hurt when they split: her or Glori. It was over twenty years ago, yet Glori still gets a scowl on her face when she talks about Dad's career. He won his first Oscar on a role she convinced him to take.

"Based solely on the amount of emails you've sent me where you've referred to me as Sloane Traverson, I know there's something to this," I add.

"You're still off social media, right?" she asks.

"Yeah. I haven't really been on since Dad's heart attack." The amount of negative energy on there was like a spout flooding me from the inside out.

"You're not gonna like what I'm about to tell you." Her hands wrap around her coffee mug. "Remember that night you were telling me all about how you didn't want to do the fifth season of your show?"

It was raining, and Glori and I were both sopping wet when we sat down for dinner at our favorite Italian restaurant in the hills. I spent most of the meal begging her to find a way out of my contract. "Of course I do."

"All of this is being published with a heavy dose of *allegedly* and *supposedly*, but *apparently* Daniel Traverson's mother was sitting next to us. She heard what you said about the show. And she told Daniel, who told the showrunner, who decided to do what you asked and ax you."

"Are you kidding me?"

"I told you you weren't going to like it!"

"Why the hell is Daniel calling me then?"

"The story broke yesterday night after your casting was announced. It's a pretty boring scandal, if I'm being honest. I'm not sure a lot of people even believe it's true. It all seems pretty ridiculous. Of course we know it's probably real, because that conversation was real. If Danny Boy is calling, it's to look out for his mommy. And himself."

Daniel Traverson's mother was a woman next to me at a restaurant. Like any of these people around me now. And instead of saying hello, she listened to my private conversation with my manager and got me fired for it. *Allegedly.* And it's so frustratingly ridiculous that it's hard to know what to do with the information other than sit and take it in and marvel at the fact that I work in a business where something like this is possible.

I did my job. I was never late. I didn't blow my lines or say rude shit to the crew. I only complained in private. After all the horrible actors and directors I've worked with, gritting my teeth and smiling through their bullshit, it's *me* who was the problem?

"Remember, it's all good press in the end," Glori says. "And personally, I think Daniel's mom comes out looking like the clown here. But that's just me."

"Except now people know I'm an ungrateful asshole complaining about my six-figure job over a two-hundred-dollar dinner and then stealing a part in my family's movie."

Glori shrugs. "We've all got ugly sides, Sloane. You happen to be in the business of constantly showing yours to the world." She waits a respectful two seconds before jumping back into her real interests. "Now tell me about Joseph Donovan. Is he single? Do you still hate him? What is the deal?"

I end up arriving late to my hair appointment, my lunch with Glori running over and my fitting taking longer than I expected. I passed the time by opening up Twitter. The first thing I saw was the Deadline article announcing I'd been cast in *Horizons*, my photo beside Joseph's. Haven quote-tweeted it saying she was truly excited for me and it was all for the best. There were at least twenty comments beneath it mentioning how my mom fired Haven to make room for me.

That was enough to make me shut off my phone altogether.

When I park, a single paparazzo yells my name from across the street. I pay my parking meter and keep my focus on the salon, watching the pap through my peripherals. He snaps shots and calls out questions like, "Is it true that Daniel Traverson's mom had you fired? Do you regret what you said? Will Daniel still play at your gala this year? Have you talked to Kearns Adam? What about Haven Church? Is it true you two spoke?"

Back in the paparazzi heyday, there were times when our family was greeted with forty or more flashes outside the grocery store, or my martial arts studio, or the gates of our old Bel Air complex. It was like being in the eye of the storm, the way they'd follow us with mere feet of breathing room, a perfect circular swarm of sweating men with flashing cameras, staying with us all the way into Dad's Range Rover or Mom's Mercedes. Not giving up until we were on a street too busy to follow on foot. They'd sell pictures of Tyler, Powell, and me in the back seat of the car, Powell crying because he was always crying as a kid, and they'd run a story saying the divorce was destroying our family. It was surreal, being followed by a herd of strangers who thought they knew my life better than I did. Mom and Dad taught me to keep my eyes down and continue on my way.

This single paparazzo is harder to ignore than forty weird strangers. He's one bored guy chasing the big C-plot news story of the day with half-hearted interest, not even bothering to cross the street, and he manages to wedge loose a tidal wave of past memories within me.

Clutching my dad's hand so tight the sweat between our palms made it hard to stay latched on. Staring at my shoelaces to avoid the lights, Mom saying that looking at the camera was giving them a piece of my soul. Powell tripping and falling into the crowd of men, for a moment swallowed up not just by their flashes, but their bodies.

My hands are shaking by the time I open the salon door.

"Sloane! We're so excited to see you!" the lead colorist says when I enter. Four members of their team are waiting for me and only me. "Champagne?"

"God yes. Please." She hands me a small flute, and I drink it down in one gulp, the pleasant fizz not as much of a balm as I'd like it to be. I feel restless. Trapped inside my mind and desperate for a break.

"Thank god. It's a lighter brown than we thought. We pulled up clips of you from your show. This color reads darker on-screen," the colorist says, combing through my hair with her fingers. "We can get you to a reasonable blond tonight." She walks me over to a chair to begin.

Who should spin around in the seat next to me but one Joseph Donovan.

"We meet again as costars," he says, doing another three-sixty for extra flourish. He's got on a pair of black cropped denim jeans and a short-sleeve chambray shirt, a pair of tortoise Wayfarers tucked into the chest pocket. The top three buttons of his shirt are undone, showing off a dog tag necklace.

I almost drop my empty flute. "What are you doing here?"

"They asked me to come in to make sure your hair color looked good against mine."

"You're going to sit through a five-hour appointment with me?"

In disbelief, he looks to the colorist. "It'll take five hours?"

"And that's just today," she says.

"I have to come back tomorrow to finish it. They want it as blond as we can get it in the time frame without breakage."

The stylist musses with my shoulder-length bob. "And there might be extensions," she adds.

"There might be extensions," I echo.

"Christ," he mutters.

"Thank god I'll have some company." I was attempting to sound sarcastic but find something far closer to the truth than I expect to hear from my own mouth, especially when it comes to my new costar.

He grins. "Right then. Let's make an Elise outta ya."

It's a long process. Everyone on the style team talks about my hair like TV surgeons talk about lifesaving operations. I can't help but feel guilty for not having the best possible texture and follicle porousness for a six-shade lightening process done on an impossible timeline.

Joseph's presence comes as a welcome distraction. He details what he's been doing with his off time. Taking boxing lessons in the early morning. Trying to rebuild the engine of a classic car for a few hours in the afternoon. That's how he got the Camaro, I learn. It was an interest of his older brother's that he picked up on out of sheer boredom as a kid. Now it's a bit of an escape for him, tinkering with vehicles whenever he can. He's also been spending his nights reading through the stack of World War II novels and memoirs he got for research.

He's someone who always needs to be busy. To be moving. It's one of the countless quirks I've figured out over the last two weeks. He eats very slowly because he's always doing something else at the same time. He seems to have a mild aversion to pigeons. And his mother was definitely his favorite person on earth. She comes up often, his grief manifesting in many fond retellings of the countless ways she filled his life with purpose and love. I notice too how little he mentions his dad, and how formal it is when he comes up. He sounds like me talking about any of the friends I made after eighth grade.

I run him through what he's missed on set. The plan for an updated shooting schedule, putting the love scene reshoots at the very end of production, tacking on an extra week. It's easier to discuss with him when I treat all of it as business. Powering through the awkward parts with the same direct energy I've seen my mom use daily.

Nothing more casual than talking sex scenes with my costar. The guy my mom thought I was so desperate to sleep with I almost gave up my life's passion over it.

"I nearly fell off my chair when I saw the announcement," he says when I finish explaining how we will need to get the second kissing scene and the sex scene done in one day.

"They didn't tell you?"

"Nope. Neither did you, might I add."

It crossed my mind more than once that I should have reached out and texted him. I even drafted a few jokes about how all our rehearsals will pay off. Before Haven's firing, we'd gotten into character backstories and world building outside of the script. We'd improvised scenes that happened at different points in Calvin's life. We'd learned these two people from the inside out.

And now we will play them together.

Exactly as my family always wanted.

"It was Method," I say. "I was embracing all the war-torn years Elise and Calvin spent apart without communication."

"But they wrote letters."

"Keep your eyes peeled for the mail in the next few days. You never know."

"Don't get my hopes up."

The lead colorist stops mixing to laugh at us. "You two are going to be great together," she says.

I give her a gracious thanks, feeling a full tidal wave of nerves crash over me. This isn't the two of us in the trailers making sure Joseph has his shit together. We can break it down into scheduling and costumes and location shoots and hair colors and script changes, but at the end of the day, this is a movie about Joseph Donovan and me as lovers.

And unlike *A Little Luck*, we're not enemies in real life anymore.

After they rinse out the second round of color, I move to a corner and FaceTime Tyler as promised. She's standing near set, Elise's apartment behind her.

My apartment. It's mine now. The thought forces me to steady myself against a drying station. Taking on this role has become something that continuously shocks me. It's all happened so fast I can't seem to hang on to the reality of it.

I show Tyler the current color. Several shades darker than Haven's, and a touch too warm against my skin tone.

"It's almost there," Tyler says. "I kind of like it shoulder length. What do you think, Guy?" She turns the screen to him. I prop my phone against one of the styling counters so I can rotate side to side to give him the full view.

He does several chef kisses. "A vision! Exactly how I imagined you when I wrote this!"

Mom appears in the background, walking closer. "Can someone get me my readers?" A PA hands her the frames off-screen. She puts them on to appraise me. "Color's wrong, but I don't mind the length. We can work with that. Maybe even an inch or two shorter? Wish I could see you beside Joe."

"Oh. He's here. So you can."

"He's there?"

I grab my phone from the counter and move to the farthest corner possible. "Of course," I say with an even tone. Joseph's off talking it up with other people on the color team, so far oblivious. "I told him it would be a good idea to see how my color looked against his hair."

"Definitely," Tyler agrees, fully fearful we're in for Sloane versus Kitty, round two.

"Have you heard what Daniel Traverson did?" I pivot.

It proves to be a good distraction, because they've been so busy they haven't heard any of it. When I'm done explaining the story, Mom says, "We should sue," right as Tyler asks, "Are you going to release an apology?"

"Do you think I should?"

"God no!" Joseph has come near me again, apparently having listened to the better part of the Daniel Traverson saga. "If all of us had to apologize for the private conversations we've had about this business, there wouldn't be a single working actor still going."

"He's not wrong," Mom agrees, her eyes flitting quickly between us. Scrutinizing. "And if you say something, it proves the story is true. I change my mind. We won't sue. I'm just in a suing mood."

"But I look like such a privileged asshat trying to get off that show," I counter.

"You *are* a privileged asshat!" Powell yells from off camera.

"So are you!" I yell back.

Joseph starts pacing. "So is Daniel Traverson for using his mam to get you removed! Is he seven years old? Christ!"

"Again, he's not wrong," Mom echoes, her mouth forming a hard line. The same expression she had when she came out of her emergency meeting with Haven and announced that she'd been released from the production. "We have to get back to work. It will all be for the best, Sloaney. Go lighter on the hair. And remember what I said the other day! See you!" Her finger reaches for Tyler's phone screen and presses, leaving us in black.

No relationship is ever worth sacrificing your talent.

As if I could forget.

Joseph is still in his own world of upset. Arms folded as he treads the same five-step path back and forth. I could brush his arrival under the rug, but it's honesty that's gotten us this far, and it's honesty that will keep this movie afloat.

"Why did you come today?" I ask him.

He halts. He must know that my family gave it away that no one asked him to be here, because he moves to form words that don't come out. One of the colorists tells me it's time to go back for the last round of the night, buying him some time to answer. Joseph takes all of it and more, staying in the back corner, his long fingers tapping along his lips as he stares off at a wall.

The lead colorist looks from him to me. "Lovers' quarrel?"

"Oh. We're not together."

She nods at me through the mirror, giving me that sage, smug face that says she knows more about my life than I do.

At once, Joseph resolves something and marches up to me. "Because I wanted to see you," he admits. "Because I think right now, you're my only real friend. Because if I spend one more day by myself in my house, I might lose it. So that's why I came. And I'm sorry I lied about it. That was shit. I'm working on it."

The lead colorist, her three assistants, and I all gape at him.

"I'm your only real friend?" My insides seem to be free-falling, and I'm fighting to find something to grab. "You don't even crack my top five."

"What about people you're not related to, though?" Before I can make up an answer, he grins. "See?"

"Daisy Montoya and I get coffee all the time."

"Rodrigo and Doyle. *The Seeker*'s most underrated pair. When's the last time you went to a diner with her at midnight, though?"

My cheeks are burning. "We do daytime meals, thank you."

"Then come to lunch with me tomorrow."

"I have my hair appointment."

"Christ. This should not take as long as it does! They wash some brown into mine. It takes twenty minutes!"

The lead colorist puts a hand on my shoulder. "If they don't want her as blond as Haven, we might be done tonight. One more round and we'll have a nice color on her."

"We're not getting lunch," I whisper, but he's not listening.

"Glorious," Joseph says. "Who can argue a nice color? I know

I can't. You tell me where you and your real friend Daisy Montoya go, and that's where we will—"

"We're not getting lunch!" I yell. "Okay?"

Even though I want to, I don't add. *Even though you're right, you're my only real friend outside of my family or Glori. Even though I think I actually like spending time with you.*

"No lunch," Joseph echoes, prideful. Almost mocking. "Fine."

Ever the stubborn fool, he stays through the last round of color, forcing his charm onto all of us in a way that still grates on me. All glimpses of the Joseph I know are gone and we are in full Brand Mode. He's clomping around, leaning on every available counter, batting lashes at anyone willing to make eye contact, saying words like *faffin'* and *jammy* and seeming to do it just to prove a point: that I know him well enough to know when he's not being himself.

When I'm ready to leave, he insists on walking me to my car.

The street outside the salon is quiet. Most of the other shops are long closed by now. It's still, only the rush of distant traffic thrumming in soft undertones. I try twice to go on the side closer to the street. Joseph loops around me both times.

"Christ, Sloane. Let me be the one to take on the possibility of a stray vehicle coming up onto the curb," he says when I try for a third time.

"Are you kidding me?"

"No. My mam was always very insistent on me being a gentleman."

I bust out laughing.

"At least I'm trying!" he protests.

"Fair, fair. You can bravely protect me from the bustling streets of Brentwood."

We make it to my Prius without any rogue cars obliterating us. "This is me."

He stands there, expectant.

"What?" I ask.

No response.

"Okay. *Fine*. Today was kind of shit. It was good to see my sixth-best friend."

"Aha. I knew it." He takes a step toward me, grinning. "I mean what I said earlier, about you being my only real friend out here. Everyone else is either a business partner or a shithead. You are neither."

I step back, my heart suddenly racing. "Easy, Joe. You have to remember what happens to people on set. We hardly know each other."

His eyes light up, blue and wide, like two open doors to oceans of possibility. "You called me Joe."

My breath catches. "I . . . sorry. Joseph."

"Don't apologize. I liked it. *It's what my friends call me.*"

"Everyone calls me Sloane."

"That's not true. Your mom calls you Sloaney when she wants something from you. I believe I heard your father call you Sloanius. Every once in a while, your sister calls you something strange. Bub?" He's leaning against the side of my car now, his elbows resting on the front hood.

There's an unexpected ease that's wiggled into our dynamic. And a deep knowing. It's still set life, I tell myself. This is what always happens. This is why I told him Daisy Montoya is my friend. Because you're strangers with your costars until suddenly you know their every tic. Fourteen-hour days will do that. You know what they like to eat and how they chew it. The way they act when they're tired, cold, cranky. What makes them cry. Who they're dating. Who they're avoiding. What their vices are and how they use them. And they know the same about you. Then the project ends, and so does the connection, and you realize it was all a larger act anyways.

It's still a job. Everyone is playing a role.

"I should get going. Another day of this tomorrow." I reach for my door handle, and Joseph wraps a hand around my forearm.

Our eyes lock. We're not Sloane and Joseph. Or Elise and Calvin. Suddenly we've become two people I don't know at all. Two people who care about each other. He holds on to me. Five seconds pass. Ten. It's a lifetime here, with his hand on my arm, his eyes boring into mine, but I don't want it to end.

"I'm glad it's you," he says, opening the door for me. Closing it behind me, then patting the top of my car.

I drive all the way home without any memory of being on the road at all. Only Joseph's hand on my arm and the way I felt when I was looking at him. Like I was alive. Like I was in danger. Like I was safe.

How in the hell am I going to do this movie?

11

My alarm goes off at the same time as always. But today I'm already awake and dressed, staring at the painting above my couch. Tyler made it for my thirtieth birthday. She said it's her and me standing at the edge of the world. Personally, I see two black smudges on a cliff of some sort, with pink and yellow flowers exploding out of the middle of each smudge. And maybe some stars overhead?

Okay fine, it looks like a mist of blood to me. The kind *The Seeker* crew would spritz onto the wall with a squirt bottle full of sticky red liquid. Tyler's painting uses blues and greens, but the effect is the same. Maybe someday I'll stop imagining the world as a place for a fake forensic analyst to solve crimes by dinnertime.

I should start trying to see it as Elise would. She's a writer. She'd instantly pick up on the black smudges being people. She'd see them as her and her mom, facing war and illness and poverty together. The stars would be memories to her. Pieces of her life scattered all around her, lighting all the dark crevices of the world. She'd see Calvin in there. He'd be the deeper blue specks. The ones that are colored like a rural sky settling into evening light. The ones that seem too far to reach without the chance of falling off the cliff where she stands.

Good god. I need to get out of my house.

I opted out of having a driver pick me up and take me to set, liking the peace of being completely alone on my way to work.

My first day is supposed to be an intense one. We're shooting a scene with my mom, Joseph, and me where Calvin gets a glimpse of what's changed since he's been away. This is the first time on-screen we see how Vera's Parkinson's tremors affect her daily life. Guy's own mother had Parkinson's, and a lot of this depiction is very personal to him, which is why I know it won't be easy. Mom has to carry the bulk of the scene, but it's important that Joseph and I show up for her.

That's what I'd tell Joseph at any other rehearsal. I'd encourage him to breathe out every expectation he has for himself and instead look his scene partners in the eyes. Let his choices come from what he's seeing, not what he thinks he needs to do to make the moment "good."

Yet all I can think about is how I have to nail this first day. They've fired a twenty-three-year-old with a huge following and cast me, a second-generation hack job who was once called box office kryptonite by a well-respected critic with no known mean streak. It's now as much my responsibility to make this movie work as it is Joseph's. And while I've fucked up takes in front of countless actors, I've never screwed up a moment for my mother.

My mother, who stepped out of the spotlight for almost twenty years. My mother, who is putting so much on the line for this film: money, pride, her identity. My mother, who trusted me to be the one to save this sinking ship. My mother, who was once shamed by this industry and saved all that shame up to place on me for no good reason.

Inside the parking garage, I recline my driver's seat all the way back and stare at the ceiling of my car.

"Siri, play the album *Fear of the Canyon*." Midway through track three, "Blush"—which has become an underdog favorite of mine for the fact that it's all about how sex with me was so unsatisfying it consistently made the both of us blush—there's a knock on my window.

Joseph peers down at me right as Kearns sings out, *"In the bedroom there's a hush. Not a sigh, only blush."*

I don't immediately put my seat into the upright position. It's better to see Joseph at this very humbling angle, looking up into his nostrils, which are ever so slightly different shapes.

"Don't mind me," I say, trying to find his face dissatisfying. I can still feel the way his hand pressed into my arm outside the salon. How everything inside me started to burn while we looked at each other.

"It's hard not to when you're putting on a free concert." He opens my car door. "His voice is even worse without the window blocking it from my ears. Tell me he didn't rhyme 'bedsheet' with 'deceit.'"

I turn off the music. "He did."

"He seems like a delight."

"He was, actually. That's the thing."

"Really?"

"Yes, *really*. He was a pretty nice boyfriend to have."

Joseph looks impressed. "What the hell happened to make him go around singing songs like that one?"

"I don't know." I'm ready to move on. It's as mystifying to me as it is to everyone else. For some reason, the way Joseph looks at me—full of open curiosity and a willingness to understand, as if maybe we can crack the code together—makes me continue.

"We broke up because he told me we'd grown apart and he was tired of everything always being the same. I was working a lot with the show, so I thought that was fair. I wasn't around enough. We never did anything fun. I thought it was a mature decision. I even respected him for it. Then he dropped a twelve-track ode to my every failing, and it turns out I'm the world's biggest fool, because after three and a half years together, he was still holding up this idea of me. Girl incapable of feeling, because life's been served to her on a platter. Even after all the time we spent together. That's all I ever was to him. The best part is that his first album was full of songs idealizing women, then tearing them down. And I thought I was *different*. I was *special*. But no, I was only a good idea that got old."

My actions catch up to my thoughts, and I realize I'm saying all of this to the last person on earth I want to be discussing Kearns with, and here I am pouring my heart out nearly unprompted. I unbuckle my seat belt and slide out of my car, avoiding making contact with Joseph's body. "*Anyways*. Let's get to work."

Joseph chases me through the parking lot and toward his trailer. "Why are you walking so fast? Wait up a minute." He manages to get around me as we reach his trailer door.

He opens it for me, and I step inside, ready to collapse onto his couch like I've done so many times prior.

Instead, anxiety locks up my limbs. This little trailer with its ugly boring furniture means too much to me. I don't want to screw this up for my mom and my sister and my stepdad, but I also don't want to screw this up for Joseph and his morning tea and his classic rock and his framed picture of his beautiful dead mother that he loves so very much.

"I can't do this." I turn to leave, but Joseph angles himself around me, pressing his body against the exit.

"Whoa, whoa. Hold on now. What's really going on?"

We're inches from each other, a phenomenon that has honestly never happened in my real life. It's something I've had to do for every love story I've ever filmed. The moment where the two people are unnaturally close, holding a conversation with their chests pressed against each other. I should move, back all the way up into the counters on the other side of the trailer, like any real-life person would. We shouldn't be talking about this with our breath blowing on each other. But it's so nice to feel his body against mine. To see the veins in his neck pulling taut. To smell his soap and his deodorant.

To watch a bead of sweat form along his hairline.

"I'm not ready for this," I tell him. "I haven't done any real research. I've never done a period piece. I won't be as good as the rest of you. No one in my family seems to trust me to do anything right. Why would they trust me with this?"

Joseph waits, letting my words hang in the air until I'm sure there's nothing more to add. Then he asks, "Do you know what I did last night?"

"Why would I know that?"

He smiles. "I watched *A Little Luck*."

"Shut up."

"I swear to God I did." His gaze softens. "You're brilliant in it, Sloane. That movie would have been a wash of hog shit if there was anyone but you with me. I'm bloated, half–in the bag, and grieving, and you still helped me to pull out a semi-decent performance." His hands work the edges of his shirt, pulling on a loose thread. "If you think you'll be anything less than spectacular in this, then you've been listening to entirely too much of that American boy's pathetic music."

"Please."

"I'm serious. I tell you what it is. He was afraid of your power. Same with Detective Colfax. Can't remember the bastard's name. Daniel Traverson. There it is. He was afraid too. Took the first chance he could to get you kicked off that show, because deep down he knew you're twenty times better than he could ever be, and that scared the piss out of him."

"If that's all true, why aren't you afraid of my power?"

"Don't give me that much credit. I'm terrified of you. Because you're the only person who has ever told me the truth when I needed to hear it."

"What is there to like about that?"

"Everything," he says, like it's the most obvious answer in the world.

It shouldn't mean as much to me as it does. Not after all I've promised myself about Joseph.

When he says things like this, it makes me believe in real forgiveness. But it feels too easy. Like a sleight of hand or a trick of light. I knew Kearns had written a prior album full of melancholic warbling about all the love he'd been denied, and I refused to accept that as a reality that could be mine.

It happened anyways.

There has to be another side to Joseph. A place where he buckles. Slides back into who he was. My attention shifts to the whiskey on the counter. I break away so we're no longer touching. "If you're sober, why do you keep this around?"

There's a folded card tucked underneath that springs up. The first two lines are visible.

Joseph, congratulations on landing such a prestigious role. I know—

"Yeah," Joseph says, seeing the card. He picks it up and reads the rest. "*I know it's not easy to take on a project with this much meaning. I look forward to hearing how it goes. Save me a drink for the premiere. Cheers, Dad."*

"Wow."

He neatens the paper crease so it folds flat. "I thought the whole thing was hysterical. Here I am, three years sober, clawed my way out of hell to get here, and my father sends me his favorite whiskey with a note that reads like a friendly threat. Figured I'd do him one better and not just save him a drink, but the whole bottle. I know it's not the best idea. But I look at it and I think to myself, 'Well, at least I don't have my head so far up my ass I'd send my alcoholic family member a celebratory drink.'" He points to the blanket on the couch behind me. "On the other hand, my youngest sister, about to turn twenty, knitted that for me when I got this part. I barely know her. She was born a few years before I moved to America. Of all my siblings, she's the most like my mam. Thoughtful. Sharp mind. She remembered that I used to have a blanket like that back home. I lost it in the move. I think I mentioned it to her maybe once in her whole life, and she made that for me."

"That's really sweet," I say. "Reminds me of Sarai. She's so much younger that sometimes she feels really far from me, but then she does stuff that knocks me over. And I realize that the years between us don't matter. We both get it."

"Exactly." Joseph looks again at the whiskey. "My dad's not a bad man, he's just a bit busy with himself. Always has been. So I keep it. Because even if it's shit, at least he was thinking of me. Which is the saddest part, I know. But you don't become an actor if you don't love to be sad."

It strikes me how well respected his dad is. How getting Michael Donovan attached to a project stamps it with the words PRESTIGE and IMPORTANT. He's one of the few people that's gotten away with being judged completely on the quality of his work, not the type of person he is off set. Michael Donovan could benefit from a touch more public accountability.

"I get it." I may not understand the details, but I know what it's like to want to be seen by a parent who's hurt you.

"I knew you would." He takes a seat on the random chair in the corner, turning it around and sitting straddled, arms folded across the backrest. "Have I done it? Have I convinced you to stick around and make sure we pull this shit off?"

I give him a few beats to worry. Long enough to watch him squirm as I appraise him, taking in the way his forearms push into his biceps.

"You have," I say.

He pretends to wipe sweat from his forehead. "Whew. Good. Let's rehearse. Elise and Calvin." He pauses. "You and me."

In the wardrobe trailer, our costume designer fastens the last button on my mustard-yellow sweater. There's a white Peter Pan collar peeking out beneath, and delicate red roses embroidered along the left side of the chest. She's paired it with a matching red A-line skirt and black Mary Janes.

With my hands on her shoulders, I step into the shoes. She leans over to buckle them for me, then gets up and smiles approvingly.

"Perfect," she whispers.

She turns me toward the mirror to see myself.

Red lips. Light blond hair, freshly trimmed and coming up under my chin from the pin curls, accentuating my jaw. This is my face. But I am another person. It's been so long since I've tried on someone new. I thought I never wanted to do it again.

But there's so much power in Elise's aesthetic. A softness I shy away from in real life that I can lean into here. At once my fears melt away, replaced by the kind of unbridled excitement I've spent years trying to find.

I want to know this woman. To fully inhabit her life. To be someone so far from my true self that from action to cut, all the difficult things in my real life disappear.

When Tyler sees me on the soundstage, she tucks her hands into the pockets of her pants. As I hug her, I can feel her shaking. Or maybe it's me. Maybe it's both of us.

"The whole time, it's felt like a practice run," she says. "This is it. This is the real movie."

"Stop it. You're going to make me cry off my makeup before the first take."

"I'm sorry. I keep thinking of us as kids."

I pull back. "You do?"

"This is what I've always wanted. To do what we used to do back then."

When we lived together, I'd occasionally drag out the home video footage and force Tyler and Kearns into a movie night. I had all of it converted from VHS to DVD years ago, and then had it all put onto my cloud when technology changed again. Tyler was always game to revisit our childhood passion projects, but the movies never seemed to hit her heart like they did mine. I thought it might be because she was behind the camera and not in front of it, so she couldn't see herself in all of it like I could.

I'll never forget her putting a ladder against the side of the house and shooting the pool from overhead while Powell and I thrashed about in the water after the *Titanic* capsized. The shot turned out so much cooler than I could've imagined on my own. Everything did in Tyler's hands. She managed to capture the scope of the chaos and the magnitude of the desperation and cold, even though we were in a heated pool shaped like a teardrop and surrounded by palm trees. When she called cut, I looked up and saw her hanging off the edge of the ladder, one foot dangling out into nowhere, making good use of the balance she'd acquired from being forced to take ballet.

Everything has been about that moment. That feeling. That trust between all of us. The silent agreement that we may fight, and we may bother each other, but when we come together, we want to create something good.

That's why I'm an actor, I remember, a simple thought that's been buried by my fears.

"Everything was going wrong because it *was* wrong. This movie was never supposed to be without you," Tyler says.

Joseph taps me on the shoulder. "Excuse me, is that Miss Elise?"

When I turn around, he sucks back an approving breath.

He's dressed in a navy-blue button-up and gray slacks, wire-rim glasses inching down the bridge of his nose. There's a magnificence to the way these clothes lie across his skin, cutting into all the right places. He looks humble and heroic, studious and strong.

That's Elise seeing him, of course.

By the time Mom gets to set, there's a breathless anticipation in the air that reminds me of live theater, the audience and the actors in a constant tango of give-and-take, both sides setting the pulse everyone moves to. We've been through a lot to get to this.

The crew sets up the shot.

We actors take our places.

The clapper announces the first take of the day.

Tyler calls action.

And so it begins.

12

Week Four of Production

It touches my heart that Melanie sits with me during our lunch break. Melanie's a formidable scene partner. Her approach is like that of a cat, sneaking up on the moment with eerie patience, then pouncing all over the emotional beats when you least expect it.

Tyler followed Melanie's Ruth in a shot that slowly pulled in closer the longer she spoke, until the camera was right there to capture her tears. Watching it back on the monitor was like sitting in the audience at an awards show as a nominated actor's highlighted clip plays on the big screen. I could even imagine Powell's score swelling in the background. Something with searing violins and a delicate piano.

"You were amazing this morning," I tell Melanie.

She swings a leg over the bench to sit, her fuzzy boot knocking into my leg. "This has been fun. I like when I get to play with the material a little. Your sister's good. She gave me my space, but she still kept her vision."

Pride wells within me. Guy has stepped back all the way and let Tyler move forward. He now spends his time tinkering with the script and giving on-the-spot revisions while Tyler has full creative control over the tone and shot list. Her quiet, intent work has a way of seeping into everyone else. It's only my second day of shooting with her, and I already feel like my heart beats a little slower while I'm acting. I want to be sure to give her the time and space to find each detail and capture it.

"You're a generous partner," Melanie tells me. "You let me have my moment."

"How could I not? You were riveting. It was all I could do not to stare."

"You are just like your dad. Feeding me a steady diet of compliments." She takes a bite of her salad. "I catch Sarai doing it too. *Mom, you look beautiful today. That's a good color on you. Your nails are so nice.*"

"That's funny. I love that kid so much."

Melanie laughs. "She's a handful, but I love her too. She's still asking me why she's not in this movie with the rest of us."

"She texted me yesterday begging me to get her in."

"Of course she did."

"Guy wanted to write a part for her, but I said no. If Sarai ever finds out, she'll be big, big mad," Melanie says.

I make a zipped-lip gesture and toss away the key.

The conversation turns to what Sarai will be when she grows up. Melanie sees her becoming a TV personality. Someone who should have her own talk show. "First of all, she's too obsessed with this business not to end up as some part of it. Second, she's nosy. But she can look you in the eye and ask the one question everyone wants to know, and the way she asks, you answer even when you shouldn't. That's a gift."

"I think I'd like doing talk shows about one hundred percent more if I got to be on one with Sarai."

"Then the next thing you know she's got you talking about why your ex-boyfriend wrote that album about you, and which song you think is the least true, and how you feel about your mom and your old stepmom sharing a love scene together."

We laugh until it hurts.

"God, that's so true," I say. "And then she'll ask why our moms both broke up with our dad."

"You know what you should say? That your parents found each other before they found their fame, and your mom was rising faster than he was, and he didn't like it one bit." She shakes her head. "And then you drive it home by saying that sometimes the people you love the most are the ones you're least likely to tell how you feel."

"I think both my parents would have me professionally blacklisted if I ever dared."

"Nah. Kitty's got a good one in Guy. He keeps her from getting too hot."

I give Melanie a knowing look. There's no way she hasn't heard about the fight between Mom and me, especially after Mom made her give me the whole speech about how the two of them found their unlikely friendship.

"Well, most of the time," Melanie corrects.

"What would Sarai say? About you and Dad?"

"If she values her life, she wouldn't say a damn thing."

We share a good laugh over that one.

♥

When Joseph's not around, I notice all the spaces he'd fill. The funny way he interrupts a silence with humming and tapping. How when someone says something he likes, he slaps his hand on his leg. How his authenticity directly correlates to his level of comfort. When he's nervous, he blazes through it with heavy-handed charm and sweet talk. When he's at peace, he's curious in the way a baby's curious, staring at things for far too long, full of quiet wonder.

I skip up the steps and knock on his trailer door. Music is playing on the other side, so I know he's here. "Joe," I call out. "It's me, Sloane."

The door opens. But it's not Joe. It's Daya—*my father's fiancée*—mussing her hair.

"Oh. Sorry. I'll . . . come back."

I rush down the stairs in a fit of confusion, turning to walk the wrong way. It'll take too much pride to course correct, so I commit, heading toward the next soundstage with full conviction, decked out in a plaid dress that's undeniably from the 1940s. It's far from the strangest thing anyone's seen around here.

I get a good ten feet past my own trailer before I remember it's mine now. I could've gone in there. I'm so used to going to Joseph's.

What was Daya doing in there? I don't want to assume the worst, but there's no good explanation coming to me. My ears keep ringing. My cheeks are hot. I can taste bile in my throat.

Was that why she invited him to our dinner?

There's bold, and then there is *bold*.

"Sloane! Sloane!" Daya's calling after me. She's almost sprinting to catch up. When I don't slow down, she says, "Do you think we could maybe cool it on the Usain Bolt pace so I can explain?"

We take a spot beside a random potted palm tree. Daya leans against the base in the shade while I stay in the sun, needing a good excuse to squint, because I'm afraid I could cry, and that would be both humbling and bizarre.

"Before you go telling your father I'm cheating on him with a troublemaking Irishman, let me assure you that I, like you, seem to be immune to the charms of Joseph Donovan."

I gulp. Immune. Yes.

"I've been trying to pitch him a comedy I wrote. I thought I'd have a minute at our engagement dinner, but I somehow forgot what those family dinners are like." She stops to catch her breath. "There's this puppy dog of a character I wrote that I really want to see Joe read for. He's *very* resistant to the idea. He doesn't think people will find him funny. I don't know, I was right about Alex. It's always hilarious when the *very serious actors* commit to something fluffy. Which makes me think I'm right about Joe too." She pauses. "He'd just gone to get some lunch when you knocked."

At the base of my throat, a balloon of tension slowly hisses out. "Gotcha."

"Girl, I promise I'm telling you the truth. Put me on the stand. Strap me to some train tracks." Her pointer finger shoots up. "Fuck. Alex is here! There's my clincher. He's here with Sarai. If I was going to step out on him, do you really think I'd do it when he's my ride home? You can text him right now. He knows about the meeting. They were off trying to find you, actually."

I don't know why I'm letting her flounder. Her cheating on my dad hardly crossed my mind as something to be mad about. "I believe you. I'm just processing."

"I get that. And trust me, it doesn't make much sense to me either, but I love Alex. I really do. I even love him after he chose a tacky-ass square-cut diamond for me. You can't tell me that isn't real."

It makes me smile to hear it. "I'm sorry for overreacting. I'm a little loopy, I guess. It's been a weird few days."

"I can imagine. This is becoming one hell of a production." She hesitates. "I mean that in the best way. This is the stuff they'd make a movie about. A movie about a movie. I'd watch it, is all I'm saying."

We start back toward the trailers. It's nice to talk with someone who knows me but doesn't know *everything* about me. "You really haven't lived until you've seen your mom make out with your old stepmom," I tell her.

"My mother is a doctor. Married to my dad for thirty-three years. I haven't lived *at all.*"

Joseph catches us on our way. The sight of him nearly tips me over, making me jittery. He's not in costume yet, just tight-fitting jeans and a short-sleeve red lumberjack shirt.

"There's the man we were looking for! Sloane here found me alone in your trailer like a kept woman," Daya says jokingly. "Don't worry. I cleared it up. Only man that's dicking me down is Sloane's dad! Hell yeah!" She holds up her hand for a high five from Joseph, who coughs out a shocked laugh.

I'm gut punched by my own mortified amusement. "Oh my god. Please never say that again."

"Besides, I'm pretty sure your girlfriend wouldn't be too pleased about it either," Daya tells Joseph as their hands connect.

Girlfriend.

Joseph's girlfriend.

My attention shifts to my feet. Suddenly it's of utmost importance that I examine every detail of today's shoes: brown leather, with a thin strap across the middle, little teardrop cutouts forming a border along the outside edge.

I think I will spend the rest of my life looking at these shoes. Great shoes.

I should go tell our costume designer.

Daya, a very keen woman, keeps the brightness in her tone. "I need to find Alex. Make sure he's picking the heart-healthy meal options." She heads toward set. "Remember what I told you about the movie, Joe!" she calls from the distance. "People would love to see it. I promise!"

She's gone, leaving Joseph and me and a million questions in the air. The sun is a laser beam to my insecurity, setting me alight. I'm boiling. Squirming. Wishing for five minutes ago, when my biggest concern was whether or not I'd be able to identify what song he'd be playing when I got to his trailer. He's gotten more obscure with the classic rock in an attempt to stump me.

"Could we go inside and talk?" he asks.

I decide to hold my ground. "What could you need to say to me that you can't say right here, right now?"

"Fine. We can talk here. Let every sound guy, key grip, and personal assistant on the lot hear this." He moves back to create more space between us. Clears his throat with unnecessary flourish, then begins. "First, am I right to say that I never once touched you?"

I squint my eyes so much I can actually see my lashes press together.

"Not in any kind of inappropriate way," he clarifies.

"Sure."

"Okay. Next, I want to say that I've done everything I can think of to prove to you that I'm not the same person I used to be."

"You've shown me that," I admit. "Three stars on your sticker chart." I try to cool myself down, but things keep springing up that make me want to set the world on fire. "It's just that one of the first things I ever asked was if your mom was your girlfriend!"

He gives me an incredulous look. "What was I to say? 'No. My mam's not my girlfriend, my girlfriend is'?"

"Works for me!" My voice sounds feral. I pull myself back to earth. "You know what? There is really no reason for it to matter that you have a girlfriend. I'd think it would've come up by now, but I know some actors like to keep their private life *extra* private. And some of them believe there are no real rules when it comes to making a movie." I'm toeing the line between sarcastic and truthful, trying to hit a sweet spot where nothing affects me. "I'm happy for you."

"Sloane. Hold on." He waits for me to still myself. "I don't have a girlfriend anymore. Haven't since about a month before we started shooting." He lets it simmer, absorbing all the confusion that's written on my face. "Daya knew her a bit. She was a costume assistant on that miniseries I did last year, and she works on Daya's sitcom. But they're on hiatus, so Daya hasn't seen her to know we've ended things."

It hits a nerve, to feel like I've been outpaced. Pokes right at the smug little voice in my head that hates to be proven wrong. "Why did you have to put it that way? Why use a hypothetical with the mom comment? Why couldn't you come out and say that you don't have a fucking girlfriend?"

One of our PAs walks by us. She tries to cover it, but her mouth quirks in reaction to what I've said. This is why we should have gone into his trailer for this conversation.

"Can we please go inside?" Joseph asks, feeling it too.

"No," I protest.

"Sloane."

"No."

"Sloane."

"*Fine.*"

We huff off together. He's all scowls and curved shoulders, and I'm all chest-forward haughtiness, clinging to my pride like a live bug on a windshield.

As soon as Joseph closes his trailer door, he's on my case again. "Why would it matter if I had a girlfriend?"

"Don't even go there."

"What do you mean? Where else is there to go? Tell me why it would matter." He takes a step toward me.

"It doesn't," I say coldly.

"No?" Another step.

"No."

"Fine then. Maybe I should give her a call. See if she'd like to go out to lunch with me, since I can't seem to find anyone else who will dine with me on off days." Two more steps forward.

"Fuck off."

"It wasn't a good match, but who knows? Maybe she'd be able to rehearse with me a bit too."

"Literally drive yourself to hell and move in."

Another step. "Those early wake-ups are tough, but I think if I explain that—"

I smash my lips atop his.

At first he's rigid, still talking, in fact. Then he melts into me, and his hands spring to life, palming the back of my head and the small of my back in one swoop, pulling me closer yet. We crash against the trailer door. His mouth breaks free from mine for a gasp of air.

He recovers and kisses me again, deep and strong. I remember the feel of him in a way I don't expect, like picking up a book

I forgot I've read before. There's a rhythm to the way we move together, a dance of pressure and touch that takes practice to perfect. We've had a whole previous movie's worth, and it's as natural as breathing, the way I tangle my fist into his hair right as he moves from my lips to the spot on my neck just below my jaw. I find the corner of his ear and nip at it, reminding him to come back to my mouth again.

He does, picking me up to move us from the doorway to the couch. He has a hand tucked up under each of my thighs, keeping a firm pressure that radiates through me. He lays me down so gently I think he's still holding me, until I realize that my legs are wrapped around him tight enough to keep me from touching the seat cushions. He has moved his arms to either side of my head, propping himself up so he can pull back to look at me.

Really look at me.

The way he leans over makes a tendril of his hair drift forward, curling up onto his forehead. "That was . . . unexpected," he whispers.

"Should I have done something else?"

"No," he says abruptly. "God. No."

There's a sudden softness to him I want to touch. To know. I press a hand to his face, running my finger along his cheek. He catches my thumb and kisses it. The strum throughout my body momentarily lulls, breaking me out of my haze.

After all I've told myself. Every promise I made. Joseph Donovan is on top of me right now.

And I would be lying if I said I wanted him to be anywhere other than right where he is.

"Don't tell me you're panicking," he says.

He starts kissing me again, short sweet pecks that move from my lips to my cheeks to my neck. "Do. Not. Tell. Me. You. Are.

Panicking." Each word is its own sentence, spoken between kisses. He takes his hands and presses into my ribs, playfully prodding at my sides. "Not. Now. That. I. Know. This. Is. Possible."

"I'm not panicking!" I yelp out. "I was worried about kissing you without permission!"

"You have it. Trust me. It's yours."

We both go still again, studying each other. His focus on me is unlike anything I've ever seen from him before. He watches me intently, a quiet, hungry appraisal that makes me feel more wanted than I've felt in a very long time. He mimics me from a moment ago and puts a hand on my face, his thumb brushing my cheek with the tenderest of strokes.

There's an aggressive knock on the trailer door.

"Sloanius! You in there?"

My *father*.

I shove Joseph off me and spring up to open the door in one fluid motion, so swift I stub my foot on the side of the couch. The pain doesn't quite reach me. Nothing can right now.

"Hey!" I say, way too loudly. It's not only my dad, but Sarai and Daya too.

My lips have gone numb and my body's tingling. I can feel my hair is askew, so I reach up and flop it to the other side with a casual, disaffected lean, pretending it's a thoughtless move, all the while holding my breath to stop my heart from racing. My hairstylist is going to kill me. She asked me to touch my head as little as possible.

I don't even want to think about my makeup.

"The blond really makes you look like your mother." Dad reaches out to touch a piece, his hand grazing the same spot on my face Joseph held moments ago.

It's the same creepy sixth sense he's had all his life. Like the time I was a senior in high school and I accidentally scraped the driver side of his car against a pole. I called Mom in a panic, and she cursed me up and down for forcing her to help, then paid a body shop a ridiculous amount of money in cash to fix it the same day. When Dad came home that night from doing a bunch of press, I watched from the garage door as he absentmindedly ran his hand along the side of the car, right where the scrape had been only hours before. "How'd it ride for ya today?" he'd asked.

In the present, I swat him away. "Don't you know by now not to touch anyone's hair without asking?" It takes everything in my power not to adjust my dress, which feels twisted to the left.

"Is Joe in there?" Dad asks.

Joseph literally leaps out of the trailer and onto the pavement. "Sure the hell am!" He starts gallivanting around with all the swagger of a John Wayne impersonator. "We were just runnin' a bit of our later scene work together."

Technically not a lie.

Daya and I share a quick glance. She knows exactly what's going on.

I can now quite distinctly feel my stubbed toe throbbing.

"Sorry to have interrupted the process. I wanted a chance to congratulate my baby girl. *The star.* Haven't seen her in person since the news broke." Dad beams at me. "I'm proud of you, kiddo. If there is anyone who's up to a task like this, it's you."

"I told him we should wait until you came to set," Daya says, apologetic. "He couldn't be convinced otherwise."

"That's not entirely true. Sarai wanted to see what the trailers look like," Dad tells me.

"I've seen *many* trailers, Dad," Sarai argues.

"And if you've seen one, you've seen them all," I say.

Dad pats my shoulder. "C'mon now. She's got a few more years before it all bores her. Let's let her see."

Daya all but winces. Joseph's looking at me, but I don't dare look back, instead painting a placid smile on my face, trying very hard not to reach down and touch my pinkie toe. Or adjust my dress. Or fuss with my hair.

Joseph jumps from the ground up to the trailer in an impressive, if not excessive, leap. "Come on in!"

"Someone get this guy a stunt job," Dad jokes. He's talking in that voice he uses when he's secretly judging someone. I can hear him on the car ride back from set, running through the visit with Daya. *What was with the Donovan kid jumping around everywhere? I thought he was gonna climb up a light pole.*

Bless his heart, he thinks we still hate Joseph.

I cannot even begin to imagine trying to explain to him how much that's changed.

Dad, Daya, Sarai, Joseph, and I cram ourselves into the tiny trailer. Five people in a space best suited for two, maximum. Nothing is particularly askew, and maybe it's only in my mind, but the energy is different. Charged. Buzzing off of every surface.

I'm considering a move to a remote island off the coast of anywhere but here.

Dad—the type of person who has always felt at home wherever he is—goes straight for the couch, plopping down and wing-spanning his arms along the back edge. "You keep it neat," he notes to Joseph.

Joseph's eyes pass over me as he appraises his place. "I try."

"How's your dad doing? I bet he was excited to see you teaming up with Guy. I haven't had a chance to catch their movie together, but I remember when it came out. It was a big deal for the both of them."

I make a note to tell Joseph not to take it too personally, since Dad hates Guy. Saying he hasn't "had a chance to catch" a movie that came out in 1979 is peak Alexander Ford pettiness.

Joseph runs his hand across the whiskey bottle. "He's in New York doing a play."

Dad nods, genuinely impressed. He loves when people do theater. "Good for him."

"How are you feeling?" Joseph asks. The unspeakable question.

Sarai gives Joseph no time to learn of this mistake. "Is this your mom?" She's picked up the picture frame from the counter, and she's holding it close to her face for a thorough inspection.

"Indeed it is," Joseph answers.

Sarai smiles. "She's really pretty."

Watching all of this unfold, it's so clear these people are my family. I have been in all of these places, done all of these things.

Daya makes a sweeping gesture with her arms. "Well, Sarai, what do you think? How's Joe's trailer look?"

"It's fine," she deadpans.

"And there you have it," Daya says. "Your trailer has been rated Fine by Sarai Davidson-Ford. The write-up will be coming in *Variety* within the week."

Our small talk continues at an easy clip. Joseph eventually cuts it off, realizing he's late for hair and makeup. All of us follow him out of the trailer.

When it's time to part ways, he does a little double head nod at me. Something I take to mean *We'll talk later.*

Later never comes. Dad, Sarai, and Daya stick around for the rest of the night to watch. The conversation feels nonstop. There is absolutely no room to even step into a dark corner, because if it's not Sarai who finds me, it's Powell. Or Mom. Or Dad. Or Guy.

Daya, for her part, tries to wrangle everyone, even going so far as to wink at me when she thinks she's finally pulled it off. Then Joseph's makeup artist swoops in for touch-ups, and Daya balls up her fists and throws them to the sky for me to see. Her attempts to help are so deeply admirable I decide that if there is anyone in this family that would be my friend without any other connection, it's her.

As the hours pass since my kiss with Joseph, I start to convince myself it never happened. That's the only way I can justify looking Mom in the face, knowing I was halfway toward doing exactly what she accused me of when all this began.

It's only when I'm home, in my bed, that I allow myself to revisit it. The feel of Joseph's hand on my back. The warmth of his mouth. How familiar he felt to me. And still so new. Someone I needed time to explore.

Someone I needed to kiss when I wasn't angry.

Someone I needed to kiss when I was excited. When I was upset. When I was tired.

Whenever.

Maybe it's okay to go headfirst into this, even after all that happened between Kearns and me. Because after the panic subsides, it's pure exhilaration.

For months, my house has felt like a hollow husk, holding me in hibernation.

Tonight, it feels like a safe place to rest my head, preparing me for an exciting new world.

13

Even on a few hours' sleep, it's easy to get out of my car and walk to Joseph's trailer this morning. Everything is completely different than it was twenty-four hours ago.

I am ready for anything.

Joseph sits out on the steps again. He's leaned back and looking skyward, worry creasing his forehead. I wonder if he's run through all the same thoughts I have, or if this is more effortless for him. As easy as the way he walks into any room, hips forward and mouth smiling.

"You're here." There's a waver in his voice, a whisper of vulnerability.

"Did you really think I wouldn't come? I'm even early."

"You look nice."

I look down at my yoga pants and camisole. "Dressed to impress." A strange quiet follows. "Should we . . . go inside?"

"Of course."

Once the door closes behind us, I kiss him instantly. There's no sense in pretending like I haven't been waiting for this moment. He holds his breath as our lips meet, barely reacting to the pressure of my touch.

I pull back and start to squirm, grasping for a way to recover. I've read it all wrong. Yesterday was a mistake.

Joseph grabs my hand and squeezes. "Give me a minute here, okay? I wanna have a chat about our boundaries."

"Really?" If I made a list of a thousand ways I imagined this going, there is no scenario where it's Joseph who's asking for us to establish ground rules. I would've bet my life that in any version of events, he'd be the one encouraging us to roam through the dark, feeling our way toward a destination.

"Well, for one, I'm not sleeping with you for the first time in my trailer."

"Who said we were gonna sleep together?"

"If we're being technical, your mam did."

It's the perfect tension breaker. My body relaxes against the wall as I melt into laughter. He takes his free hand and props it against the door behind me so he can lean forward, very conscious of how much we're touching.

After the laughter dies down, something foreign replaces it; an unnamed hurt that starts to bloom in the center of my chest, webbing and weaving through every open vessel, determined to take hold. "So we're keeping it above the belt and casual around here. Got it," I say.

"Who said above the belt is casual?" He's more serious than playful. "I never went below the belt with the lass I fancied all through primary school, and it took me years to get over her. Never even kissed her. We hugged once." He pretends to be lost in the memory. "Shannon Cleary. Wonder what she's up to these days."

"You're confusing me," I admit.

He wraps his other arm around me to hold on tight. "All I'm saying is when it comes to you, I've done most things wrong. I wanna be sure you're thinking this through."

The hurt takes a clearer form. It feels like I can't be trusted to keep this thing cool. Like I'm the obvious choice to ruin this, considering my history. I buckle down and commit to being more casual than him. "I think we keep it above the belt at work, and we make sure my family doesn't know, and we're good. Yeah?"

"If that's what you want." His expression is unreadable.

"It is," I lie. I have no idea what I want.

He licks his lips before he presses them atop mine. There is purpose now. And passion. Almost too much. Too personal for something supposedly casual.

This time it's me who pulls back. "You said no sleeping together in this trailer. I'll take that to mean intercourse. Right?"

His cheeks turn bright red. "Christ, you're as forward as ever."

"I want to make sure I'm understanding what you mean." I make a point to look down. "Because lucky for us, you're not wearing a belt today." His eyes grow wide as my finger traces a line from his jaw to the button of his jeans, working it open. "There are *plenty* of other things we can still do."

Late in the afternoon, Tyler pulls me aside while the crew sets up for a new scene. She has her hands in her pockets and she's not meeting my eye. Immediately my stomach flips. She knows. Somehow. Even though Joseph and I haven't so much as looked at each other between takes.

"I want to talk to you about something," she says.

She has a sixth sense, and she's figured it all out, and I have to stand before her humbled, forced to admit a truth I'm barely ready to face myself. At least it won't be a lie when I tell her it's nothing more than a casual thing.

"You're not gonna like it," she prefaces.

"Oh my god. Say it please. I'm sweating."

"We figured out a way to add more days to the schedule without adding on too much extra time on the lot."

"Oh." I relax. "When?"

"Well, originally we'd had days off before and after your gala . . ."

The panic inside me is replaced with the first flames of anger. "No."

"Yeah."

"Fuck, Tyler."

"I know." She stops staring at the ceiling to look at me. Her expression is solemn. "If we use those days to reshoot the stuff we did on the first two days and the sex scene, we might be able to get out of this mess without it costing a fortune." She's near tears. "Please, Bub."

This is the fourth year we've held the gala, and it's a well-oiled machine. It's less than two weeks away now, and while I've been so focused on *Horizons*, the gala has been my respite. I've been telling myself that when it comes, I will have three days where this movie doesn't consume me. Three full days dedicated to the life I have outside of this set. Three full days to sort out what's happening to me here.

Now it's only one. One busy, hectic day making sure everything goes as planned, then it's back to my red lips and Mary Janes, fighting the urge not to undress my costar between takes.

"You're not asking me. You're telling me," I say to Tyler.

"Mom says we will be hemorrhaging money for no good reason if we don't."

Tyler should look familiar to me in this moment. She should look like the sullen little girl from my childhood, always the one chosen by our parents to deliver the worst news, because she's the one we were all least likely to attack. But she looks brand new. A full-grown adult that's sprung up before my eyes, hosting secrets and pains and wishes she no longer shares with me, a whole life outside of this place that I know nothing about.

Tears flood my lower lashes without warning. "Fine."

I march off toward craft services to grab a piece of fruit I don't want.

"Bub, please don't be mad," Tyler calls out.

"I'm not." But I so obviously am that I don't know how to hide it. So I stare at the bananas and the oranges and the random wayward mango in the fruit bowl, waiting for my tears to dry up.

Joseph comes up beside me. "Is everything all right?" He places a gentle hand on my shoulder. Nothing too far over the line, and yet the least casual thing he's done yet, because the urge to fall into his arms is almost hypnotic.

It proves to be the one thing strong enough to pull me out of my fog. I wipe my tears with the back of my palm and compose myself with a small smile in his direction. "It will be." I step away from his touch to grab a granola bar, sincerely hoping with every fiber of my being that what I've said is true.

14

It's not my alarm that wakes me up, but a text message from Joseph.

Will we be rehearsing as usual today?

Of course, I respond, my eyes half-closed.

More of what we worked on yesterday?

Yes. Make sure you're prepared.

I will be.

There's a little pool of spit on my pillow and my hair is in a baby-pink silk bonnet to protect it from breakage, and still a shiver runs down my spine. This is, without question, one of the worst decisions I've ever made—attempt to casually continue learning all about Joseph Donovan without anyone outside of Daya knowing it's happening—and yet the only way this train can be stopped is by collision.

Until then, I may as well enjoy the view. Headfirst, no panicking, coasting on exhilaration.

Joseph is waiting in his car when I pull onto the lot. "Good morning, Sloane," he says in the most professional voice I've ever heard him use.

"Hello, Joseph."

We walk side by side to his trailer, literally talking about the weather, breaking down the difference between cumulus and cirrus clouds. Too much time has passed since our bodies were smashed together.

His trailer door shuts behind us, and Joseph presses against me before I can even set down my coffee. Not that I need it. Caffeine could never wake me up this quickly. His mouth settles on mine and his hands run over my body, roaming along the sides of my waist. One hand moves to my chest. I let out a little yip of satisfaction and he decides to further explore, kissing his way down to my clavicle.

"So," he starts. "I've been thinking, and I suspect Calvin is holding something back from Elise."

"Is that so?"

He works at the bottom edge of my tank top, starting to lift it up. "Nothing that's in the script. Just a personal theory. It's small. Like a memory he has that he's not ready for her to know." He pauses to get my shirt over my head. Steps back to relish me in this very casual, certainly-not-overly-complicated yellow lace bra.

I run my finger from his Adam's apple all the way down to the buckle of his jeans. "You wore a belt today. Bad choice."

He looks at me in my bra and my yoga pants. "You didn't, though."

Soon his shirt's gone too.

When we press together again, the cold of his dog tag necklace gives me a little shock. This dance between us fluctuates between something primal and something tender. I know which side scares me more, and still I find myself riveted, not able to comprehend how it is we're chest to chest, holding each other in a soft embrace.

"Why do you think he hasn't told her?" I ask.

My hands tuck into the back pocket of his jeans. His breath smells fresh, like copious amounts of mouthwash, which strikes me as sweet considering the conversation we once had about *A Little Luck*. I like picturing him getting ready this morning, leaning over the sink with a robe wrapped around his hips, spitting a second round of spearmint Scope down the drain.

"It's something he has to wait to say. He has to be sure it's the right time, or it will ruin everything between them."

Today we're shooting the midway point in the movie. Calvin and Elise sit at her desk, talking about a story she's been writing. The first crackle of something more between them really shines through as Calvin helps Elise break a plot point that's been eluding her.

"Crucial foreplay," as Guy calls it.

Horizons has lots of important conversations and slow glances, particularly in the first half. Today's scene is when everything shifts, and the pace picks up as we work toward that first chaste kiss, then the deep, climactic kiss and ensuing love scene.

Teasingly, I whisper in his ear. "Does she know by the end of the movie?"

"Oh yeah. But not by the scene we're doing today. Maybe right after."

I know he means Calvin. This is truly the exact way we've always talked about these characters.

Still, all I hear is us talking about ourselves.

Soon my leggings are on the floor and his hands are on my inner thighs and his mouth is working so fast and so well that there's not much to think about at all.

In between takes, we hatch a plan to meet in his trailer during our dinner break. It's risky. The both of us gone for dinner might raise suspicion. Our solution is to have Joseph leave first. I'll sit down and eat a little bit, then "remember" that I've left my phone in my trailer.

When the time comes, Joseph winks at me before he says to no one in particular, "I need to do a little reading," holding one of his World War II novels in his hand and tipping his head toward the outside.

"Joe! Joe!" Out of nowhere, Guy catches Joseph's arm to stop him. "Hold on a minute. I've had an epiphany, and I need to talk it over with my core players!"

"Right now?" Joseph gives him a look best described as deadly.

"Now is better than later." Guy points to Mom, Tyler, Melanie, and me. He beckons us over to the dining table farthest away from the rest of the crew. "I need all of you."

We relocate. The exhaustion among us is palpable. Tyler doesn't collapse into her seat, but melts. Mom drags her fork through her quinoa bowl like she's digging a hole. Melanie folds one leg atop the other and rubs her own foot, yawning. Even Joseph's constant motion has a newfound delay to it. He sits sideways on the bench, his outward leg not so much jittering, but swaying.

"As the days go on, Tyler grows stronger in her vision," Guy tells us. "I can start to see her style emerging in a way that excites me. But the writing is still *my* baby. And there's a gap in this story that must be filled."

"Honey, there's not much time to make changes." Mom may as well pull out a nail file, she's so uninterested in where this is going.

Meanwhile, Tyler turns noticeably rigid. Her shoulders pinch together hard enough she could hold a pencil between the blades.

"I know, but this is a film about all the ways we love each other. Yes?" Guy doesn't wait for an answer. "It's about the resilience of the spirit when the world turns against you. How our heart can want and our mind can deny us. And while we have Elise and Calvin riding off into the sunset after their long, tumultuous years apart, we should set Vera and Ruth's love story apart. They cannot end up in the same place as the other lovers."

Mom is listening now.

"Vera has this exquisite romance with Ruth. The footage is radiant. Everyone should be proud of what we've shot so far. Tyler had an eye for it that I never would have. To use color in such a way! Magentas and violets. And the tender focus, following their hands instead of their mouths. She understood the two women's love in a way I simply couldn't. And she's already woven in this beautiful imagery with the vase of chrysanthemums slowly decaying. New beauty emerging at each stage. I think we can take it further. Push the love these women share even deeper."

He's circling the point at a typical Guy Cicero pace, platitude upon platitude.

"What is it you're thinking?" Mom urges.

"The closure for Elise and Calvin is the realization that they must be together. Vera and Ruth learn this much earlier on. Their story doesn't really move beyond that. What we need is to see Vera pass on. Let this romance be her swan song. The last good days before—"

Tyler cuts him off with an aggressive "No."

"What's that, dear?"

"We are *not* killing Vera." All the bluntness she wished to inherit from me comes out twofold. She's leaning over the table, staring Guy in the eye.

"I know. You love this character. I do too. She's modeled partly after my mother, after all. But this is a movie, dear. I've heard you speak of these moments as paintings. What is it that we're showing in the gallery? The entire collection should have a theme. And this will complete it. Think of the orange chrysanthemums in the vase! A flower of optimism. Of hope. They will be dead by movie's end. Wilted but still beautiful. And that shot we've planned, when Elise moves out, and she finally puts the flowers in the trash. But she keeps the vase. Doesn't that tell you everything?"

"No." Tyler's sparse answers are like kindling she adds to a pile. She's daring Guy to set it all alight.

His face betrays his confusion. He didn't expect to receive any pushback. This is a man who basically got a blank check to do with what he pleases. But he didn't hire a yes-man in Tyler. He hired a codirector. Her word carries as much weight as his, and the tension between them here is painted into the fine lines that crease around his eyes. "It will really strengthen the love between Elise and Calvin," he adds weakly.

"Because there aren't one hundred and seven other pages of script that do that," Tyler mocks. "It's the death of our gay character that will finally *sell the hetero romance*."

I have to do something before she loses control and the flames burn down everything she's worked so hard to create. At the very least, she needs to know I'm on her side. No matter what, I'm *always* on her side.

"The problem is that if you kill Vera, you're feeding right into a pretty exhausting trope. A few, really," I say. "So while I get what you're saying about the themes and the galleries and all that, I still think the movie will actually be even better if you let them live in their joy. This is a queer interracial couple in the 1940s. Having them end up together is already the difference. Not everything has to end in tragedy to be satisfying or important."

It's a stark truth I stumble upon accidentally, and it takes my breath away.

Joseph turns so that both his legs are under the table. "You know I'm a bastard who is lucky to still have this gig at all, but I wanna say that Tyler and Sloane are right. The story's better without anyone havin' to die."

His support trips a wire in my heart. Everything he does feels like he's telegraphing our recent activities to the crew. Old Sloane would've found a way to knock him down. But this is too important. I give him a noncommittal nod, aiming for something that reads as cautiously appreciative.

Melanie takes a big bite of her salad. "It's not a good idea."

Only one vote remains.

Guy turns to Mom. Our family has always been ruled by Katherine Porter. She runs the back of her hand along Guy's cheek.

We've lost. Mom is choosing Guy. Vera's going to die and it's all going to be an even bigger mess than it already is.

"Honey," she coos. "I see where your head's at." She pulls her hand back. "But there is more on the line than your own reputation here."

Tyler perks up. The two of us lock eyes, stunned at this lead-up.

If Mom delivers the fatal blow, we win. That easily. It will save hours of tears. Maybe even years, considering once the movie is out, it's forever. This story will be attached to our names for the rest of time.

"I know this isn't easy to hear, but it won't work," she says plainly. "We're fighting against the clock as it is. There's no room in our schedule to shoot additional coverage we haven't planned for, dear. I've already made Sloane quite upset by taking time from her gala to do reshoots. Besides, Melanie won't be available to us beyond our already reworked schedule."

Melanie slowly chews her kale, not looking up. Tyler's eyes flicker from me to Guy. She's waiting for pushback. Or for me to voice my frustration that she tattled on me to Mom.

Guy kisses Mom's hand. "I've been alive for all these years, and there's still so much I don't know. Lucky for me, I have people who are willing to teach me."

He looks around the table, holding silent communion with each of us. This is the reason Guy's reputation has stood the test of time when so many of his contemporaries have fallen. Guy Cicero is willing to stretch. To bend. To understand.

"I'm sorry for stealing your dinnertime. Sometimes inspiration strikes. And sometimes it dies!" He grabs a piece of bread off Mom's plate and takes a bite. "It's the bravery that counts, isn't it?"

Joseph makes a point to look directly at me, and I don't even want to think about why. If he thinks he's being discreet, he's about as subtle as an air horn. Now that he's looked at me like that, I stare at my dinner plate and take several focused bites.

"This reminds me, honey, who's playing at the gala this year?" Mom asks me.

I'm about to say *Daniel Traverson's jam band* when I realize that of course he can't play at my gala. He can't be anywhere near this event with his custom powder-blue Les Paul and his ability to strum three clumsy chords. Last year Daniel got Keanu Reeves on bass at the last minute, which was huge. We needed a second guitarist, so I threw Kearns in there. The entire car ride home, Kearns ragged on Daniel's playing.

"Keanu and me carried that whole fucking thing," he'd said, and I laughed at him. No one cared how it sounded. It was about the fun of watching all these random famous people do Beatles covers. That's what sells the tickets and gets the donations.

No one on the gala email chain or at our monthly meetings has asked me about who is playing, because it's assumed I've got it covered. Putting together the celebrity jam band always requires a bit of magic and patience. The foundation team must be thinking I'm pulling my usual tricks.

The truth is I haven't even thought about it. Once Daniel agreed to headline it for me every year, he started waving the wand on my behalf, picking his own backup. He always came through in a major way, and usually at the very last second.

To buy myself time, I list the other usual gala performers. "Powell's doing his drag act, of course. Dad's gonna do jazz covers again. People liked it. Maybe Daya will do stand-up. I should ask. I've got a week and a half," I say with a gulp.

"I'm talking about the jam band," Mom clarifies, as if I didn't know.

"Oh. Yeah. You know, it's always a random group."

"It's always Daniel Traverson and a random group," Tyler challenges. Does she have leftover adrenaline from the Guy dustup and she's using me to let it out? After I've stood up for her, no less.

"Obviously there's no more Daniel Traverson," I say.

"He was never that good anyways," Mom tells me.

"I can do it," Joseph offers, overlapping.

Mom's fork pauses halfway to her mouth. "Do you play?"

"A little guitar. Probably about as well as that twat." He gets an appreciative laugh out of Melanie of all people. "Isn't the idea for it to be someone who doesn't normally do this kind of thing?"

"That would be wonderful for the film!" Guy cheers. "Could help refocus the minds of the vultures on something more worthwhile, such as Sloane's beloved cause."

Joseph sweetens the pot. "I could get my dad to play with me."

While everyone else asks some variation of "You could?" I ask, "You would?"

This thing with Joseph. It's new. It's fun. It's supposed to be casual. Joseph hasn't told me a whole lot about his dad, but everything I know is enough to understand the relationship is tenuous at best.

"His play is ending this weekend, so he's free. He'd love a chance to remind fans he can do it all," Joseph says. "He's a drummer. It's gloriously annoying. People will devour it."

I want to say no. That this goes too far. But to have both Michael Donovan and his son performing would be a great late-addition draw.

"I'll have my people call your people," I joke. Except I'm serious.

By the nod he gives in response, so is Joseph.

"Sarai can play the tambourine," Melanie adds. Surely this part is the joke.

Mom puts her hand on her heart. "That would be so sweet! And don't let Sloane get away from this! She can sing! It's about time she showed people! And Tyler can play the violin! You know, all my babies are musicians. Powell just took to it the best."

"I'm not playing the *violin*, Mom," Tyler says dryly.

It does not seem like any of this is a joke.

Mom scoffs at Tyler. "Well, I'd love to see Sloaney up there making use of all those voice lessons for once."

"What songs should we do?" Joseph asks me.

At once the dinner table is pitching options for us. The conversation moves like a tornado, with me in the eye of it all. My family hammers out every detail big and small. Joseph on guitar. His dad on drums. Sarai on tambourine. Me on vocals.

Who will be our bassist? the group wonders.

Joseph thinks a three-song set is doable given our time frame. It will have to be songs his dad knows. Which means classic rock. But not the Beatles. We can't do what Daniel's done. We have to set ourselves apart.

I protest nothing, instead watching. Marveling. Astonished at the fact that all of these people have come together to help me—to save me—and they're doing it without hesitation. Without knowing how screwed I'd be if they didn't pick me up in this very moment and save me. Or maybe knowing exactly how screwed I'd be, and doing it for that reason.

But still, this is patently ridiculous. We cannot possibly be doing a fucking musical performance together.

Can we?

By night's end, we've picked two songs for sure. Joseph is confident he can play "Listen to the Music" and "Night Moves." He's pledged to spend his off days practicing guitar. We're on location most of next week and he's only needed for one day. Plenty of time to rehearse, as long as he comes over one day to do vocals with me.

I agree, praying my cheeks aren't bright red.

By the time I leave set, I'm wondering how Joseph and I spent hours without touching today and yet he feels the closest to me he's ever been, like he's inches above my skin at all moments, his breath hot on my neck and his words dancing into my brain, a pleasant melody I could play on a continuous loop for days without once growing tired of the sound.

15

Week Five of Production

"Sloane? I'm Lucas."

My costar for the day has jogged from the tents over to me. He's a generically handsome white guy in his midthirties who I've seen in more than one period piece playing this exact role: the guy the girl doesn't choose. He's got the face for it. Sweet but maybe cloyingly so. The type of man you'd discover has a weak handshake and an inability to read the room.

The sight of him makes me long for Joseph. For his prosthetic scar and his crooked smile. The way his grip tightens around my waist, so sturdy I know I could dip backward and he wouldn't falter. He'd let my back arch in his hands until my head almost touched the ground. He's not here today, which is a small relief. Seeing him has become like looking directly at the sun.

"Hey. Nice to meet you." I extend my hand to Lucas for a

shake, surprised to learn his grip isn't weak at all. It's friendly and steady, with a lot of direct eye contact.

"How's it been going so far?" he asks.

"It's been an adventure. We've settled into a groove now, thankfully."

"I'm excited to be here. I *love* Guy Cicero."

Of course he does. Of course the draw isn't Tyler, or my mom. It's Guy.

I love him too though, so I play along. "It's been a lot of fun to work with him and my sister."

"Totally," Lucas adds.

"It's been really fun," I say again, catching my echo too late. Great. I'm the one who can't keep a conversation alive. "Well, I should go to the makeup trailer. See ya in a bit."

He looks at his phone to check the time. "Oh. I should too."

Naturally there's only one trailer, and we're the only two here aside from extras, so we walk there together. Get ready together. Force ourselves through all the standard talking points together.

Lucas tells me about his last project. His food allergies. His growing interest in woodworking. I tell him about my gala. He says he'll look into getting a ticket or donating. He won't, but it's okay.

Talking to him makes me remember all the ways it's different with Joseph. How when I leave work, I replay all of our conversations, combing through each interaction. What does he mean when he says he forgets to be late? Why is it that his compliments feel more genuine than other people's compliments? How is his collarbone so much sexier than other people's collarbones?

I can say with confidence that I won't spend a single minute of my free time revisiting this exchange with Lucas.

♥

Our workday consists of his character, Stuart, asking mine out on a date outside the grocery store. Lucas's bright-eyed enthusiasm gives the right hint of something vaguely sinister beneath the surface. His nervousness is a surprisingly hard beat to play without seeming like a parody. He improvises a bag fumble that Tyler loves so much she asks him to repeat it for every take.

If Joseph and I dance, then Lucas and I swim, lapping around each other in casual free strokes, our characters hiding their abilities to glide underwater like sharks. Tyler has a way of making me find Elise's backbone sooner. To let her enjoy seeing Stuart sweat a little. It's freeing to embrace Elise's confidence. My instincts were to make her a little shy. Tyler won't let me.

Elise is a shark. A smart, capable shark who chooses exactly who she allows near her.

In between takes, sitting in my designated chair under a tent—sweaty and bored and fully out of things to discuss with Lucas outside of the work itself—I contemplate texting Joseph. Something about saying hello on an off day feels like revealing too much.

Maybe I'll ask how his guitar rehearsal is going.

But I can't let on how desperately I need him to come through for me this weekend.

I opt to open Instagram instead. Someone on Joseph's team made him an account, and I would bet my life he's never logged on to it himself, but it's still something that feels like him. He must at least approve these posts. The latest one is from a week ago. It's a short teaser trailer for a movie he shot last year. *Swiped*, a techie action flick in which he's wearing a long brown wig and has a light goatee. I play it without the sound, watching his face mouth words I can only imagine are of a similar quality to my dialogue on *The Seeker*.

Seeing him in this ridiculous clip isn't the same as talking to him, but it's close. Enough to tide me over until I decide how to nonchalantly slide into his messages.

I'm about to click out of the app altogether when I see something on my timeline that makes me toss my phone up like a hot potato.

It's a post from Kearns.

In what can be viewed as either a move of great dignity or great pettiness, I refused to unfollow him post-breakup. That felt like too much of a concession.

The fist-clenching rage that swamps me at the sight of his face—casual, laughing, in calculated profile—is a stark contrast to the pure dopamine hit that came from looking at Joseph in a dorky-ass wig pretending to know shit about coding. It's unsettling how this person who used to take up so much real estate in my heart has now become someone who can make me actively angry on sight.

I do a furious swipe up to escape Kearns's presence. My eyes still manage to catch the last lines of his caption. Something about a benefit concert. I scroll back up, trying to make it so I can read the text without having to look at him.

My face must turn pale. Or maybe my entire body has gone so still it pulls attention toward me. Because Tyler is at my side within seconds.

"What's wrong?" she asks, panicked.

I show her the screen.

Kearns is holding a benefit concert in Los Angeles. The same night as my gala.

"Are you kidding me?" Tyler asks.

My hands have started shaking so hard I can hardly hold my phone. Tears threaten to fall, but I cannot give him the dignity. Not anymore. Not *ever.*

Instead I take as many cleansing, slow breaths as I can, my eyes clenched shut to redirect the tidal wave inside me. "We will make him pay," I say, hardly recognizing the low-toned threat in my own voice.

Tyler's grin is sly. The face of a person who has been waiting for a statement like this. "Tell me what I can do to help."

"You can message Emmy Carter," I blurt.

The idea that comes to me is immediate and fully dimensional. Emmy is a folk singer. Kearns's ex-girlfriend. The subject of his first album. I've never spoken to her before. Something tells me that's okay. She will be more than happy to join my impromptu plan.

"Ask her if she'd like to be a part of my gala performance," I say.

While Tyler drafts a message to Emmy via Twitter, I find the resolve within me and text Joseph.

How's rehearsal going?

Within minutes he sends back a video of him playing our third song choice, "Rock'n Me." It sounds perfect. A little unpolished but bursting with sincere effort.

Kearns may have taken the low road, but I will build a tunnel beneath him until I emerge so far ahead he can see me as nothing more than a distant mirage he can only dream of reaching.

16

W e finish our last half day on location with pickup shots. Elise reading the newspaper at a coffee shop. Her walk from the apartment to the grocery store. And finally, her frantic, running escape from her date gone wrong. There's no dialogue for any of this, which should make it easy. Unfortunately for me, sprinting barefoot down the sidewalk while holding back tears, over and over, isn't as effortless as I'd like it to be.

By the fifth take, I'm winded and unexpectedly overwhelmed. In the scene before this, Stuart has betrayed Elise. Pushed too far and tried too much too soon. Elise takes off physically unscathed. The emotional impact still hits. She wants a safe place to lay her head for the night.

In the next scene, she finds her mother isn't home. That's what pushes her to knock on Calvin's door and ask if she can sleep beside him. Just sleep. She's afraid to be alone.

This is, of course, when it turns into more.

Elise has no idea she's sprinting headfirst into the very thing she's spent years convincing herself she doesn't want. All she knows right now is she's terrified and alone and running through the dark without a hand to hold, but that's better than being touched by someone she doesn't care about.

While they reset the take, Mom comes and wraps a blanket around me. She holds me as I lean into her, both of us unsure why it is I'm crying. She doesn't need to ask questions, though. Sometimes the work is like this. Sometimes a scene guides you somewhere far deeper and darker than you intend to go, and it's all you can do not to be swept up inside your own imagination.

After my whimpers die down and I seem to be mostly all right, Mom finally speaks. "You used to do this when you were little."

"Do what?"

"Sob. Wail. Scream and cry. There was nothing we could do to comfort you. We tried everything. After a while we realized you would stop when you wanted to stop, and the best thing we could do was sit with you while you rode the wave." She's rubbing the side of my arm like she's hoping to at least keep me warm. "Tyler was easy. If I put her in a room with you, she was happy. And Powell was a little lover. All I had to do was hold him and he was kissing my cheeks with tears still running into his mouth."

I can see it so clearly. Tiny Powell with his head shaped like a block, smothering Mom with more affection than I've ever had the energy to give in my entire lifetime. And baby Tyler with her fingers in her mouth, dark eyes staring at me with alarming focus.

"I thought when you learned to talk that would solve it," Mom continues. "I gave you all the words I knew to teach. You still never told me how I could help you."

"I'm sorry," I say.

"Don't be sorry. It's who you are." She kisses the side of my head. "I think if you asked your father he'd say it's because you're just like me. Naturally, I think it's because you're just like him."

"Sounds about right."

She smiles. "I saw the way you and Joseph were looking at each other when we started this shoot, and I swear I thought I was having a flashback to me and your dad. We hated each other at first. Did you know that?"

Of course I know it. It's a famous part of their canon, how they were at each other's throats when they filmed *Touch*.

They were engaged three months after production wrapped.

But I let Mom tell the story anyways. When she gets past the details I could recite along with her, she says, "I know now that I was wrong for assuming you would make the same mistakes I did. Not that loving your dad was a mistake. He brought me the three greatest joys of my life. But I also spent way too many years still playing that game with him. Comparing my successes to his. Ranking my worth against his. Believing that everything I did had to be in some kind of response to him. It always starts as fun. Then suddenly you're looking in the mirror counting your wrinkles and going to bed counting your husband's and secretly making appointments to get yours injected so that you'll age slower and look better and be more beloved than the person you've chosen as your life partner." She wells up. "I'm sorry. I put all of that onto you when you've done nothing but show me that you're *not* me. In all the good ways."

After a thoughtful beat, she adds, "And you're not your father either. You're you."

I keep my mouth clamped shut and accept the apology. It's everything I've ever hoped to hear from her. She doesn't need to know that Joseph's coming over to my house tonight to rehearse for the gala, and while I'm terrified over whether or not we can pull off this performance, I'm excited to see him.

The truth is, I know I'm not her. In my bones I know it. Besides, this thing with Joseph and me? It's only casual.

Joseph shows up at my doorstep with his guitar slung across his back and flowers and chocolate in his hands. "Thank you for letting me come over." He's about to lean in for a kiss when I inform him that Sarai is already here, and Emmy and her husband are on the way.

He hands me what he's holding. These are not grocery store impulse buys. It's one of those $150 boxes of pink roses that can live for up to three years. And an eight-bar box of Compartés chocolates. Nearly a hundred dollars as well.

"You can't show up at someone's house empty-handed, and I didn't wanna buy booze," he explains, reading my startled expression.

"Of course. Thank you." I kiss his cheek in the most formal, courteous manner I can muster, using the opportunity to externalize my panic for a single second, frantically looking out into the dark beyond my entryway. "Come on in."

Sarai's in the living room with her tambourine, playing "Listen to the Music" on her phone and practicing the rhythm against her leg. "Hey," she says to Joseph, an ease in her voice that reads like she's known him for years. "Did you have enough time to learn everything?"

"Sure hope so."

His hands wrap tight around his guitar strap as he walks through my living room, going right past the banana leaf chair that everyone comments on when they first arrive. Instead he heads to the bookshelf beside my TV, pausing to tilt his head and read each title, saying nothing. Then he wanders from there to looking at Tyler's painting above my couch. Then the picture frames on my side table and the small, weird figurines and random art pieces I've amassed from years of going to the Melrose Trading Post.

His quiet appraisal of my home surprises me. He's always the type to immediately claim the energy of any space with the sheer brute force of his charm. But he's gently padding across the hardwood like a tourist in a museum, drinking it all in with an almost meditative focus. It's a funny contrast to Sarai hammering on with her rehearsal, tapping the tempo of the song with her heel while she hits the twos and fours on her tambourine.

When Joseph is done looking around, he makes a decisive turn to give me one small head bob of approval. I've spent so much time remembering how this home used to belong to Tyler and Kearns that I forget how everything that remains is only mine now.

"Would you like something to drink?" I ask.

"Water, please. And a tour of the kitchen, if you'll give it."

"Oh. Sure."

He follows me with the same light, cautious steps. Watches me open my refrigerator and take out my filtered water.

"What's new?" I ask, trying—and failing—to mimic the same ease my eleven-year-old sister just had.

He laughs at me, musical and lilting. "My fingers hurt." He shows me the blisters he's gotten from playing guitar.

I take his hand in mine to look closer. "When was the last time you played before this?"

"I had a band with my mates in Ireland when we were in primary school."

Joseph is nearly thirty-three. A quick round of mental math tells me that has to be at least fifteen years ago.

"We called ourselves Boys a Dear. Never played a single show, but we practiced a few times a week at my buddy Cian's house. Fancied myself to be a bit of a rock star in those days."

My doorbell rings, startling us both. I drop his hand and scoot back, a new wave of nerves rushing over me. "That must be Emmy and her husband."

"It's a good thing you went and got us a few real professionals." There's a truth behind Joseph's joke that I recognize, because I feel it, too. We are in so far over our heads with this performance.

Sarai answers the door, another of the countless gifts she gives me through her existence alone. "Welcome to the show!" I hear her saying, and I know without having to see them that Emmy and her husband are smiling. Sarai's presence is an injection of happiness into the veins. She loves to meet new people more than anyone I have ever known. It's comforting and startling, her ability to find the fastest route to a stranger's appreciation. She's shaking hands with Emmy and her husband, Garrett, when Joseph and I come to the door.

It feels unsettling to know so much about a girl I've never met. Someone whose name I've heard spoken like a curse. Whose music has caused more than one forced exit from various coffee shops.

Emmy has long red hair that grazes her exposed navel. A nose ring and a hypnotic rasp to her voice. It's even more pronounced in her singing; her music sounds like Janis Joplin doing lullabies.

"It's so nice to finally meet you. Thank you for helping me." I start for a handshake and she opens her arms to embrace me, which feels like the largest olive branch anyone has ever extended me. Her hug is tight and intentional, saying everything words couldn't. *I understand how you got here. It happened to me too. I'm excited to make him pay.*

Everything we've hinted at through texting wrapped up in one tight squeeze.

Her husband has the same gentle way about him. Dulcet toned with long shaggy hair and a Ramones tee that doesn't seem overwrought or even ironic. There's an honest-to-god coolness about the both of them that radiates. A quiet love humming in the space between their bodies, the kind of thing that seems sacred. Instantly I think of one of Kearns's songs about her.

I spent years searching for
A truth I'd never find
You gave me access to your heart
Never access to your mind

I hope it's the kind of line that makes Garrett laugh when he hears it.

We all come into my living room. Emmy immediately compliments both the banana leaf chair and Tyler's art. Garrett notes the copper light fixture overhead, the first thing I ever picked out for this house. It's these small kindnesses that bowl me over, filling me with a need to overcompensate. The fact that they've agreed to do this isn't lost on me. It's such a big gesture, as nice as it is satisfyingly vengeful.

There's not a ton of small talk to be had in a group like this, which is good. It lets us get to the work sooner. Garrett will be our bassist. Emmy backs up Joseph's guitar and harmonizes. Sarai on tambourine. Me on vocals, praying with every note that comes from my mouth that this will magically get easier by Sunday.

That my decades of insisting I don't sing will somehow dissipate and I'll be reborn as the kind of person who hops into a song and belts a high E because they can, then sits back down and eats their dinner with everyone else, shrugging off the barrage of compliments.

After the amps are all set up and everyone is plugged in and ready, we start with "Night Moves." I want to ask Emmy to sing with Joseph and let me fade into the background. Then Joseph looks my way when he starts the first verse and gives me this expression of utter gratitude, like there's no one he'd rather fumble through this with than me.

Joseph's dad can't get into town until the day of the show. Lucky for us, drums don't kick in until well into the first verse, and Sarai can hold down the tempo with her tambourine.

The second song we practice is what will actually be our opener, "Rock'n Me." Joseph's insistence we don't do any Beatles songs proves to be a smart choice. These songs are fun and joyful and lend themselves well to a group performance like this. And Joseph is a decent guitar player. Emmy and Garrett legitimize the whole thing, of course. We'd be drowning without them. With their help, we sound pretty damn good. As good as Daniel ever was.

We need a drummer for this one, but it's not too bad without him for now.

Joseph and I came up with a system for switching verses while sharing the choruses, and there's at least ten seconds where we're singing together and I'm not actively dreaming of finding a lightless cave to reside in for the next ten to twenty years.

When we finish the song, Garrett whoops out in appreciation. His seal of approval is a high I think I can ride for the remaining days until the show.

"This is going better than I expected," Emmy adds. "Should we become a real band?"

It's another ego stroke that bolsters me up.

We can pull this off.

We really can.

And then we move on to our first run-through of our finale.

Sarai hits the twos and fours of "Listen to the Music" with gusto. It doesn't matter, because without a drummer here, Joseph's having a hard time holding a consistent tempo. Emmy and Garrett are true professionals, eyes on Joseph's hands, trying their best to match his speed and salvage this. There's nothing I can do to help the situation. When a musical boat starts to sink, I only know how to watch it go under, so the verses I sing are fragmented and impatient. I can't hear where we're going and it's obvious.

A line of sweat forms a perfect river down the center of Joseph's head, over the slope of his nose and onto the rug under my coffee table. When the song slows, and it's only occasional strums while he sings the last bridge before the final swells of the chorus, he has an almost evangelical look about him. Feverish. Desperate to solve this. Emmy is supposed to take the fancy guitar riffs near the end, but she can't leave Joseph hanging, so she strums along with him to our disjointed finish. The instrumentation peters out and Joseph squeezes his eyes closed, wincing as if he's waiting for a scolding.

Sarai pulls the song up on her phone again. "We could play along with the real version until your dad's here," she proposes, so soft and kind I want to squeeze her. "I think that will really help me." She says it like her tambourine was the problem. Like she's the one who needs saving. It's a gesture so much bigger than her years and executed with the kind of simplicity that only seems to come from the hearts of children.

We run the number again, streaming the original track through my TV speakers. Having a driving beat behind us makes it so that when Joseph can't keep up, he's able to stop and let the song carry itself until he can jump in again. My two distinct vocal cracks are masked by the actual vocals. It's obvious this is the one song we really need Joseph's dad for, which means we will have to find time to rehearse during setup. Or wing it.

If I'm guessing, it will be the latter.

"It's supposed to be a fun thing anyways," I tell everyone, unsure who it is I'm trying to convince.

Emmy wouldn't have come to this if she wanted us to flop onto our faces. We want this performance to be worthy of reposting on our social media accounts. Something to give sound bites over. Something to draw attention to my foundation and pull in even more outside donors after the fact. Something to think of every time a Kearns song gets licensed for a commercial or a TV show.

The fact that Daniel Traverson used to fly by the seat of his pants every year truly astounds me now.

We rehearse a little while longer. When even Emmy starts missing some of her parts, I know it's time to call it. Everyone's come to this after a long day. There's no sense in making this even more frustrating for all involved.

Even with the lows, it's exhilarating to have created together. Made music with our voices and our hands in the middle of my living room, a place I once sat and cried with a cold plate of bucatini while hate-watching the movie Joseph and I shot in Ireland.

Emmy and Garrett head out, waving once and then linking hands. Sarai goes into the bathroom to get ready for bed. She's spending the night in Tyler's old room, then coming to set with me tomorrow, insistent that she doesn't mind the early wake-up.

Joseph makes a show of heading toward the door. "Better be going," he says, fishing his keys out of the back pocket of his jeans.

"Hold on."

I grab his arm and pull us to the little alcove of my front entryway, which is out of the eyeline of the rest of the house. Eleven-year-olds are nosy by nature, and it's not at all out of Sarai's wheelhouse to have her ear pressed to the bathroom door, listening to this conversation. I saw the way she clocked the chocolate and the roses and the quick glances between Joseph and me.

"Thank you. For all of this."

He waves me off.

"No. Don't make this a small thing. You've gone so far beyond what anyone's ever voluntarily done for me. I got an email today about your donation too. Which I really thought was a joke until the money came through. It means a lot."

"I told you. I owed you."

It's a strange thing to say, and it nags at me. "We're past the point of settling old debts and you know it. Don't act like you did it because you had to even the score."

"I'm not acting like anything, Sloane."

"Really?"

He grimaces. Takes a step back and then two forward, suddenly holding my face in his hands. It's the exact kind of indulgent gesture all the best actors used to use in theater school, and I hate that my mind goes there. Hate that I can't divorce my job from my real life in moments like this, when Joseph's looking at me with so much consideration that I can barely breathe.

"I just don't know what to do with you," he whispers.

"Don't think too much," I say, giving the one piece of advice I can never seem to follow, knowing full well that I'm playing this like a scene myself, landing every beat in a way that would have made my classmates softly applaud.

The truth is, to let go of my thoughts would be to let go of what keeps this from spiraling out of my control.

Then Joseph kisses me deeply, long enough to make me forget everything about performances and thinking and whatever else I had on my mind. He still has my face cupped in his hands, and the pressure between us is intense enough to bruise.

The bathroom door squeaks open.

"I'll see you tomorrow," Joseph says, walking off.

I can't resist one more lingering look to the darkness beyond the trees, needing some kind of acknowledgment from Mother Nature over all of this, because truly, there is no other way to handle how Joseph Donovan makes my heart race.

"Did Joe leave?"

Sarai stands in the hallway watching me. She's taller yet again, I notice now, even though in my head she's perpetually two years old with apple cheeks and an adorable way of saying my name. *Thone. Wanna play?* If she's anything like me, which I know she is, she'd hate that I'm not seeing her for who she is now. For all that's happened in her life since she was a bright-eyed toddler.

"Just now." I slowly close my door and walk toward the bedrooms. My attention has to shift to my sister or I will think of nothing but how my mouth tingles. "Ready for bed?"

Flicking on the light in Tyler's old room, I'm struck by how sparse it is without Tyler's crystals and rings scattered across the dresser. A stack of her boots beside the door. All the funky pillows she collected over the years. In her absence, I made everything cream. Life is simple in cream. Uncomplicated.

Boring.

Sarai takes one look at the room, then one at me. "Can I just sleep with you?"

I laugh. "Of course."

No matter how old she is, she'll always have a place in my room. There's something sacred about that, which she understands on an instinctual level.

By the time I'm ready for bed—night creams and serums and oils all applied to stop the hands of time—Sarai is still up, scrolling through her phone.

"Why aren't you asleep already?" I ask.

"I dunno. I was waiting for you I guess."

It warms me as I climb under the covers to lie beside her. We haven't had many chances for moments like these. There are so many years between us. But I am grateful that she still lets me in. Still wants to know me as much as I want to know her. I don't have to compare our closeness to my relationship with Tyler, because this is its own thing. We make the rules.

We lull ourselves near to sleep, talking about everything and nothing at all. We've had a long day, and we're both feeling it. But anytime one of us is close to closing our eyes, the other says something that shoots through the room like a lightning bolt, cracking us both up.

The later it gets, the easier it is to do. At one point all I have to say is "Fuckin' Powell," and Sarai is near hysterics.

After our longest bout of silence yet, I roll over to face her, finding her eyes are closed after all. "Sarai?" I whisper. "You still awake?"

"Yeah," she says in a hush.

"Thanks for helping me."

"You needed it."

"You're right," I tell her. It's the truth, and it's also exactly what I would've wanted to hear at her age. The way she smiles at me says it's exactly what she wants to hear too.

Eventually her breathing turns into gentle snores. My eyes well with tears. There are so many things happening in my life that I don't understand, but this simple truth will always exist: I will always need one of my sisters beside me under my covers, whispering into the darkness with me.

17

They say déjà vu is when something happens and it feels like you've lived it before. What's the name for actually reliving a moment from a different perspective? Because here's Joseph in suspenders and brown slacks, wire-rim glasses and a little swoop to his hair, crossing the set and saying, *"Elise. Whatever it is that has you avoiding my eye, you can tell me. I can handle it."* The very same line he tripped over on our first day of shooting.

Only now it's the end of the fifth week, an extra day tacked onto this already jam-packed schedule, and it's me in the powder-blue shirtwaist dress, red lips, and pin curls, pointedly staring at the floor, eyes brimming with tears. I'm the one who says in response, *"I tried so hard to do things right."*

Joseph—no, *Calvin*—puts a hand under my chin. *"Look at me, Elise. Please."*

I stare straight into his pupils, focusing on the pitch-black orbs instead of the wave-crashing irises around them. Treating the moment clinically. Avoiding the feelings bubbling over the surface, responding to his touch. The gaze holds.

And holds.

And holds.

Long and loaded and shifting from clinical into meaningful into something hopeless and unstoppable.

"And *cut*," Tyler whispers.

Joseph doesn't break from me right away. His stare lingers, hand still under my chin. After he lets me go, I have to actually shake my head side to side like I've been lifted from a trance.

When Joseph and I did *A Little Luck*, I plunged completely into that world, believing in my love for him. Then our director would call cut and I'd shoot right back up to the surface of myself, fully in my own body, scowling at my drunk costar.

Now, I'm waffling, caught between two places, seeing nothing but Joseph in moments when I'm supposed to see his character. Watching the way his arms flex as he moves, knowing things about his body that Elise doesn't know about Calvin's yet. The ways he likes to be touched. How he breathes when he's worked up. Heavy and drifting. The low, dangerous growl in his voice that comes out only then. Sometimes I get scared it's written all over my face, so I pull back further than I should until I'm not Elise or Sloane but a third-party bystander to the scene.

Tyler rests a hand on my shoulder, moving us away from Joseph. "We've been talking a lot about exchanges of power. How Elise leads with the knowledge that she has the upper hand. Right? But this is the moment it switches. For one moment, Elise accepts that she can't stop this. And I see the war of that in you, but I don't see the surrender. Give in a little. Not all the way. That's for the moment after the Stuart date. This is a tease."

She leaves me to give her notes to Joseph, preferring to talk to us separately, always loading our heads with secrets and leverages to use against each other in the scene. How can I make Elise give in a little when I don't know the line anymore? What's a little when I've already gone so much further than that? Above the belt isn't casual. Joseph was right. Not that it matters, because we've blurred that line like we've blurred every other. I'm afraid my version of giving in a little is actually giving in too much.

I shouldn't even be thinking like this. I'm the one who told Joseph not to think too much, and here I am thinking myself into a corner. I should just take Tyler's note and insert it into Elise's world. This is right before her date with Stuart. Before everything goes wrong and she takes off for home and falls into his arms. And it's a scene we absolutely need to finish today.

The professional in me leaps to the forefront, determined to get this right. When we run it again, I stand rooted in the world of Elise, leaving Sloane so far behind I don't even talk to Joseph between takes.

At the end of the scene, Joseph presses his lips onto mine. Soft and wanting. It's easy to push him back, because if I don't, I won't stop. Forget the lights and the dozens of crew people scattered about. This is what will make me lose it.

This exchange is meant to be cut off. Left hanging.

And it is.

It has to be.

When we break for dinner, making such great time we're likely to wrap early, I signal to Joseph that we have to go to his trailer. I have reached my limit of pushing back against my own desire.

I follow behind him, not bothering with our usual spaced-out getaway, instead rationalizing this as us needing to talk about the gala tomorrow. Which we do. Whenever a scene has felt too close to home, I've jolted myself out of it by allowing a little room to panic about the celebrity jam band. Not the best of acting choices, but effective nonetheless.

He closes his trailer door and we meet each other with lips parted, teeth bared. It's almost ridiculous how quickly the top half of his clothes come off. His *costume*. The parts that are the most Calvin, shed, finally giving me only Joseph. Above the belt, at least.

He lifts me up under my legs and presses me back into the door, my legs wrapped around him. My lipstick smears onto his cheek, something we discovered yesterday to much panic. Most of my shades are nontransferable, but this one is not. Luckily I was able to sneak off to the makeup trailer and get wipes and a fresh tube of red for such an occasion. Now the products live in one of his cabinet drawers.

He pulls back to let me see the lipstick imprints, knowing how much it made me laugh the last time. After we'd solved the crisis, of course.

I take to kissing every part of his face, aside from where the prosthetic scar has been carefully placed. Each eyelid. His nose. The space in front of his earlobes. I go until there's no more lipstick left to transfer.

It reminds me of being fifteen, my first boyfriend and me meeting up together at the park, having no real idea what to do with each other's bodies but feeling pretty confident with the mouth half of things, so just kind of living there, kissing each other in the most creative ways we could come up with in a public space.

While I know exactly what to do with the other half of myself these days, it's refreshing to subsist on silly things like covering Joseph's face in lipstick.

Still, after we move from the wall to the couch, him on top of me, my right hand gets curious, reaching beneath his belt buckle.

"Easy," he says, breathing heavy as I stretch past layers of fabric.

I play coy. "What?"

He laughs, lipstick stained and throaty. "This was your rule, miss."

"Was it?"

He pins both my hands at the side of my head now. "It was." He plants kisses on me in the same way I did to him, though he leaves no mark on my skin. Still, I feel it. Everywhere. Even in the places he doesn't touch.

"Are you ready for tomorrow?" I ask. "Because I'm not."

This makes him collapse beside me, nestled into the tiny sliver of space left for him on the couch. "My father should be in by late afternoon. He's asked for me to pick him up. From LAX."

"Wow. He really is an asshole, isn't he?"

Joseph laughs. "At least he's doing this for us."

The way he says it so easily—*us*, as in me and him—stops my breath. "It's very nice. People are really excited."

"What about Mr. Twat's Guitar Benefit? Any word from him about why he's gone and done such a shitty thing?"

"Not really. Someone on my team sent me a clip of him saying something about how there are a lot of days on the calendar to have a charity performance. As if I'm the one overlapping with his plans."

"At least he's raising money and not doing it solely for himself."

"So he says."

Too much talk of tomorrow has me jittery.

I get up and reapply my lipstick. Then take out the cosmetic wipes.

Immediately, Joseph sits upright, hands on his knees and chin jutted forward, ready for me to fix his face. Eyes closed, he waits for my hand to brush his cheek. To wash him. Serene and sure, trusting completely that I won't interfere with the work of our makeup team. That I will be able to clean up my mess without a trace left behind.

When I look at him like this, I know I am falling.

Falling and falling with no landing in sight.

18

Week Six of Production

I f you're in a gown, it means you're about to have either one of the best days of your life, or one of the worst," Mom says, checking her lipstick in the compact mirror she's stuffed into her handbag.

She's wearing an iridescent gold, one-shoulder number, draped lamé with a cinched waist and a leg slit that stops at her left upper thigh. I can close my eyes and drum up at least ten other variations on the gold dress and soft blowout she's done throughout her career. The major difference this time is the lip color, a deep plum that she's looked at in the mirror three times on the car ride over to the Hilton.

I fiddle with the diamond bracelet I've been lent. "Let's hope this one is good then."

"*Choose to make it so,*" she says, reaching over to stroke my cheek.

Six days a week of Producer Mom almost made me forget about this version. Lightly whimsical and bizarre, spouting off fragmented remembrances of her favorite inspirational quotes. It draws into focus how true it is that set life isn't real life; it's a heightened facet of our personalities, professionally lit by a director of photography.

"I've never had the pleasure of wearing a gown, but I've enjoyed every event in which you've worn one," Guy tells Mom from the second row of the SUV, turning his head to look at her.

It's ridiculous, but it helps me stay calm, the both of them seemingly free of the stress they've worn throughout the shoot. Of course I've picked all that surplus up—with some extra for added flair.

We get out of the car and head inside. This is the same venue where they hold the Golden Globes, and it's something I can't fixate on for very long, because our red carpet isn't even the length of a swimming pool. It's a ten-foot-long step and repeat near one of the bigger ballrooms of the Beverly Hilton. The white canvas backdrop is about eight feet high with the words 4TH ANNUAL SLOANE FORD FOUNDATION GALA printed across it in a repeating pattern, along with all of our top-tier sponsors. A fence of red velvet rope sections it off from the photographers. Their lenses capture an elegant nighttime affair. Our eyes see a handful of people standing in low lighting in the place you'd accidentally wheel through with your luggage, lost on the way to the elevator.

I was here at the hotel this morning, checking in, helping with setup and overseeing the final details. Usually Kearns and I would spend the previous night at the Hilton and I'd get ready there with him and a small team, then come down early and get the carpet stuff out of the way. I still have a hotel room booked for tonight, solely to hold my outfit change for me.

No date, though. I thought going with my mom would be a nice way to feel better about everything that's changed in the last 365 days.

Naturally, Mom insisted we be late to my own event, which is something I should have anticipated when I asked if I could ride with her. Mom is old school. So is Guy. The two of them together seemed to be locked in a battle over who could take the longest. When our SUV arrived, Mom went inside to get the gel insoles for her Louboutins. She came back out, and Guy remembered he hadn't rinsed with mouthwash.

I felt so thoroughly fifteen by the time we actually got on the road that it's a miracle I didn't ask for the driver to put on my Emotional Pop-Punk Classics of the Early 2000s playlist.

Now we're here, and it's happening, and all of that melts away when I see the small crowd waiting to walk the carpet and go into the ballroom. There's always a shadow thought plaguing me, saying no one will show up. Year after year, the people come. The prior year's contributions are celebrated. More money is raised. All of the monthly planning meetings, and the subcommittees, and the sub-subcommittees—and dear god, the never-ending email chains—are worth it.

Dad and Daya are having their photo taken as we walk up. My dad has the look of someone who relishes the exposure of a flash, someone who can gaze into a lens and know what looks back without having to see. His arm cradles Daya's waist, and she's matching his energy, though where his smirk says, *I've won Oscars and we all know it,* hers says, *This charade is ridiculous and I'm loving every second of it.*

"Good. We beat him," Mom comments.

I stare at her. "Are you sure you didn't want to head back to the house and run the garbage disposal really quick? Check that all the smoke detectors are working? Rearrange your closet by date of purchase? Then we'd really destroy Dad by missing the event altogether."

"Oh, honey. You have lipstick on your teeth." Mom stretches out a finger and rubs my left incisor.

On the near side of the red carpet, there are a few attendees waiting in small groups, held back by members of the foundation team. Our step and repeat is so small that people have to go down one or two at a time. Mom glides past all of them, deciding to impede upon Dad's moment as only she can. For all her acknowledgment of their unhealthy professional pettiness, she refuses to let it die.

I give a rushed hello and sympathetic look to our carpet attendant as Guy and I follow Mom, knowing instinctively that even though I'm the reason we're here, she's the one we put in the middle. That way I can break off for solo shots and they can do pictures together.

We start with the typical, delivering yard-long smolders. Guy and Kitty move down, and I'm left to pivot and twirl alone. My least favorite part. The gauzy red dress I'm wearing has a neckline so plunging that I have to turn with precision or my boob tape will come loose.

It's always better to have another person to play off of, to wrap your arm around when the nerves reach their peak and you can't for the life of you remember how it is you normally stand.

As I'm midpose, my eye snags on a familiar sight, a tall Irishman rushing toward me with a guitar slung over his shoulder. There's a little flutter inside my chest that makes me reach up and press my hand to my heart. Not that I doubted he would come. He has proven to be more than reliable. But the reality of his physical presence swells underneath my skin.

My involuntary chest clutch reads like a coy photo op. One photographer calls out, "Love it, Sloane! Turn this way!" My attention stays placed on Joe until his face says, *There you are*, and it's enough to make me beam, losing all sense of the smirk I've manufactured for moments such as this one.

He passes his guitar to our attendant—she's truly great at her job, because she accepts it like she's been waiting all night to hold an instrument—and he joins me on the red carpet.

All of it happens so quickly I have no way to stop it. Rationally I know that pictures like these are great press for both the movie and the foundation. That 4TH ANNUAL SLOANE FORD FOUNDATION GALA watermark is in every single shot. More than that, I want this chance to have his arm wrapped around me in public and have not a single person wonder why.

He's wearing a deep blue tuxedo with a black velvet collar and black velvet piping down the side seam of the pants. The blue fabric must be threaded with something metallic, because when it catches the light, it's wonderfully vibrant, striking against his sharp white undershirt and classic black bow tie.

He leans down to me and whispers, "You look unbelievable."

A dozen flashes go off at once, capturing my measured thank-you and his easy pullback. He places a light hand on my mid-back, leaving a good three inches between our bodies.

The entire extended moment doesn't read as too intimate. Everyone greets one another with close whispers while in front of cameras. It's like how baseball players always talk to each other through their gloves. But my ear tingles where he touched it, and my skin sparks against the feel of his hand on the exposed part of my back.

"How are you?" I ask through my teeth as we grin for the cameras.

"Nervous." He moves us down a bit farther on the carpet. "I have something to tell you."

"Right now?"

"Yes." We angle ourselves toward the right. "My dad isn't coming."

My plastered smile flattens. "What?"

"I'm so fuckin' sorry," he says, still gritting his teeth and posing. "He never showed at the airport. I called and called him. He finally rang back on my way over here to say he missed his flight."

My limbs start to float away from my center. My mouth tastes like vinegar. I rush us through the rest of the photo ops, grateful I chose not to have any interview element on the carpet this year. Usually I'd want all the attendees to give nice sound bites about why they support the foundation. This year my personal life has so fully eclipsed all my community contributions that even though I'm running the event, I know the line of questioning could slip away and push me toward any of the handful of loaded topics surrounding me: Kearns's album, his benefit concert, Haven's firing, my departure from *The Seeker*, Dad's heart attack. It's a real Choose Your Own Adventure of awkwardness, and it would only take away from the night's true focus.

At least that's what I tell myself to help me sleep at night.

The second Joseph and I step out of the lights, I state the obvious. "We need a drummer."

"I know. I was calling people. Turns out I don't know any drummers. Other than my buddy Cian back in Ireland. Don't think he can get to the states in the next few hours." The way he talks—hand insistent on my back, mouth tight and careful—tells me how upset he really is. I know him so well now. I can see the tension etched into the space between his brows. Feel the way his jokes are as much to calm him as they are me. "Christ, Sloane. I really fucked it all up."

"No you didn't," I assure him. "You *helped* me. We will figure it out." I guide us toward the ballroom doors. "Here goes nothing."

The lights inside are mostly purple and blue. It always feels a little like a wedding in here, which is something donors tend to respond to in a positive manner. Weddings are events that bring a lot of giving. A lot of celebrating. Our event designer leans into that, while doing away with the more obvious matrimonial touches. No floral centerpieces or romantic candles. Instead, each circular table features a school that has been helped by the money we've raised in years past. On the projector screens that flank the stage, photos play on a loop, reminding people exactly where their donations go. A silent auction wall takes place along the left side of the space, filled with nearly a hundred donated baskets and items from local businesses, perfectly catered to the interests of an audience full of actors, directors, producers, musicians, and other entertainment-centered people. And an open bar sits along the right side, along with mountains of appetizers and small desserts.

The stage is dead center with two screens on either side of it that will eventually livestream what's happening up there, ensuring the people near the back can see the action up close.

Joe looks utterly zombified, staring forward. "Fuck," he whispers.

"Fuck," I repeat. It cuts through the tension enough to make us both laugh.

We're screwed.

We really, really are.

After much pre-event mingling, the gala kicks off with video packages from the various schools we've helped. Teachers we've worked with and the kids who've been given access to the world of performing arts. Last year was our best yet. We were able to renovate two music rooms, give funding to start a theater program at a middle school, save another program from folding, and provide camera equipment to four different high schools.

I watch the whole video from the shadows, waiting along the side of the stage to walk up and give my opening speech. This is the first relief I've felt in hours, standing here alone while our highlight reel plays. The work we do with this foundation really makes me proud. When I'd started it, I wanted it to be an extension of me, a kid who got to grow up immersed in a world of performing arts. There's no telling how much that shaped me, because there isn't a single corner of my life that hasn't been affected by the fact that I have always been in this position. Always had privilege and wealth and access. If I spent my whole life never trying to share that, to redistribute some of what's been stacked in my favor since my first wailing breath, then I'd be truly selfish.

It's not enough. Nothing ever could be. And I really shouldn't have named the foundation after myself, I know now. We're rebranding after this year. It's too me-centric for something that's really about other people. That's the price that comes with learning in public. You wear your mistakes like forehead tattoos, and even if you find a way to get them removed, everyone still remembers what used to be there.

The video ends and I walk out to speak, for the moment embracing the fact that I am Sloane Ford at the Sloane Ford Foundation Gala. I crack well-written jokes crafted by an expert team, even throwing in a few of my own improvisations. Mostly about my family. It's an easy and effective route. I make eye contact with people I don't know, people who've known me since I was a cantaloupe-size bump in my mother's belly, and every type of person in between. They've all come here for me. For this. And it's my job to encourage them to keep coming back. To write us those checks and spread around their excessive wealth too.

After my opening speech, which Guy calls "rousing and inspired," and Dad says "was a little hard to hear at first, but they got the sound worked out by the middle," I take my seat at our table.

We're seated at a circular twelve top right in front of the stage. Counterclockwise it's me, Tyler, her girlfriend Mara, Powell, Mom, Guy, Melanie's husband Terrence, Melanie herself, Sarai, Dad, Daya, and the twelfth seat. Right beside me. At the last minute, Powell decided not to bring a plus-one. That's how Joe ended up here, rounding out the last spot on the clock, his elbow pressing into my side.

He leans in. "Did I tell you already that you're unbelievable?"

I bite back a blushing smile. "I believe you did." I don't turn my mouth toward him. My family can read my lips if they want. We're not saying anything worth hiding.

Then his hand slyly reaches for me under the table, landing on my inner thigh. He gives one squeeze, and there's a sudden pulsing between my legs.

"Making sure." He pulls back, and it leaves me desperate with want, which is the number one worst feeling to have while at a table with every single member of my immediate family.

Glori begins her effortless work as the event emcee, offering a welcome distraction. Her aggressive brand of hustling people and casual ribbing is tailor made for this setting. She leans against the podium and does her first of many bits of the night, pretending to auction off the most famous people in the audience, ranking them by their IMDb STARmeter. I wasn't sure about this gag. I asked her to come up with something a little less controversial. She sells me on it in the moment, somehow putting the audience at ease while shining a spotlight on the most elite among us, making sure they're ready to open their wallets and contribute.

This is why she's one of the best in her business. She can nudge you toward working on a romantic war drama with your entire family, and less than a week from wrapping the production you realize it's the best decision you've ever made in your entire career, and you can hardly put your finger on all the reasons why, because there are so many.

After Glori finishes her opening remarks, we break for dinner and chatting. Sound doesn't carry well in a space like this. Joe, Daya, and I end up in our own conversational subgroup while we eat our meals. Powell has already left to prepare for his drag act. I should have followed him and changed my dress before dinner, because now I have to curate my every bite until it is so small there's no way I can drop a single morsel. At the very least, the gaping V running down the center of this halter gown means that one of my boobs has a higher chance of catching a stray roasted potato than the dress itself.

Normally I'd wash everything down with a healthy swig of champagne. Watching Joe nurse his club soda and lime has me reaching for my water instead.

Daya carries the weight of my secret with such ease I'd all but forgotten the day Joe and I first kissed. That's how well she holds herself back, giving nothing away. I really do want to know her better after this movie wraps. She may be the only person in my life who has ever made me feel as though my every word will not be broadcast to the family at large, be it accidentally or intentionally. In fact I can't remember a time in years that I've wanted so badly to be someone's friend.

She's asking Joe about doing her movie again. "What are you

so worried about? I'm telling you right now. You're the only person I want for this."

"I dunno. Falling flat on my ass," Joe says.

"Hey now. We all saw that new trailer for *Swiped*. It doesn't get worse than that."

If the joke is punching down, she's landed it in a place that doesn't cause harm, because both Joe and I crack up. I reach up for his head and grab a fistful of his hair, remembering that ridiculous lace front he wears in the trailer. "If you do it, put in your contract that you refuse to be wigged."

"No. We'd have to do a wig," Daya adds on. "My movie is set in 1994. It would be a crime to turn our backs on the option to give Joseph Donovan a floppy bowl cut."

I move my hand from Joe's hair to his jaw. "He's got the bone structure for it."

It's only when I pull back that I catch the twinkle in his eye. My hands had reached for him so instinctively.

Casual touch, I assure myself. The result of two people who've spent the last five weeks of their lives together for nearly every waking moment. It happens with every project. Some nights on the set of *The Seeker*, Daniel Traverson would all but breathe the same air as me and know that I needed another coffee. Context is different. The idea is the same.

Isn't it?

"Do you play the drums?" I ask Daya, seemingly out of nowhere. Thinking of Daniel led me to the jam band, which led me to thinking of the top layer of my suppressed panic, the one I am not dulling with copious amounts of champagne like I normally would.

"When I tried to play Sarai's tambourine, I sounded like I was cannonballing into a pool full of glass. Alex was in the other room.

He ran in to see what happened. He said, *Sweet shit! I thought you broke my awards display!*" Daya does a pitch-perfect impression of my dad, down to the goofy swearing and completely selfish concern that the glass case around his two Oscars may have been compromised. "Why do you ask? Do you need a drummer?"

Joe and I both go so still she immediately switches from playful questioning to full concern.

"Wait. Is your dad not coming?"

Joseph shakes his head.

We do not mention it for the rest of our meal.

Powell is the first performer of the night. His drag act is an exaggerated version of Mom: Katty Hoarder, a feline-obsessed queen who never lets go of anything. It's the kind of absurd that circles all the way around to being amazing, and Katty's performance to "You're So Vain" has so much going on that everyone is absolutely transfixed. It feels like it's about Dad because it *is* about Dad, and yet the whole time Katty Hoarder also references the infamous *Cats* movie—complete with a bedazzled catnip shaker. She has a Dolly Parton–meets–Kitty Porter wig on with cat ears over it.

I look around our table to take in everyone's reaction. Dad's stern but not unmoved. Even he has to laugh when Katty starts magically pulling dozens of random things out of the pockets of the gold skirt she wears over her unitard.

Daya and Guy hoot and holler like two rowdy concertgoers.

Mom is actually crying, dabbing her eyes with her napkin. I'm unsure if it's pride or amusement. Probably both. Tyler and Mara are making the exact same expression—stunned appreciation. Melanie is in hysterics, clutching her husband's arm. Sarai sings along and marks some of the choreography. And Joe bobs his head with fervor, his hand striking down on the table every time Katty nails a beat.

When Katty finishes with a death drop, then revives herself, only to death drop again, the entire room erupts in applause. Everyone gives her a standing ovation, to which she graciously comes to life for a bow and then slinks off to stage left, down the stairs and out a side door to transform back into the Powell we know during the day.

It's a high that leaves the room buzzing, everyone milling about, heading toward either the silent auction items or the open bar, then swapping sides.

She should've been the closer, I think, watching everyone bid on waxes they don't need or movie night packages for films they've produced. At least there will be a good amount of distance between Katty Hoarder and the jam band. Daya's stand-up will make everyone laugh. Dad's jazz songs will soothe everyone. Then the jam band will . . . well, we will definitely be there.

That's for sure.

One hour and twenty-four minutes later, I'm standing behind the stage, wearing a green sequined minidress with my hair down in loose curls. It's nice to be free of the boob tape and the inability to breathe, but all this exposed skin makes me prickle with nervous goose bumps. I rock back and forth, shaking and stretching and hoping that the tension in my throat will dissolve and the notes I'm soon to sing will not sound strained. I spent too many of my conversations tonight trying to casually find out if anyone was not only a drummer, but someone who wouldn't mind coming onstage during a performance and playing three songs without any rehearsal. No surprise to find that my very niche request was not fulfilled.

One by one, the rest of our jam band meets me on the floor behind the stage. Sarai first, her tambourine matching the sparkly silver mock-neck jumpsuit she's wearing. She's got a young Diana Ross look to her, curly black hair big and flowing, a hint of shimmer on her cheeks.

"This is gonna be so fun," she tells me. I hug her, praying to absorb even a fraction of her candid excitement.

Emmy and Garrett appear next. One of our attendants has been monitoring their instruments all night, and Emmy and Garrett take their guitar and bass respectively, slinging them over their shoulders and then making all kinds of little adjustments.

"Whew," Garrett says. "No sound check. Okay." He starts jumping up and down to excite himself.

Emmy closes her eyes, lids bare except for two dramatic swipes of liquid liner, and begins humming. She's in a full monochromatic ensemble, a burnt-orange flared pantsuit the exact shade of her hair.

I spoke to her earlier in the night, not having the heart to admit we don't have a drummer. Watching how seriously she prepares, I know it was a mistake. She came here for revenge. For solidarity. For the cause. Above all, she came here because she loves music.

She is not going to love this.

Her eyes open to stare right at me, like she can read my mind. "Where's Joseph and his dad?" she asks.

"I . . . don't know," I say, because truly, I have no idea where either of them are. Joe was at the table when I went up to my room to change after Dad's jazz set. He knew to meet me back here.

I peek around the corner to scan the audience. His seat at our table is empty. He's not recognizable among the crowd. There's fear coursing through my veins. There's also a sense of longing. All night, he's been the one person I can spot within seconds. Every time, he's already been looking for me or at me, no matter our proximity to each other.

Without saying a word, I charge through the ballroom and out the front doors, my gold pumps clomping and sucking against every step, the back of the shoe struggling to stay wrapped around my heel at this speed. I turn left outside of the venue, and there he is, slouched against the wall.

I plant myself in front of him, sitting on my feet with my hands atop his knees. "What's wrong?"

His face is blank.

"I promise you, it's okay that your dad isn't here. We are gonna get through it."

"No. It's not that. I'm . . . I . . ." He lifts up his hands, which are violently shaking. "I guess I should've told ya I have a bit of stage fright."

"Oh." A million feelings whirl through my head at once: disbelief, confusion, worry, sadness, determination, pride, fear. I think of him sauntering through life, swaggering into each room. Then I think of all the times he's been on edge. A constant jitter to him that's come to be so commonplace I've stopped wondering why.

"It's not so bad when I'm acting," he explains, answering the question most would ask. Not me. I've been around the business long enough to know that more than half of all actors are terrified all the time. "It's the playing and singing that gets me. The two things at once."

I take his shaking hands in mine and hold them. "Is that why Ireland was robbed of the opportunity to see Boys a Dear live?"

"We were supposed to do a set at my sister's birthday party. I passed out before we ever went up." He almost laughs. "It was in our backyard."

This is too delicate to rush, but I can hear Glori onstage, prepping the crowd for our performance. Thankfully she can vamp with the best of them. There's maybe two minutes to convince Joe to find a way to make his courage louder than his fear.

"I like you so much," I blurt out. It shocks not only Joe, but me. I power through, hoping that maybe this will show him exactly how to be brave when bile is building in the back of your throat. "Don't tell anyone inside. You're officially number one on my best friend list."

His hands are still shaking, but a hint of personality returns to his face. "Number one? Can I get that in writing?"

He's attempted a joke, which means there is still hope. "Only if you come sing with me," I say, pulling him up to stand with me.

"Okay," he says weakly.

With my hand wrapped tight around his, I open the door and march us through the entire ballroom. There's no time to worry about this gesture or how people will receive it. If I let him go, he will leave. His grip is fixed on mine like he's hanging from a cliff.

We head around to the back of the stage, where the rest of our band waits for us impatiently.

"You scared us," Sarai tells me. "We thought you left."

"Nope. We're here. But I have some bad news. We don't have a drummer." There's a collective gasp of horror, everyone surely remembering our one and only rehearsal. "It's okay. I have an idea."

Before I can elaborate, Glori begins announcing us one by one, starting with Garrett. He has no choice but to leave this conversation hanging and round the corner with a wave, disappearing from sight. Emmy follows. From where Sarai, Joe, and I wait, we can hear the two of them plugging in onstage, little guitar licks and bass strums to check the volume levels.

Glori calls up Sarai. She smiles at me, then jogs off around the corner, shaking her tambourine the whole way. "Hope your idea is good!" she calls out as she goes.

It's only Joe and me now.

Glori calls his name and he doesn't move. He's still holding my hand, tighter yet, a new wave of panic all over his face.

"Sloane," he says, deadly serious. "I really don't think I can go out there."

I figured I was on borrowed time, but I thought I'd be able to at least get him onto the stage with me. Finding a more permanent solution will be difficult to do with roughly fifteen seconds to spare.

"Normally, I'd have a good, stiff drink," he explains. "Or hell, in my twenties, even a bump or two."

"We're *definitely* not gonna do any of that."

"I know." He winces. "Fuck. I'm scared outta my mind."

I stroke his cheek with my free hand, praying I won't need to find a bucket for him. "Close your eyes."

Glori's calling Joe's name again, this time a little more sternly.

"Don't worry about that. Close your eyes."

He does, probably thinking I'm about to do some kind of visualization exercise with him. Maybe I should. I don't know what to tell him to see, though. This is so far out of my wheelhouse.

"My favorite thing about you is your ability to change," I start, improvising without a destination in sight, letting out an anxious breath of my own. "You've shown me over and over that you are more than willing to become someone better. I'm not saying you can just *decide* to not have stage fright, but I know from experience that you are the best person in the entire world at winging things. If this situation was reversed, you'd have figured out a way to get me up there that I can't even imagine right now because I don't have that gift, and that's why we're standing here doing this in the first place."

He nearly laughs.

Good.

"Tyler says I say what I mean and I don't feel bad about it, but I don't want to just say the first thing that comes to my mind," I tell him. "I want to say the *right* thing to you. Because when I've been so scared on set these last few weeks, you've been the one who makes me feel safe enough to try anyways. I watch you fail and pick yourself up and keep going until you get it right, and you do all of that with a smile—which is a fucking great smile, by the way—and it's everything to me. You are absolutely everything to me right now, Joseph Donovan."

He opens his eyes to contemplate me. His lips are pursed, and his breaths are coming out in short puffs, but he's looking at me the same way he holds my hand. Like he's still dangling off a cliff, and I am the only person in the world who knows how to save him.

I think of all those times on set where I was his obstacle. How scared I made him. And how hard it has to be for him to put all his faith into me in this moment. How brave it is for him to show me that he's terrified.

"I'm going to be honest," I continue. "I am really, really scared right now too. But I know if I get to go up on that stage with you, it won't be so bad. Because I will look over at you, and you will already be looking at me. And you will somehow make me forget that I really hate to sing. Like fully detest it. Like 'refused to do drunken karaoke at my brother's twenty-first birthday' level of hate."

He bounces from foot to foot. Either this is almost working or he's about to sprint to the nearest trash can.

"To go up and completely bomb would be mortifying," I admit. "If we do it together, somehow I know it will be okay. Because it's you. And it's me. And we are pretty damn good at making the most of bad situations together. So please, please come with me. If you suck, I suck. I promise."

Abruptly, he lets go of my hands and sprints around the side of the stage.

It all happens so fast I can't process what's going on until I hear him say into the mic, "Don't mind me, I'm a jammy bastard, stealing up a few last moments of rehearsal time with our star." There is not the slightest waver in his voice. He is all brogue and charm.

My eyes well with tears. I'm glad I'm still backstage, because I need a moment to process how it is we've gotten to the point where the sound of his persona makes me want to cry.

He's doing this for me, putting on the full Joseph Donovan Brand.

"You have to forgive me," he says to the audience. "She is the woman of the night, after all. A lass that's made more of a difference in people's lives in one day than most of us have done in a whole lifetime. When she cares about something, she gives it everything she has. So it's time for the lot of you to show her some love back. Please give it up for the one and only Sloane Ford!"

He's stolen Glori's intro from her, which she's quick to let me know as I pass her onstage, walking on as she walks off. Joseph hands me the mic, no trace of the nerves he showed me only a minute ago.

Our fingers brush.

It's electric.

He smiles, encouraging me forward. "You suck, I suck," he whispers in my ear.

My nerves are replaced by a warmth that spreads through me the same way alcohol does. I feel buttery somehow. Loose. Free.

"Good evening, everyone," I say into the mic. The crowd roars in response. "Thank you again for coming out tonight. You already know how much this foundation means to me, so I don't need to say it again. Instead, I have a favor to ask of you. We've had a little last-minute snag, and we're without a drummer."

The audience goes quiet.

"Exactly. Not much of a show to do without the percussion, right? So I'm wondering if there's someone out here in this very talented crowd who is brave enough to come up and play with us?"

The shell-shocked silence continues.

"Come on! It's only three songs. You'll know them when you hear them. And! You will be up here making a memory to last you a lifetime."

Still no takers.

"I don't know if all of you know this," I start. Bless the looseness of my limbs. Otherwise I'd surely keel over. "Last year, this jam band featured two men who were pretty important in my life at the time. And Keanu Reeves, who is always important in my life, but not really the point of what I'm about to say."

Thank god they laugh at that.

"If you've read any news about me lately, you'd know that those other two, non-Keanu guys haven't done me much good this past year. And I've been working really hard to overcome all of it. Lucky for me, I've had a lot of amazing people in my corner helping that along. Coming together to solve what could have been a real disaster. A celebrity jam band with no celebrities to jam! What horror!"

The audience laughs again.

Little by little, it's working.

"These people you see behind me, ranging from my superstar baby sister, to my wonderful costar, to a Grammy Award–winning bassist, to an unbelievably amazing musician who happens to share a certain ex in common with me. They all came here tonight with the sole goal of helping me out. It would be a real shame if we couldn't play this music for you the way we intended to, with a drummer behind us to drive it all home. All for a cause that's really incredible, if I do say so myself. So I ask again, who wants to come up and play?"

The silence stretches again.

Breaking through the hush is a clear, confident "I will."

My eyes roam the crowd for the source. Then I see. The wide-legged gait. The backward pageboy cap and the gap-toothed smile. Guy Cicero ambling his way onto the stage.

The crowd starts to slow clap. "Don't bother with that yet!" he yells, waving them off. "Save it for my finale!"

"You play the drums?" I whisper once he's up here with us.

"My dear, my father was a drummer." He grins proudly, then moves himself behind the drum set. Takes the pair of sticks from atop the seat and spins one through his fingers. "Get ready for the ride of your life!" he tells both the audience and all of us onstage, though honestly, I don't think there's any way to get ready for what's about to happen.

Garrett turns his back to the crowd to whisper to Guy, telling him our songs and talking about time signatures and other musical stuff that's going all the way over my head. It might be over Guy's head too, but he is nothing if not consistent, full-wattage grinning and nodding as if this is exactly what he woke up this morning planning to do.

Joe starts fiddling with his guitar, strumming random chords, tapping his foot and doing little hops and walks.

Meanwhile, Sarai of all people has taken to vamping now, leaning into her mic and asking the crowd how they're doing. "You people excited to hear us perform now?" She has the measured confidence of a seasoned pro. "When I say 'jam,' you all say 'band.' Ready? Jam!"

The crowd echoes, "Band!"

"That's right! I hear you! Jam!"

"Band!"

We've got them now, all the way in, desperate to discover if we're going to sink or sail.

Once our band seems settled, the audience is so in tune with us that an understanding hush falls over the room.

Garrett counts us in.

Off we go into our first number, "Rock'n Me."

The song literally starts with a drum roll, which Guy nails like he's rehearsed it a thousand times before. Joe misses his entrance he's so stunned. Guy repeats the intro again, unfazed. He has that perfect head-bobbing drummer swag to him, more at ease than everyone onstage combined, looking around at the rest of us like *Come on, guys, let's play!*

Joe doesn't falter this time. Emmy sweeps in to back him up, the both of them gliding through the intricate opening while Garrett's bass kicks in, thumping along as fast as my heart beats. When it comes time for Sarai's tambourine, she's so fully inside the music that her head sways back and forth as she shakes along to the beat.

Joe starts the first verse. His gruff tone has an intoxicating urgency to it. I leave my mic to share his, desperate to climb inside this moment with him. He turns his head to sing sideways, eyes on me as he rocks us all the way to the chorus, neck muscles pulling taut as he reaches into his upper register and growls out the high notes. I get up on my tiptoes to meet him at the mic, my lips inches from his.

The song ends with Joe and me harmonizing into a fade-out, softer and softer until there's nothing left. All I want is to press myself against him and never let go.

He feels it too. Leaning closer. Inches turning to centimeters.

Then the crowd cuts the tension with their applause, snapping us back to an appropriate distance.

The next song, "Night Moves," flies by in a heady daze, soft and sweet and so easy I'm able to wander the stage as we sing, sharing a mic with Sarai and Emmy and even Guy, who jumps on to the vocals the same way he jumped behind the drum set, eagerly and without fear.

By the time we reach our finale, there's a gloss of sweat coating my skin and a pulsing all through my body. It's so utterly alive, this feeling, deep enough to get lost inside. I can't remember being nervous. Or scared. Any of it. There is only raw adrenaline coursing through my veins, making me certain I could lift cars.

Guy kicks in with the drums. His beat is as alive as the feeling inside me. I turn around to see Emmy has a wild, free-floating way about her, eyes squeezed shut and hips gently swaying. It's the same look I've seen in the performances I've watched of her on YouTube, the comment section full of her fans assuring me that this is how she gets when she's really feeling it. Sarai has it too, shimmering and twinkling, slamming that tambourine on her hip. Garrett's looking at me, bobbing his head up and down in approval.

And Joe.

Joe is as I said he was.

Everything to me.

We sing together like we've always done this. Like we wrote this song for us. Like this is our favorite activity. Not the very thing that had the both of us pale faced and worrying ourselves near sickness.

Near the end I am so feverishly happy I start to cry, wrapping an arm around Joe, swaying the both of us side to side while we take it home. All the bad things, the strange moments over the past year that I once saw as tally marks of failure, come to me now as stepping-stones. Rocks I've had to climb over to get to here. To see this view.

It's a great fucking view.

When we finish, Joe wraps me up in his arms, holding me tight enough to lift my feet off the ground, kissing my cheek over and over. Sarai piles onto the side of me, squeezing tight. Then Emmy and Garrett. Then Guy. He tries to be on the outside of our circle, and we have to reconfigure, because he is undoubtedly our hero.

We rearrange into a kick line, turning toward Guy with our hands pointing in his direction, encouraging the audience to cheer for him and him alone. Then we wrap our arms around each other's backs and take a collective bow. The DJ plays the album version of "Listen to the Music" as an outro, and we dance our way offstage to it, the crowd still standing.

While the rest of the jam band goes to their seats, I pull Joe behind the stage. Out of the audience's sight. I kiss him as hard as I ever have. Leg wrapped around him. Hands in his hair. I have never felt this desperate to be breathing someone else's air.

"We are not at work," I say, pulling back. "Do you know what that means?" I reach my hand into the pocket I had sewn into this dress—a stunning feature—and slip my room card into the front of his pants. "I have a room upstairs. You'll go up ahead of me. When I get there I'll knock six times, so you know it's me."

"Sloane," he hisses out, breathing heavy on my neck. "Are you sure?"

"If my parents weren't ten feet away, I wouldn't bother going to the room at all." I can feel him straining. "It shouldn't be long now. Just goodbyes, really."

The event winds down with countless hugs. Last-minute pledges and final bids on all the auction items. Early projections from my committee say this was our biggest year yet. Guests leave, and the remaining stragglers work their way out of the ballroom and into the open area outside. The step and repeat is gone now. It's an expanse of hotel flooring again. A funny place for a drunk crowd of industry people in formalwear.

"You really saved the day," I tell Guy.

He blushes. "Please. I think I need an ice bath now."

"If I'd known you could play like that, I would've asked you right away."

"It's been decades since I've played like that. But I felt a wave of inspiration I couldn't ignore! I knew I had it in me."

Mom rubs his back in small, appreciative circles. "You coming home with us?" she asks me.

"Oh. No. I think I'll sleep in my room upstairs."

"The one you booked to hold your dress?" She looks deeply confused. "Why don't you go to the front desk and see if they'll upgrade it to one of the suites, at least, if you're actually going to stay there."

I don't know what to say to that, so I say nothing, instead

giving them big hugs and kisses. Melanie helps me by grabbing my arm and gesturing to Sarai, who is animatedly telling a story to Tyler and Mara.

"You gave that one the night of her life," Melanie says. "I'm never gonna be able to keep her out of this town now."

Sarai breaks from her conversation to squeeze me tight. There's no hint of self-consciousness in a hug like this. We rock back and forth, holding each other, whispering declarations of love and praise. Eventually Melanie has to break us up, saying it's so far past everyone's bedtime that they have to leave now or they'll end up sleeping in the lobby.

"See you tomorrow," Tyler reminds me, slipping into the open space Sarai and Melanie and Terrence have left.

"I'd say I hate you, but I'm mostly grateful it's a ten a.m. call," I tell her.

"It was the least I could do." She gives me a side hug. "I'm really proud of you, dude."

"Yeah," Mara adds. "This whole thing was amazing."

Mara—with her perpetually solemn energy and her penchant for laughing without moving a face muscle—has always been a tough nut for me to crack. It makes her small validation that much more satisfying to me. She and Tyler slip off holding hands, Mara leaning her head on Tyler's shoulder as they walk.

"Another great one, Sloanius," Dad tells me. It's a never-ending receiving line where I stand. I haven't moved once.

"It was so much fun," Daya says. "I didn't expect that."

"Thank you both for performing. You were excellent."

"It was an honor!" Daya pulls me in and whispers. There's a faint smell of liquor on her breath. "And you and Joe? Holy shit. Girl. You don't even understand."

My cheeks warm. "What am I even doing?" I ask her.

She's got that drunken kind of honesty glinting in her eyes. She takes in my face, then leans in again to whisper, "Girl, if it's worth exploring, then you better explore it. Better to get your answer than to always wonder how things would've been. Right?"

"Thank you," I say, hoping I sound casual. "You and I are doing lunch when I wrap the movie. It's not an option."

Powell comes up behind me and attempts a jump scare. We both outdo each other with praise until it's settled that he was still the best performer of the night. Even better than me. "A close second, though," he says. He hugs me and heads out, turning around when he's about ten feet away to give me one last bow.

For a moment, I'm left unbothered.

I scan the sparse crowd, looking for Joe. He's not here, which means he's already upstairs. I take full advantage of this lull and slip off to the elevator, leaving my gala behind.

19

An echoing expanse of patterned carpet covers the length of the hotel hallway. The lights above are a warm yellow, brightening the green sequins shimmering on me like scales. I knock five times on my hotel door. And then six. By the time my last knock lands, the inside bolt is already unlocking.

Joe appears to me as he has so many times before, smiling and eager, filling up a doorframe. Only now he's barefoot, his white dress shirt unbuttoned to right above his navel. Shoes already off. A tendril of hair slicing down the center of his forehead.

"Hello, you," he says.

"Hello right back."

"And what brings you to my door?"

"I believe I made an appointment."

"Ah. Yes. How could I have forgotten?" He leans out to check that the hallway is clear. Then he scoops me up and tosses me over his shoulder in a fireman's hold.

I feel calm, the way I do when I've finally made it home after a very long day. It's a sharp relief that requires a contented sigh, which might be ridiculous to do when I'm halfway upside down, my head pressed into the middle of Joe's back, but I don't care. I do it anyways.

Joe sets me onto the bed with a gentle hand, holding me close until I'm in a comfortable upright position. Then he kneels on the floor, propping my left foot onto his knee.

"The woman of the night," he says as he slips off my heel.

"And being treated accordingly, I see."

He switches my leg and slips off the other shoe.

The television isn't on. There is no music playing. Only Joe and me immersed in hotel room quiet after a long, loud night. I allow myself to relish this peace, collapsing back onto the bed with my legs hanging off the edge, staring up at the ceiling and seeing nothing but my own happy memories. After the gigantic roller-coaster drop that was the gala, we have to ride up again, cautious, leaned into the incline.

The bed shifts. Joe rests on his back beside me, fingers stitched together across his chest, staring up like he wants to see exactly what I see.

"Can you believe we survived?" I ask him.

"Honest to god, I came in here and splashed my face with water. Still not sure how it's possible I not only did that, but did that sober."

"Same."

I start to match his long, full breaths, finding contentment in this quiet mirroring game. I scoot closer until I can fit my head into the crook of his neck. He smells faintly like expensive cologne, something smoky sprayed into the air and walked through once. He also has that scent that's undeniably him, sweat and skin and soap. I nuzzle in, draping an arm over his body.

"I didn't even think about how I sounded up there. Haven't thought about it until right now," I say.

"You were glorious." He readjusts to tuck an arm beneath me, stroking my shoulder with his thumb.

My pointer finger brushes up against one of the few remaining buttons of his dress shirt. With one hooked swoop, I unbutton it, granting myself access to more of him. "Maybe Emmy is right. We should start a band."

He lets out a gentle snicker. "I don't think so."

On a looping figure eight, I get the last two buttons, one of which fights to stay tucked into his pants. My finger pushes downward to hook around it until the shirt opens completely. Satisfied, my hand rests on his belt, an intentional, baiting gesture. "Why not?"

"For one, luring me onto the stage will get old. Eventually you'll run out of good things to say."

"Hmm. I guess I should pad out my list then." I lift myself up, putting a leg over until I'm perched on top of him, sitting on the open expanse of skin above his belt. My dress hikes up so much it's pooling in front of me, sequins spilling onto his abdomen.

"Let's see. What is good about Joseph Donovan?" I lean over, pressing my fingers into his chest, my loose curls hanging toward him. "You're right. This is very tough already. His face? Impossible to look at. And his stomach? For one, it's hard to sit on."

His hands are quick to grip the sides of my thighs.

"Ah, yes. That's much better," I tell him. "I guess his humor has a way of getting me."

"Finally. Proof that I amuse you."

"Sometimes." With my pointer finger, I draw lazy circles on his chest. "I very much appreciate the way he loves to learn."

He wears a half grin, faint smile lines creasing into his cheeks. "I am a great study."

"*Hmm.* What else?" I squint my eyes. "Honestly, if I can't come up with anything, I can always borrow some of my lines from *The Seeker*. I had a great monologue about trust in the season three finale. Something tells me he'd love that as much as my own words."

"When Colfax leaves you at that warehouse and says he'll be back, and you think he's not coming after all, and then he does?"

"What is wrong with you?"

"Many, many things." He lifts his head to kiss me, teasing with a light peck. Desperate for more contact, I lean closer. After a lingering beat, he pulls back to gaze at me. "Do you remember the day we went to Haven's apartment?"

It's hard to stave off the rising pulse beneath my skin. He is a master of patience, but he will not be better at pacing than I am.

"Pretty sure I won't be forgetting that for a very long time," I tell him, thinking of how he watched me our entire ride back to the lot. The steady pressure of his stare, so unabashed. I can feel it even now, goose bumps emerging at the base of my neck.

"Tyler said something that day. About being able to sell it with a look. That's how I feel about you. Like all I have to do is look."

His words shoot right into the space between my ribs. "What do you want to see?" I ask, careful not to get swept up yet.

"Anything you want to show me."

The cause is lost.

I lift my dress up over my head, ravenous, helped by his eager hands. My chest is bare. I'm completely naked except for my underwear. I could wait for us to appreciate each other like this, but it's been too long.

My lips meet his. He wraps me up and flips us over in a graceful roll so he can give his all to the admiration. His mouth moves from my lips, to my neck, to the space between my breasts.

"Is this what you had in mind?" I tease.

"Precisely."

He slides down and down until he's at my underwear, all the while whispering something that sounds faintly like worship, praise for all the soft places so few get to touch like this. His fingers move the fabric, and his tongue works exactly as it does when he speaks, quick and smart and eager to make corrections.

"Hold on," I eventually pant out, too worked up to find more words. He stops, eyes gazing up from the space between my thighs.

This is our one shot. Our place outside the rules of the trailer. All he has to do is look.

He holds close to me as he slides his way back up my body, slowly, methodically, making sure I feel every inch. My hands reach for his belt while our eager mouths work together. I unhook the buckle and slide the belt out from the loops. Then I rope it behind his neck to pin us closer yet.

"That's better," I say.

"Is it?"

He laughs into my hair, laying his head against the side of mine for a moment. All the while he is struggling, and failing, to pull down his own pants. I toss the belt to the ground, and he rolls off me to situate himself.

There are so many things I cannot believe, but the first is that I am sober, and I want to be sober, and I want to always feel lit up like this, like every breath we share is a bolt of electricity. The second is that we are both laughing, and it's such a good, true laugh. The kind of frenzied excitement that says we are *here*, and we're rushing a bit, but it's better than we ever could've imagined, because it's real.

These moments, the small exchanges between the big things,

are the ones that always manage to stay with me. And Joe's face—amused and desperate and so full of adoration for me—is an image I know I will never lose.

It doesn't hurt that he's now properly discarded his clothes and gotten the condom from his wallet.

When we come back to each other, I have my hands on him, working in a way that makes his pupils dilate. He has his arms on either side of my head, so much like that first moment in the trailer. But we are not those versions of ourselves anymore either. The Joe I see now is the one I like best. He kisses me, full of wild hunger, and I'm already sure that the Joe I meet when I wake up in the morning will be even better.

But right now.

Oh. Right now.

"Are you sure?" he asks, wanting, but serious. Deadly serious.

I could tell him with a look, except I need to say this out loud. "You are the only thing I want."

At that he leans back. Slowly slips my underwear down my legs and off me completely, then tosses them onto the pile of clothes we've built on the floor.

"My god, you are marvelous."

He kisses all the soft parts again, treating each stretch of skin like it's sacred.

He slides the condom on, then comes back to me.

We share one last long look.

And then we are together, learning this new rhythm as we've learned every other. Finding the way we work. Pressure. Patience. Touch. Honest questions and honest answers.

I show him where to hold me. How to touch me to make this work best for the both of us. He tells me the sound of my voice is his favorite sound, so I whisper words only he gets to hear, hushed and right in his ear. As pleading and insistent as the beat we create together.

After a while, moving and working and building, building, there are no more words to whisper. I am gasping. His body and his hands and his insistence to get this right. Everything comes together, crashing over me in a seismic wave. All I can think, until I can't think much at all, is he is mine.

He is mine.

Mine.

Falling to pieces, I whisper *mine* into his ear until both of us collapse, his body draped over me like a blanket, warm and safe and holding me to this perfect moment.

Okay, Sloane, I need you to climb on top of Joe." Tyler stands off to the side, her headphones resting along her neck, hands in her pocket trying to force a casual energy.

Our intimacy coordinator comes forward. "How are you feeling right now? The intention is for your robe to be off. To be sure your breasts are only in profile in the shot."

"I'm great. That's perfectly fine," I assure her. I tried joking with her once, and she let me know her sole role on this set is to make sure everything we do is comfortable and consented to, and humor only makes it harder for her to know my boundaries.

"Joe? How are you doing?"

He bites back a smile. "I'm wonderful. Thanks."

Tammy the AD projects as loudly as possible to the sparse few here on set with us. "Only the necessary eyes right now, people!" Even she averts her gaze as soon as I remove the robe.

Our intimacy coordinator takes it. "Still all right?"

"Yes, thank you."

As instructed, I, mostly naked Sloane Ford, climb on top of mostly naked Joseph Donovan. He looks not at me but at the ceiling beyond my head.

"I'm sorry," Tyler says. "I know this is really weird. Sloane, can you lean forward a little and place your hands on his chest?"

I do, and she moves back to the monitor to look at the coverage and talk it over with our DP.

"I'm so sorry again. Would you mind doing some light thrusting so we can see how everything moves?" she calls out to me.

The intimacy coordinator makes sure I am okay with this too.

I answer them both by rocking back and forth atop Joe, hands on his chest.

Tyler takes a breath. "I'm really sorry. Joe. Can you hold her?"

"No need to apologize," he says. "Of course."

This is what makes us break. His hands on my hips. He starts laughing, honestly kind of a giggle, and so do I. Lucky for us, it seems like it's because we're about to burst over how awkward all of this is.

And it is. So, so awkward. My weird flesh-colored underwear piece thrusting against his. My sister watching me on a monitor.

"It's normal to laugh," the intimacy coordinator tells us in a gentle tone. "The further we go, the more important it is that you two continue trusting each other. When the cameras roll, every motion should feel familiar and expected."

Joe raises up a hand to salute her. "Yes to familiar and expected."

I can't help but blush.

Our coordinator is doing a phenomenal job of making sure we feel cared for and safe, but I have to say, discussing the technical aspects of sex is never really easy, especially when humor has been nixed. I want to laugh again, but I know it's really because there is truly nothing weirder than pretending to have intercourse for the first time with someone. Add on the fact that you actually just had sex for the first time less than twelve hours ago, and now you have a small audience of people pretending not to watch or pretending not to think it's strange, and wow, the whole thing turns into a textbook example of the most awkward situation in the world.

Joe straightens his expression. "Do anything fun last night after the event?" he asks me.

"Hung out in my hotel room," I tell him, still thrusting. "How about you?"

"Yeah. I stayed inside."

"Sounds relaxing."

"It was rather glorious." He cuts me one quick look, then puts the shield back up, ever the gentleman, paying no gaze to my bare chest, a sight he was sure to relish more than a few times last night.

"All right, that's good," Tyler tells us.

The intimacy coordinator hands me my robe. I climb off of Joe, who can't help but let out one more laugh.

"Shut up." I smack him lightly on the arm.

"Thanks for being good sports," Tyler tells us. "Everything is looking amazing so far. You're really selling it."

"Thanks," I say while Joe overlaps with "Why thank you."

Back to work we go, fake sexing our way through the day.

20

A few different news outlets will arrive on set throughout the next two days of filming, coming to capture behind-the-scenes footage. After our disastrous start, the plan was to do all the on-set press stuff during the last week of the shoot. Everything would be settled by then, we all thought. It would be a weeklong celebration of our hard work.

We were right. But this movie is almost over when I swear we started only a few days ago, and I'm sad to think we will spend some of our last moments already talking about it in retrospect instead of fully living it.

Even my morning ritual is stunted by some of the documentary-type camera people here. They're filming several featurettes, one of which will be on my transformation from Sloane to Elise. Mom made it very clear I'm to arrive at my actual call time today instead of getting here early to meet with Joe.

A cameraman and a producer greet me, ready to follow me around the lot.

"That's Joe's trailer," I say when we pass, fulfilling their request that I narrate my experience. It's a bit like letting strangers read your diary as you write it. "Usually I'd go there for an early

morning rehearsal before he's off to have his prosthetics applied."
I point to the trailer next to it. "And that's mine," I say, no other
elaboration to give.

They set up a time-lapse video for my hair and makeup. We
do standard coverage too, and I talk them through Elise's aesthetic. Her penchant for blues and greens. How that plays into
what our set designers have done with the apartments, and the
fact that Elise tends to match Calvin's home better than her own.
How all of it looks so lush thanks to Tyler's idea to make the lighting and colors as uniquely vibrant as possible in spite of the bleak
circumstances of their lives. How Guy has taught her to embrace
that stylishness while searching for the quiet, impulsive beats, the
small visual truths that make a movie sing. I go through some of
the specific lip colors we've used for Elise. Niche stuff that ap-
peals to makeup junkies and film buffs who appreciate a peek
into this side of the process.

It makes me laugh when I hold up the one that once covered Joe's face. "This one is a beautiful color, but it's definitely
not longwear."

Today's shot list is all over the board. Production wanted the
outside crews to have something fun to cover. We've held on to a
dance scene between Elise and Calvin for this occasion.

It's past the midway point, after the breakthrough writing moment between them. Elise has come to Calvin's apartment to
shoot the shit. They're sharing drinks while Elise finally fills Calvin in on the granular details he missed while he was away at war.
Something about telling him these mundane stories feels the
most intimate of all. She admits she was taking dance lessons for
a while. Calvin, a little tipsy, asks her to show him. He has no
record player, so he offers to hum his way through a tune at any
speed she'd like. Elise explains she isn't very good. Calvin is

persistent. Eventually, Elise gives in to trying. She attempts to teach him what she knows as he makes up a song that fits their clumsy, blooming rhythm.

I would've loved to run this with Joe this morning. There's a lot of quick-flitting dialogue and a good amount of blocking to cover. Without one last practice, it really will be like improvising. Guy was firm on not wanting this to be too planned, anyways. Tyler agreed.

On set, we dance. Making up our moves as we go, guided by a choreographer hired to keep the movements period appropriate. Joe spins me. Dips me. Holds me. Hums a song suspiciously close to the one his dad made up about his siblings. We sprinkle our dialogue throughout, swift as our feet, covered in one long take that dances with us.

Tyler calls out encouragement in the soft moments. "Keep going, Calvin," she says when he starts to swirl me. "Make her dizzy."

The world around me spins. There are a hundred eyes on us, following our every step. With us through our laughter and our missteps. Through our shuffles and swirls.

We have them.

"And cut."

I tip into Joe's arms, too dizzy to stand straight.

It takes a long time to set up the shot again. An entertainment news correspondent pulls Joe and me off to the side for a casual interview while we wait. Half of Calvin's apartment is in frame behind us. The other half shows the wooden slats holding up the back of the walls and the soundstage floor.

The correspondent's team pins lapel mics on us, and we're off to bantering.

"You guys are having a lot of fun dancing out there," she comments straightaway.

Joe runs a hand through his hair to wipe sweat from his brow. "Oh yeah. This is a great time."

"I'm a much better dancer than Elise is, though," I joke.

Joe looks straight to camera. "All lies," he deadpans.

The correspondent giggles. "What's it been like here on set? I know this movie has had a bit of a bumpy road up until now."

My nose wants to scrunch up. We've all been briefed that no one's allowed to ask anything specific about Haven's firing. Vaguely hinting at it will always be the name of the game, though.

"I'm quite sure everything's worked out for the best," Joe tells her. "Except my American accent. That might be a bit painful for the locals."

"All lies." I look straight to camera as he did moments ago.

The correspondent eats all of this up. "You two have worked together before. What's it been like to come together again for this?"

"A dream come true," Joe tells her right as I'm saying, "Pretty amazing." He puts a hand on my forearm. "Sorry. You go."

"It's been incredible." I amp up my enthusiasm now that Joe's called it a dream come true. "Joe's the best."

"Watching you two today, you seem so comfortable with each other. How do you create that kind of trust?"

Joe gives her a wry smile. "Loads of rehearsal."

"I bet. Sloane, tell me how this experience with Joe is different than your last?"

There's a subtle shift in Joe's posture, feet turning in toward me, shoulders rounding forward to get a bit closer to my level.

"For one, we know each other so much better now," I say. "We didn't come into this as strangers. We're definitely better at communicating this time around. It's easy. Acting with him doesn't feel like work."

The interviewer nods. "And Joe?"

"She really said it. But I'll add that she's brilliant at getting me out of my own head. Our first flick, I was in a bit of a personal hell, if I'm being honest. Life's a little steadier now." He places a hand back on my arm. "Sloane is my anchor."

"Wow," the correspondent mutters, surprised. "Can you—"

Tammy the AD interrupts. It's time to wrap up and come back to filming. The correspondent is devastated, clearly hoping to follow this line of questioning as far as we will push it. Which, according to our answers, is pretty far, I realize with a dawning horror.

Later, as sunset turns the outside sky a dreamy sherbet pink and orange, Joe and I let the camera crews follow us as we walk the back lot, running our lines. It's a more interesting location than his trailer, we've been told. If we want to rehearse, we have to do it here. I keep fighting the urge to reach for his hand while we pace back and forth through brownstone facades and iconic stretches of street used in countless movies and shows.

Our last scene to shoot is the second kissing scene. It was Mom's idea to move it to today. To my surprise Tyler agreed, no longer finding a closed set necessary for kissing. Our intimacy coordinator talked it over extensively with Joe and me, making sure we understood that we don't have to be uncomfortable just because the team wants outside crews to see this. We assured her it was fine.

As production inches toward wrapping, mindsets are slowly shifting out of creative mode and into marketing mode already. Everything has a spin, and the tension of this sequence will build great buzz among the industry people here to watch. We both understand that, and we trust each other enough to know we will get through it just fine.

This scene is Elise in her slip, after running down the street. She's explaining her fears to Calvin. Why she's pushed him away.

"I could never leave you," he tells her, realizing for himself that it's true. How did he ever think he could? "Why do you think I came back to this town? I was happy being your friend."

Joe says the lines without feeling it, the both of us focused on getting the text right instead of nailing the emotion. The emotion will come when we shoot it.

"Can't you see? I . . ." Elise balks, unable to say it. *I love you.*

They're supposed to get closer. Calvin says if he touches Elise, he won't be able to stop. So she kisses him everywhere but his mouth, not allowing him to touch her back, driving him mad.

Joe and I talk about this with *blah blah we're kissing here* practicality, eyes on our feet as we walk in sync.

Next, Stuart pounds on the door, looking for Elise. She begs Calvin to hide, saying she will handle it. Calvin says, "No. Trust me, you hide. I can fix this." He tells Elise to go change while he takes care of Stuart.

While Calvin talks to Stuart, Elise hides, watching. When Stuart leaves, she emerges in her slip once more.

"I didn't get dressed," she says, walking up to Calvin. Scared and shy.

He asks why.

"Because I wanted you to see me."

"Please," he says. "Can I touch you?"

She nods. Calvin reaches his hand out to slide the slip off Elise's shoulders. "Don't you know it's always been you? I love you, Elise." He works from her arm up to her mouth, their lips finally pressing together into the kiss that sets off the sex scene we filmed yesterday.

We shoot everything up to the climactic kiss. Lucas is here, his last day on this job. Between shots, we film a few behind-the-scenes things together, which is funny because I truly barely know him, other than the woodworking thing. A stark contrast to everyone else in this cast, who is either my family. Or Joe.

Lucas has Stuart's dark desperation nailed. Joe captures a tenderness in Calvin, the way he takes down Stuart to assure Elise she is safe here. It's not done with the machismo I expected. That's Tyler's touch. She brings a different edge, urging them to do away with the chest puffing. Play it with the love, not the anger, she tells them more than once.

After that coverage is done, Lucas sticks around to watch the rest of the scene. Powell's stopped by, sitting beside Mom, the two of them with their heads constantly pressed together, whispering what I assure myself is praise for my stunning performance.

We pick up at the moment before Calvin eases down the strap of Elise's slip. The coverage is on me first, but Joseph gives me everything he has, down to the soft, eager eyes I know well, a storm of desire building behind them.

"*Please. Can I touch you?*" he asks.

I nod.

He steps closer. His thumb brushes the strap of my slip until it falls off my shoulder.

"*Don't you know it's always been you?*" He presses his lips to the skin where the strap once was. "*I love you, Sloane.*"

He continues kissing my shoulder—*my* shoulder—waiting as

if it were me making the mistake here, forgetting the next beat. I'm supposed to stroke his cheek.

I am frozen. He has said my name, not Elise's, and he hasn't even realized.

The crew knows. My mother knows.

I try not to look at anyone. Not to move. Not to breathe.

"Uh, cut," Tyler interjects, lobbing it toward Joseph like it will wake him up. He pulls back and shakes off the moment, prepared to get notes and deliver a better performance in the next take.

Tyler gives me a helpless, shocked look that I pointedly avoid.

Finally, in this excruciating, infinite stretch of uncertainty, Joseph realizes. He says, "Oh, my bad," blushing, creating a sizable distance between us. More than is necessary. He knows no one is buying it. Not the behind-the-scenes guys. Not the entertainment correspondents. Not Lucas the woodworker.

This isn't the kind of slipup that just happens. I know it isn't because almost every movie I've done has had a love story. No other actor has ever said my name in these moments when they've meant to say my character's. Every person on this lot has worked on one or a dozen or a hundred romances, and they'd all say this isn't a thing. Not in this particular context.

I know it isn't because of the way he's looking at me.

Because all it takes between us is a look.

What I don't know is what to do. How to sit inside the gravity of what seems to be a genuine admittance on his part. And a public one at that.

"Let's take a five," Tyler says.

The crew disbands, everyone acting like they have some small side job they need to do *right now this very instant*. *Acting* being the key word. Everyone that's not a professional performer is putting on a show for the two people who are being paid to pretend.

The extra film crews, notably, keep rolling.

I tell myself not to storm off. Instead I remove my mic and say something about getting my phone from my trailer, even trying out a laugh with it. Oh-so-breezy Sloane Ford, known for being effortless and cool. With each step I take away from set, the tension builds. By the time I'm off the soundstage, I have to keel over, hands on my knees, nearly dry heaving. I'm barefoot, I realize with a distant amusement. And in a peach slip.

"Sloane! Sloane!" I hear, almost outside of myself. Joseph's leading us to his trailer, always to his trailer, and I'm following, only because I don't know where else to go.

We get inside, away from the cameras, and he tries to explain. To act like it's fine. It's so preposterous that he's doing this, so monumentally ridiculous that it snaps me back into myself. Where there was confusion there's now anger, near boiling.

"What the *fuck*?" I spit out, interrupting his empty monologuing on how no one thinks anything of what he said, and it happens all the time.

He stops, stunned. He has never seen me mad. Not like this. Not in my claws-out way. At least not that he remembers.

That's not true. I never gave him the satisfaction of this vitriol in Ireland. It wasn't worth my energy.

Now it is.

"I told you we had to keep it cool at work," I say, whisper-yelling. "I know there's a lot happening between us, but fuck. We have one fucking week left of this shoot. One! And now the entire cast and crew of this production thinks you are in love with me!"

"Because I am!" he whisper-shouts back, instantly on my level. A worthy, passionate opponent to my rage, both of us battling between wanting to scream and trying to ensure no one hears us. "Of course I love you, Sloane! Christ, every goddamn thing I've done is because I love you! I make the mistake of saying it, and *that's* the deal breaker for you? That I slipped up a line of dialogue in the heat of the moment?"

"Everybody is on set right now! It's not just our crew today! *Fuck.* My whole family is here!"

"You think me saying I love you is what's gonna clue your family into what's going on? Not your fingers in my hair at the gala, or the way you sang each word of every song directly into my mouth, for chrissake! Or how you held my hand and marched me through that entire room? Or the way you look at me, like every word I say is something you're not gonna miss, no matter who else is talking? You don't think any of that means something?"

"Don't get smart with me. If we're talking things people do, who showed up with three hundred dollars' worth of flowers and chocolates to a band rehearsal? That sure as hell wasn't me."

"God, Sloane. You're right! Gestures of affection. What a repulsive thing to do for someone I care about! Someone I *love*."

"Will you stop using that word for one second?" I say, rubbing my temples. "I get it. You think you love me. Understood."

"I don't *think* anything. I know. I was listening to every word you said to me before we sang. And everything you said to me in that hotel room. *Mine. Mine. Mine.*"

"Don't," I say, putting up a hand.

"If you're expecting me to take it back, I won't be doing that. It wouldn't matter if we never touched again. I told you that when we first started this. I told you everything. Not always with words, but . . ." He peters out, hoping to drop us down a level.

"And I told you that set life isn't real life," I argue. "This is all fucking make-believe."

He paces back and forth in the small corner he's marked as his side of the trailer, his side of the fight. "I tried to see you outside of this place and you wouldn't let me! You create all these rules for yourself. You don't do period pieces. You won't go below the belt here. I can't say this or that. Then you break all of them anyways, and I follow your actions instead of your rules, and you're too stubborn to admit I'm right!" His hands reach for his hair. "I'm fuckin' right!"

"Says the guy who won't do a comedy because he's afraid no one will laugh at him!" On my side is the whiskey from his dad, which I pick up and shake. "Maybe you're the one who holds on to too much. Did you ever think of that?" I put the bottle back down. "Sometimes it's better to let go." He has no idea what to do with that. The upper hand is mine, and for a moment I relish in it. "Just because you love me doesn't mean I have to love you back."

He laughs. Full and throaty, louder than we've been for the entire fight. "You think you're slick. Trying to hit me where it hurts."

"It's been six weeks, Joe. People don't fall in love that fast."

"There you go again. Another rule."

"Cute."

"You know full well we've known each other for years." His eyes narrow. "I want you to tell me why this can't happen. Truly. Say it with your whole voice, Sloane. And if you use your family as an excuse, it's bullshit. Those people will love you through it all, judging by the fuck-twat with the guitar that was your last suitor. So your mam thought you wanted to sleep with me. What's it matter? Costars sleep together all the time. This is more than that and you know it. I know you do." He's shaking his head, staring at the carpet as he stops treading ground to instead tap his fingers together. "You want to be the one to ruin this, don't you? That's what it is. You wanna make sure you get out of this ahead of me. No matter how much good there is between us, you only want to see the bad."

That's not true, I think, remembering the way he laughed when he couldn't get off his pants. Such a ridiculous thing to recall right now. To think of him so candid. Guard down, ready for anything. The memory is barely a day old and it already hurts me. It's miles away from where we stand in this moment.

Hot tears push up from the center of my throat.

"I take it back. You must be right. It must be better to let go, because right now I don't wanna be anywhere near you," he says.

"Hold on," I force out. His hand is on the trailer door, ready to make an exit.

"What?"

He's looking at me, waiting for me to tell him why it is I think that we won't work. Or to fight for why we would. But I'm such a coward. I can only say what I mean until it really matters. Then I don't have any words at all.

Joseph nods, tears rimming his eyes. "Right then. I'll see you back on set, Sloane."

He leaves me alone in his trailer, collapsed onto the blanket his sister made, staring at the picture of his mother.

After a mild existential crisis, I stifle my confusion and return to set, ready to be not only Elise, but a version of myself who can be in the same room as Joseph Donovan and not feel two seconds away from a full breakdown.

Everyone studies me. The camera crews. My mom. My sister. My brother. Fucking Lucas the woodworking actor, picture wrapped but still here to watch the rest of the night. I want to scream at everyone to go home. Leave us alone and let us work in peace.

It's now a show within a show for all of them. Personal drama and theatrical drama.

Lucky for me, if there is one thing that has always buoyed me up in the middle of personal tsunamis, it is my pride. I ignore all their inquisitive stares and the long, breathy pauses that come in conversational transitions, each one of them contemplating exactly what's appropriate to ask.

Am I okay? No.

Is there anything they can do about it? No.

This is all my fault and I know it.

If there is one person on set who is better at this than me, it's Joseph Donovan, of course. He delivers every line of dialogue word perfect, including the *I love you*. He kisses my mouth like he really means it, then laughs with cameramen while the shot is being reset.

Only *I* notice that when I am not Elise, I am invisible to him.

So utterly unacknowledged that you'd never, ever know he loves me.

And you'd never know that I don't hate him either.

21

For the second time in as many days, Joseph and I do not begin our morning with a rehearsal. I walk straight to my trailer instead of his, where there's not a single personal touch beyond my phone charger. It's empty, it's boring, and all I want to do is press my ear to the wall and hear what songs Joseph's playing.

There is only silence on the other end.

Everything about this project has been wrapped up in the two of us. What I put on when I leave for work. The mood I'm in when I start each day. Where I sit for meals. What I talk about between takes. And I'm supposed to get in front of cameras and explain that?

There's a gaping hole between Joseph and me now, a gigantic chasm that's swallowed up all that movie magic and replaced it with hurt. He proved last night he's a better actor than I am. He can do this. He can make everyone believe nothing is wrong.

This last week isn't about celebration anymore. It's about survival.

I lie down on my couch. Put on my headphones. Sip my iced coffee. Listen to my Emotional Pop-Punk Classics of the Early 2000s playlist and prepare myself for the day ahead.

♥

They've tucked me into a far corner of the set. I'm in costume, a forest-green turtleneck and brown pleated skirt, one pearl barrette pinning back the curls on the left side of my head.

An interviewer sits beside a single camera, two studio lights flanking either side, shining on me. "We're going to start with broad questions here. Be as descriptive as possible without giving away too much plot."

"You got it."

When the camera rolls, I'm asked to tell as much about my character as I can. More featurette fodder. They want this to be a little gratuitous and actor-y, which is good. It's easier to survive when I can be cerebral.

"I play Elise Morgan," I start, smoothing down my skirt. "She's a schoolteacher in the 1940s who lives in a small city apartment with her mother, Vera. She lost her father when she was a young teen, and the two women have been inseparable ever since. Their neighbor Calvin used to be their go-to handyman. For Elise, he was also one of the only people who knew what her home life was like. There's about two years age difference between them, so as she was still growing up, they developed a strong friendship. Then he got drafted into the war, and Elise had to take on all of the jobs he used to do for her and her mother. Now Calvin is back, having been injured, and there's all this unresolved tension between the two of them. They're older now. Full adults. But they've both changed so much in the years they've been apart. Vera can no longer work. Elise has to make ends meet for the both of them. Elise has hardened a lot since Calvin left. She's not quite ready to let him back in. And he's got all of his own baggage too, obviously. They're both very hurt in different ways."

There's a hitch in my breath. Something that feels suspiciously close to tears. I swallow it down, exhaling, looking to the interviewer for the next question.

"Great," he says. "Can you go a little deeper into her relationship with Calvin? How does it change as the movie goes on? That kind of stuff."

The first thing I ever learned about interviews is to start my answer with the question again. "Elise and Calvin's relationship is constantly evolving throughout the film," I explain, finding a small comfort in knowing this is the first of a thousand times I will say a variation of this sentence. Somewhere down the line, we'll do countless press junkets and magazine interviews and red carpets. Summarizing this movie will become like reciting state capitals.

All I have to do is get through the first round.

"They're old friends, but it's clear that something more has been bubbling beneath the surface for a very long time," I continue. "They can't start there, though. They have to relearn each other. For Elise, she's content with their friendship. She's committed to making life comfortable for her mother. That's her number one priority. The problem is Calvin is as steady and loyal as he ever was. After a while, she has to confront that. She fights hard." I laugh. "Very, very hard."

"Why do you think that is?"

"Elise fights a romantic relationship with Calvin because it feels so permanent. The kind of thing that will swallow her whole. She has so many other things to figure out. How to best help her mother as her health declines. How to get them out of this crumbling apartment. What to do about her own dreams of becoming a writer. Of course it's Calvin urging her toward the solutions. He's the person she most needs in her corner."

Anxiety balloons in me, shoving into every open space until it's hard to breathe. Small sips of water help, so I take them readily.

The interviewer watches, stoic, waiting to ask the next question. "Can you talk a little bit about what it's been like to work with your family here?"

I sigh, relieved the conversation has shifted away from Joseph and into more comfortable territory.

"Working with my family has been a dream come true. I am so impressed with my sister Tyler's vision for this film. She and Guy have worked really hard to create an environment that's safe and exciting. It's an actor's dream, really. Guy's always been known for trying things off-the-cuff. I've heard old stories of him picking up a camera, slinging it over his shoulder, and shooting the footage himself. He brings that kind of energy to this set. You feel like you can go for whatever with him around, and he'll follow you. Tyler balances that really well. She has a patience about her that puts people at ease. And a clear vision for how it all should look and feel. This movie is so warm. That's all Tyler."

"And your mother?" the interviewer asks.

"My mother is unbelievable in this movie. She hasn't acted in so long. People are going to love her work as Vera. Particularly the love story between Vera and Ruth. It's done with such care. Melanie and Kitty are complete pros. Watching them reminds me why I got into this profession. To get to work with actors of their caliber."

"Great. Can you talk about it in character terms too?"

"Of course." I sip my water. "Elise spends so much time trying to save her mother throughout the film that she misses the fact that her mother doesn't need saving at all. Vera's disease doesn't hold her back from having her own desires and finding her own happy ending. While Elise is discovering what she really wants, Vera has already figured it out for herself, and she's going after it."

"What about Joseph Donovan? What has it been like to work with him again?"

I take a deep, cleansing breath, then paste on a jovial smile. "Working with Joseph Donovan has been amazing," I start, finding myself out of words to follow. Everything I want to say feels like a conversational land mine.

The interviewer crosses his legs. "Could you elaborate?"

"Sorry," I whisper, breaking some kind of fourth wall between the interviewer and me. I take another long sip of water and start again. "Working with Joseph Donovan has been amazing. We've had a lot of fun figuring out what makes Elise and Calvin tick. He is a really caring scene partner." My mouth goes dry. "Sorry," I say again, in my Real Sloane voice, not my Interview Sloane voice. "One more time."

"Sure," says the interviewer, still stoic.

I clear my throat.

Close my eyes.

Take a long breath and start once more.

"Joseph Donovan has pushed me to learn more about my character than I ever would have done alone. And it doesn't feel like work. It feels like being a kid again. Getting to play. I can so clearly imagine all the places Elise and Calvin have been before the movie starts. I can feel all the beats they've lived between the scenes we see on-screen. Because Joe and I have done all that backstory together. We've built a fully dimensional world for these people, and shooting this story together has been like trust-falling from the top of a mountain and knowing he'll be able to catch me."

Suddenly I'm breathless.

"I'm really sorry," I say. "I need a minute." I take off my mic pack and place it in the interviewer's lap.

His expression finally changes. Utter bewilderment. I wander away from him, heading toward the soundstage door. No idea where I'm going. Anywhere but here.

My legs start tingling. My throat is constricted. *Why is this costume so itchy? How is the sun so bright? Why won't everything stop?*

Suddenly Tyler's hand is pressing into my back. "Sloane, it's okay. Take a deep breath."

"I'm already trying to take a deep breath!"

"Shh. Shh. It's okay. It's gonna be okay."

"No it's fucking not!" Hurling harsh words at her feels vaguely satisfying, releasing the pressure in one way. Building it up elsewhere.

"Let's sit down in the shade." Tyler guides me toward a golf cart parked near the stage door. We climb in, and she rubs my back, saying nothing. It's the first thing to ground me, calling to mind what my mom said about how as a kid I would cry and no one could help me.

Why can't anyone help me? Why do I never ever let anyone help me?

The tension within me breaks, and I'm crying. Heaving. Snot-filled, sharp, staccato breaths. "I'm sorry. I'm a mess." I wipe my nose with the back of my hand, grateful for the pressure leaking out of me but feeling more drained than ever.

"Dude. You really are." Tyler stops my hand from touching

my costume, instead wrapping it up in her black tank top and wiping it clean. It's funny enough to make me give her something resembling a smile, which makes her laugh. "You cannot believe how ridiculous you look right now."

"Is my face blotchy?"

"You don't want me to answer that." She runs a finger under my eye, then pulls it back, showing me a watery smudge of eyeliner and mascara mixed together. Then she takes it to her own face and paints a line under each eye.

"Now *you* look ridiculous."

"And people always say we don't look alike!" She grins. When I don't cave, she turns serious again, dipping her chin to get me to make eye contact. "Talk to me. What's going on?"

I tell Tyler everything. The whole truth about Joseph. No more hiding. I'm exhausted and overwhelmed and I fucked everything up by trying to control it all, like I always do. I'm terrified about what happens when this movie is over and we have to go back to real life. I'm scared I've pushed everyone away.

Tyler and I haven't talked like this in months. I keep trying to pin it all on her, but I've pushed her away too. Like I've done with everyone else.

It all makes me a babbling mess, apologizing and sobbing and saying things like "I ruined everything" and "I should've told you sooner."

"This is probably the wrong time to tell you this, but everyone already knows about you and Joe," Tyler interjects.

"Because of yesterday?"

"Um." She's hedging, afraid to say more.

"What?"

"We're always listening to you guys talk on the headsets in

between takes. And I mean, I lived with you and your old boy-friend. I know you when you have feelings for someone. And then the *gala*." She loads the last word with meaning, no longer meeting my eye. "When you finished your set, Mara turned to me and said, 'You didn't tell me Sloane and Joe started dating.' Mom overheard her and said, 'Oh yeah. For at least a few weeks.' Then Daya was weirdly insistent that it wasn't true and you guys were just friends. Then Powell said something about Sarai telling him about some flowers and chocolates Joe gave you or something? Then you guys came back to the table and we stopped talking about it."

She has the guilt-stricken look I know well, like the time she admitted she spilled black nail polish onto a favorite shirt of mine I thought I'd lost.

"I figured you'd tell me when you were ready to, and everything we were shooting was turning out so great that I didn't press it," she finishes.

"So everyone knows?"

"Maybe not Glori?" she suggests, hoping for a laugh.

We sit without speaking for a minute, letting a cool breeze wash over us. Tyler's gnawing on her fingernails, a nervous tic Mom only halfway scolded out of her as a kid. I'm twirling a piece of hair around my pointer finger, wrapping and unwrapping until it forms a proper coil, the hitches in my breath slowly evening out.

"Do you ever think about why we don't have any friends?" Tyler asks suddenly.

This is what finally makes me laugh. This and the two black mascara smudges still under her eyes. "Literally every day."

"Do you think it's from growing up with a life full of strangers always making assumptions about us? Like it's easier to be around people who've lived it. Then we don't have to worry about always trying to explain things. You know?"

"I do."

"I think we forget that sometimes we have to explain things anyways. Even to the people who've lived it with us."

"Probably. Yeah," I mutter.

She turns to me. "Shit. Okay. I'm working on being direct. Like you. I'm trying to say I'm sorry for how I stopped showing up. That's what I mean."

"I really needed you after Kearns left," I find myself saying, surprised this comes up first, bursting out with no warning. "It wasn't that he left me. I know now that was a good thing. It was that I was alone. For the first time in my life, I was completely alone."

My tears resurface. God. It's so exhausting to cry. It takes such effort, every facial muscle squeezing and tightening and contorting to accommodate all these emotions. This is why I do the single teardrop stuff on camera. The reality is way too draining.

"And you were falling in love," I continue. "So I didn't press it. I didn't ask you any of the questions I should have. I stopped showing up too."

Tyler's crying now. She wipes a hand across her cheek, forgetting about her mascara war paint. Now it's smudged all the way to her earlobe.

"We never used to do this," I say. "No matter what. It was always you and me."

"Why did it change?" she asks. Forever trusting that I have an answer.

Even though I don't—not really, at least—I give one anyways. Because that's who I am to her. Her big sister. The one who is brave and says what she feels and finds solutions in impossible places. "It didn't change. We just got lazy. Wrapped up in our own stuff."

"I wanted to be there. I didn't know how," she admits.

"Hey." I lick my thumb, then wipe the mascara smudge running along the side of her face. "It really wasn't all you. This is my fault too." I think for a minute, looking at her sad eyes. Knowing how much she hates to be this broken. How she only does this for the people she really trusts. "Here's what we do. Once a month, you spend the night at my place. The two of us."

Her expression shifts, something hopeful blooming in the hairline cracks between us.

"And then every other week, or maybe more depending on our schedules, you and Mara come over for dinner. And Opal. The whole squad."

She breaks into her real, full grin, the one she shows to so few people that seeing it is like being handed a piece of the stars. "I'd *love* that." Then she licks her finger and tries to run it across my cheek.

"Ew. I don't want your spit on my face!" I yell.

"You just did this to me five seconds ago."

"That was different."

"Different how?"

"I don't know. Different. Get your gross hands away from me."

She pulls back, another genuine smile plastered across her face. "Thanks, Bub," she says, as if she's the one who stormed off set, in desperate need of saving.

"No. Thank you." I hit her shoulder. "I hate you. Don't forget it."

She walks with me to hair and makeup, an arm wrapped around my shoulders. One of our makeup artists silently puts an ice mask over my eyes to take down the puffiness while a hairstylist runs her fingers through my pin curls, basically giving me a head massage.

These are luxuries I'm taking as commonplace. I'm being cared for by people who don't know why I've been sobbing, though I'm sure they have a pretty good idea. They only know that it's their job to make me shiny and new. They care for me with such delicate hands it makes me want to cry again, which would be the rudest possible choice to make. It's *my* job to keep going. To make sure everyone here can leave set knowing we've gotten the necessary work done. To not be the spoiled daughter who got this role through sheer nepotism alone, doing whatever she pleases.

Tyler leans against the makeup counter, cleaning her face with one of the makeup remover wipes. The sight of which should not incite as much of an emotional response in me as it does. I let it pass, feeling the cool ice soothe my swollen eyes.

She kicks my leg with her boot. "Can I say one more thing?"

I have no idea what's about to come out of her mouth, but from her tone, it's going to be personal. The hair and makeup people are always the first to hear the real gossip, so I give her a quick nod of approval, throwing my rules out the window.

"We all went to a full-on movie premiere the day after Kearns broke up with you," she reminds me. "And you were so happy. The best mood I'd seen you in for months."

It's less revealing than I expect, while also being more insightful than I'm ready to deal with at the moment. It's not everything, but it explains a little why she didn't think I needed her. Though I don't think that's the point she's trying to make.

"What am I supposed to do?" I ask.

"Whatever that line is Dad told you that you always quote. Put pride behind your happiness, or something."

"Never let your pride get in the way of your happiness."

"There it is." She tosses her wipe into the trash. "Do that."

"As if it's that easy," I say. Then I shake my head.

No more bitter rejection of uncomfortable truths.

"I'll try," I tell her. "I promise."

22

I knock on his door. Once. Twice. All the way to six times. Then I stand waiting, plunged in the half darkness of a morning on the verge of coming awake. The trailer door swings open a quarter of the way.

Joe waits out of view, only his fingers in sight, curled around the locking mechanism.

"Can I come in?" I have to ask.

"That's why I opened it," he says, almost disdainful.

Inside, all his personal effects are gone. Blanket, whiskey, picture of his mother. Even the teakettle has been put away. There's no coaster set out for my iced coffee, which is fine. I didn't get one this morning.

Joe leans against the counter with his arms crossed, while I position myself onto the side of the couch, awkwardly propping up my left leg to feign some sense of normality. "How are you?" I ask. "Can you believe it's almost the last day?"

"I'm fine. And I can."

"I heard you're bringing an ice cream truck onto the lot later."

"I am."

"That's really nice."

"Thank you."

"And I think I heard you are donating your A *Little Luck* salary to an organization that helps families of alcoholics?"

"That's correct, yes."

I pretend to take another inventory of the space, even though I clocked all the changes immediately upon entering. "Already cleared out, huh?"

"Why are you doing this?" Joe asks.

For a beat we only stare. There's an instant, squeezing pressure in my throat. It hurts to look at him. His sweet face, always so open, replaced with a steely frown. "I'm here to say sorry."

"For what?"

I swallow down the urge to say, *You know what.*

He remains unmoved, arms tightly folded.

"For how I handled myself the other day. I wasn't expecting you to be so, I don't know. Vulnerable, I guess. I'm not used to that." His insistence on remaining stoic makes this whole thing feel like punching a concrete wall. "I reacted out of fear instead of appreciating the fact that you were willing to tell me the full truth."

For the first time, his posture changes. Only it's to shake his head, as if disapproving.

"Is there something you want to say?" I ask him. He has a right to be upset. It can't be that easy for me. A part of me selfishly hoped it would be, anyways. That these past two days of ignoring each other as soon as Tyler calls cut have been enough to make him want to cave.

"I'm quite good not saying a single word to you," he answers.

It's so final, blunt as the broad side of a boulder, tumbling down to crush me. "I fucked up, Joe. I know I did. I don't know how to make it up to you, but I want to try."

"This is all make-believe. Right? So let's wrap this picture and then we can stop *pretending* and go on with our real lives." For as still as he wants to be, I make note of the way his index finger presses into his bicep, wiggling the skin pulled taut by the tight fold of his arms. That's enough to encourage me forward, putting pride aside for happiness.

"I'm sorry I ever said that," I tell him. "You're right. I was trying to find a way out."

"What do you want me to do, Sloane? Forgive you? Wrap you up in my arms and continue on with our private business? What happens when we finish? Will I be allowed to see you? Will your family be able to know?"

"Of course. Most of them already do, I guess. We weren't fooling anybody."

"This'll sound like a load of shit, but maybe we were. We had a truly fucked beginning. I will never stop feeling terrible for how I treated you when we first met. I think I'd spend the rest of my life trying to prove to you that I'm not that guy anymore. But the truth is, I'm going to screw up anyways. I know I am. Not like I did. Of course not. There's a very good reason I'll never drink again. But I still won't always be able to get every single thing right. And the way you reacted to what I said. Christ, Sloane. You were ready to brawl. All because I put into words what you already knew."

He buckles here, his brow furrowing, mouth squeezed into a tight line. His arms break free from their fold, and he's off to pacing, worrying a well-worn path. "You're only seeing one side of me. For all the time we've spent together, who knows if you'd even like me outside of here. You were the first person to make me truly believe I could be more than what I've been. Then I showed you a side of myself you didn't like, and you went sprinting away from me."

"I guess I've been showing you a side of myself that you might not like too. And to be honest, you're not having a perfect reaction either." It's impossible not to call attention to it now that it's dawned on me. "You were the one who told me you weren't afraid of my power. Maybe that's because I'd never used all of it on you."

This reunion is turning on me, souring in places I thought would be sweet. Boxing gloves instead of roaming hands.

"Here's the proof you wanted," he tells me, gesturing to the air. "That all of this is a fairy tale. We had a nice stretch, but it was nothing more than two costars caught up in the story they were telling." He takes a long pause. "We don't know each other at all."

Joseph Donovan remains the only person capable of outpacing me. In all ways. I lost to him playing my own game, and we both know it.

He opens the trailer door for me. "I don't think we're in need of any rehearsing today," he says. "I'll see you out there."

In stunned silence, I take his cue and exit.

23

Mom has tears in her eyes, looking over Elise and Vera's apartment, all of it packed up into boxes. We saved the last scene of the movie for the last day on set, and there's a tangible bittersweetness to the mood here, knowing that these characters are leaving this place behind right as we are, all of us heading into new unknowns.

Mom squeezes my side and plants one quick kiss on my temple. "Thank you for doing this. I know I didn't make it easy."

"That's an understatement," I quip.

"It's been a long road, Sloane. Lots of therapy. And I still haven't learned how to stop myself from giving out the same treatment I got."

I watch the words come out of her mouth, and I still can't believe she's said it. Ultimately they are only words, and hopefully her actions start to match up, but her admitting this much is still better than any empty inspirational platitude she's ever spouted.

She wipes her tears, then shakes it off. "Whew. I need a smoke." When I give her a disapproving glare, she throws her hands up.

"I know, I know. I'm quitting after this. You try managing your children on a set and tell me it doesn't make you wanna set your lungs on fire. Okay?"

She excuses herself to vape, and it's only me, basking in a rare reflective quiet.

This is it, I think as if narrating it for Elise and for myself. *Time to let go.*

This movie has held a magic to it I never could have anticipated. Bigger than anything I ever imagined as a kid, because for all its magnitude—the millions of dollars spent, dozens and dozens of crew members—it's also felt like a secret. A corner of the world only the lucky few of us got to know about, right here on a studio lot of all places. No matter what happens from here on out, for the first time in my professional career, I am proud of what I've done, without expectations.

Whether we sink or we sail, we made it to the end. In spite of it all.

Someone places a hand on my shoulder. For a moment, I allow myself to hope it's Joe, having the same end-of-production feelings as I am. Contemplative and emotional, ready to surrender. It's going to be so painful otherwise, shooting a happily ever after when we don't even speak between takes.

Guy stands behind me instead, wistful, smirking like he's known all of this would happen in the exact way it has. This is how we started this production. And this is how we will end it.

"The thrill," he tells me. "It never gets old. Not if you've done it right."

I half laugh. "I definitely haven't always done it right."

"That's okay. Neither have I. I got there eventually, and I never looked back."

"All I do is look back," I admit. It's hard not to mimic the way

Guy speaks. Like each sentence is its own Hemingway baby shoes story.

"My dear, don't get me wrong. The rearview has a spectacular shine. Without it, you'd never know which way to go next." He puts a hand on his heart. "The trick is to pack up the necessary things and take them along. Then everything you need is right beside you." From his pocket he digs out a small box and hands it to me. "A wrap gift for you. From your mother and me."

I open it and find an antique-looking gold chain bracelet with a delicate orange chrysanthemum painted onto a porcelain plate at the center.

"Flip it over," Guy says.

The other side of the flower is backed with gold. There's an inscription that reads *It's always been you.* Calvin's line to Elise, right before he says he loves her. What Joe said right before he told me he loved me.

I suck back a breath of surprise, the wind knocked out of me. "Thank you."

"I've said it once, I will say it again," Guy starts. "This part was always meant to be yours. Thank you for playing it as you have."

"It's been my honor."

"The honor is all mine, my dear." Guy bows to me. "You made her real."

Acting out these final scenes is as easy as it is hard. Tapping into the sadness requires no effort. It's right on the surface for all of us. Even Joe's eyes glisten with tears every time we shoot Calvin and Elise carrying their belongings out of their respective homes and meeting in the hallway.

Between takes, there's no longer the silent hostility that's been storm-clouding over us these last few days. It's now a soft drizzle of hurt, slowly filling the space of words, gaps that grow wider with each shot notched off the list.

Mom and Melanie finish with Vera and Ruth sitting side by side on Ruth's couch, listening to the radio together. It's only when Tyler announces a picture wrap for both of them that they simultaneously sob, laughing through their tears. Their work gets a long, deserving ovation from our crew, the two of them hugging and waving, drinking in the fanfare.

It's up to Joe and me to take it home.

The last moment of the whole shoot belongs to Elise and Calvin. The infamous dead chrysanthemums in the trash. At a different point in my career, or even a different point in this production, I'd have asked why there's still a garbage can in this otherwise-empty apartment.

I don't have to now. Not every detail needs to be examined with a magnifying glass.

Joe—*Calvin*—waits in the doorway. Elise gives him one last look. All it takes is a look. She throws out the flowers, holding on to the vase, and they leave, ready to carry their individual boxes to the new home they will share together.

Our final take—an extra one Tyler's asked for to be sure— begins the same as the ones before it. I throw away the flowers, then walk toward Joe, who is supposed to place a hand on my back and guide us out into the world beyond the apartment. A world the viewer won't see.

Joe doesn't reach for my back. Instead he spins me toward him. I have a hand around the vase, and it nearly slips out, saved only by the sudden lack of space between our bodies. Chest to chest, I can feel his heart pushing against me, pounding. He looks down, head tilted, eyes asking for permission, which I grant by lifting up onto my toes to meet him.

Our kiss is every word unspoken. All the pain we have to leave behind. The hurt we cannot fix and the hope we need to face tomorrow. It is slow and bittersweet, lip to lip without a breath.

This kiss is a goodbye.

When he pulls back, once again we're in limbo. Not Elise and Calvin. Not Joe and Sloane. At least not the versions of ourselves we last left. We are the two of us in that perfect place, the magic of set life, where nothing is quite real and everything comes easily.

He reaches for my hand, and we walk out of the apartment with fingers interlaced, going until we're off the set and into the back, the land of black paint and wood slats holding up prop walls.

Tyler calls cut.

Joe looks at me, our fingers still intertwined.

Suddenly it's a blur of cast and crew, everything happening faster than I can process. Tyler announces we're picture wrapped on *Horizons*. Mom kisses me. Guy hugs me. Tyler wipes a tear and nods. Joe's hand is free from mine and I don't remember when it happened. There was a gentle surrender between us, released like a breath, gone as quickly as it came.

This movie is officially done. Until we meet again for the inevitable reshoots we will need for small beats, of course. And the ADR sessions to cover spotty dialogue.

That's for later.

In this moment, everything has come to its end.

24

A Few Weeks Later

I can't believe we're finally doing it. Brunching like the millennials we are." Daya picks up the sugar ramekin and pours some onto her spoon, then dumps it into her coffee. "Thanks for agreeing to come all the way to Burbank for this, by the way."

"It's no problem. We could've gone anywhere. I've got nothing but time these days." I take a tentative sip of my iced coffee. "Love to be an out-of-work actress."

We're seated along the front wall of a jam-packed breakfast spot, tucked into the corner of a generic strip mall, as so many of LA's best food spots are. The restaurant is loud and a little cramped. The clinking of glasses and plates provides a constant percussive symphony. Our view overlooks a parking lot, where Camrys and Benzes and Priuses battle for diagonal spots down one-way lanes.

"Girl, I remember when that was me, but for *real*," Daya says. "Be grateful you will never know the struggle of paying for three dollars' worth of gas in dimes because your parents refuse to support your misguided dream of being a star."

"I am definitely grateful for that." Daya has a knack for keeping me aware of my place in the world. After a lifetime of constant accommodation, it's refreshing. "I'd still like a job, though. Very much."

"I'd tell you to come read for a part in my project, but you-know-who came in for it yesterday."

My stomach drops. Suddenly the idea of eating the matcha pancakes I've already ordered sounds impossible. "Oh." I feign nonchalance, taking my second sip of coffee in the span of ten seconds.

"Oh no. It's like *that*?"

"We're fine. Cordial."

"Legitimately have never described a relationship as cordial in all my trips around the sun. I'm gonna try it out now. I feel like that's me and your mom. Cordial." Daya tests out the weight of the word with several different intonations.

"My mom hated Melanie until she was best friends with her. You'll win her over eventually. She's not as tough of a sell as she seems. I think I finally got her to like me on the day we wrapped. Give yourself another thirty years with my dad and you're set."

"Perfect. Alex will be edging ninety and I'll finally have the begrudging approval of his first ex-wife!"

I laugh. "Sounds about right."

We eat over friendly conversation, Daya filling me in on how this season of *Lucky Strike* has been going so far. "Exhausting," she says. "Never write your own show and then star in it. Except do. It's a blast. But learn to love being awake more than you love the sight of your own pillow."

We talk about her life before she had her break. She tells me about her parents. How they're extremely proud of her now, but she had to bust her ass to earn it from them. She shares that when her show premiered, everyone in her entire family made T-shirts with her face on it. Anytime she visits relatives, at least one of them is wearing it.

We go over some of the projects I've been in to read for lately. Glori and my agents have been scraping together a truly mixed bag of auditions: a recurring spot on a cable drama, a guest arc on a multi-cam sitcom, the lead in a paranormal thriller, even the older sister part in a Regency romance shooting in England next year.

My name carries a strange weight these days. Getting written off *The Seeker* and then replacing Haven in my family's film has everyone wondering if I'm trouble or if trouble has a bad habit of following me. It's palpable in every casting office I enter, the conversation always starting with something like "It's been quite the year for you, hasn't it?"

My hope is that when they see *Horizons*, it will prove something. Show that even though I'm not hiding from my parents' legacy, and I know that nepotism has sailed me to the front of many lines, I'm still in the business I am meant for. I understand who I am.

Daya laughs generously at all my carefully considered jokes, especially the one about her being my favorite soon-to-be stepmother of all time. Still, she checks her phone several times throughout, a habit that seems born from nerves I don't think I'm giving her. For how warm she is, there's a slight edge to her demeanor. A well-disguised panic that only appears when she lights up her lock screen.

"Everything all right?" It takes courage for me to ask, closer to the end of our meal.

She's been so understanding, keeping the conversation away from Joe even though her curiosity had her gripping the edge of the table when I told her we were cordial. I don't want to push too far and upset her.

She sighs, biting back a sentence.

"If it's about Joe, you can tell me. I promise I won't be weird," I assure her.

"It's not him. It's Alex."

"Oh. Are you breaking up—" I pause. "With my dad?"

"No. It's—" She shakes her head, then makes a clear decision. "He has a big doctor's appointment today. They thought they noticed something abnormal with his heart on one of his follow-up exams, so he had to come out to a specialist in Burbank to get it checked out. I wasn't supposed to tell any of you."

"Fuck." Now I'm as panicked as she is. "What do they think it is?"

"I don't know. I'm so bad at remembering all the names and stuff. He told me he'd text me when he was done, and he hasn't yet, so I'm getting worried."

"Are we close to where he is?"

"Very close."

I take out my purse and fish out three twenties. "What are we waiting for? Let's go."

My dad loves attention. Always has. His mother, my gammy, who died when I was thirteen, always called him her golden boy, because he shone like a star in every room he entered, demanding to be noticed. Even in this doctor's office, he can't help but smile through his supposed disappointment that he's been exposed.

"I'm sorry, babe. I caved," Daya explains, kissing him on the cheek.

Dad pretends to cower, then opens his arms to me for a hug. "My Sloanius. Always squeezing the truth out of people."

"Excuse me. Why didn't you tell us?" I'm as mad as I am grateful to see that hint of a smirk on him, a little wink to this audience of two that he's not the least bit upset by Daya's reveal.

It's hard not to love Alexander Ford. I read that once on the cover of a magazine from the nineties, captioning a tight shot of Dad's laughing face, eyes crinkled up and hands on his cheeks. It's true. It's hard to do anything but love this man.

"You know me. I didn't want to give everyone a scare," he says.

"Too late now. I already told everyone," I inform him.

"No you didn't," Daya says, mortified. She's learned quite a bit about us, yet she hasn't figured out the most basic truth of our family. There are no secrets, even when we want them.

Someone knocks on our door. It's not the doctor coming in with results like we expect. It's the front desk receptionist. "Excuse me. There's a woman here with short black hair. She says she's your daughter." She looks at me. "Your *other* daughter."

First it's Tyler, who wasn't lying when she said she was close by. Then Melanie and Sarai. Then Powell. And eventually Mom and Guy roll up, Mom taking a clean five minutes to decompress from all the traffic they battled to get here.

The staff kicks all of us, except for Daya, out of Dad's room and into the waiting area. It's not every day an entire family rolls up for a scheduled appointment. We Porter-Davidson-Cicero-Fords spread ourselves out around the waiting room, killing time by telling stories and making each other laugh.

Tyler and I team up against Powell, ripping into him for leaving an earnest comment on Celine Dion's YouTube page of all places.

"I don't understand how you even found that!" he protests, cheeks red as raspberries.

Sarai springs up. "It was me," she admits. "Your iPad was unlocked when I was over last week. I texted them."

"You two finally corrupted her." Powell sneers at me. Tyler and I are in stitches. "I hate all of you. Including you, sweet precious baby Sarai."

Sarai beams. An official member of the Pick On Powell Club.

Daya comes out to give an update, which isn't much at all. They're being a little tight-lipped yet optimistic, she says, and they want Dad to come back for another appointment soon. Everyone here takes in this news with a hint of solemnity, processing for the second time this year that something really could happen to the golden boy of our family. The glue that's pieced these strange fragmented groups together.

My whole life has been about movies. But real life doesn't always end in periods or exclamation points. Real life throws out questions with no intention of ever answering them. My perfectly healthy, relatively young father got dealt an ellipsis with the heart attack, and there are a million ways that sentence gets finished. No matter where we end up, we will face it as a family. A big, strange, imperfect family, showing up when needed.

Mom finds me as we're all leaving for the day. She links us up arm in arm to walk me to my car. "Any good parts coming your way since we wrapped?"

"I'm kind of into that period piece I went in for last week," I tell her. "Shoots in England at the start of next year."

"That would be fun. I love Europe in the winter." She turns me toward her. "Have you talked to him?"

My defense mechanism rears up, chest puffing out, chin held high. "Who?"

Mom reacts with the fearsome look I became well acquainted with on set, the face of a woman so allergic to bullshit she can make it disappear through sheer willpower alone.

"No," I admit. "I haven't."

"If that's because of me, then why on earth have you chosen now of all times to listen to your mother?" She sweeps my hair—still blond, but darker now—out of my eyes.

"It wasn't you. Joe and I were caught up in the whole 'set-life costar make-believe' thing," I rattle off. "It wasn't real."

"Oh for fuck's sake, Sloane. Look at who your parents are! Of course it's real!"

I want to react, but there's nothing to say.

"You should know this," she tells me. "The first thing Joe ever did when he came in to read for the movie was apologize to all of us for how he treated you in Ireland. He did it so effortlessly, I really thought it must've been less of a deal than you'd made it, because in all my life, I've never seen a man be *that* humbled that easily. He spoke very highly of you that day. Even told us all what he really remembered from that shoot was the music you used to play in your trailer. He said listening to it always made him think of you. American rock, he called it. I wanted to tell him it was white dad rock and your father didn't let me play enough Joni Mitchell for you as a child, but I let it be."

It's so much to take in at once. My mind scrambles to reassemble my relationship with Joe, layering in what my mom's just told me with everything that happened during our shoot. All those visits to his trailer with classics playing. That night in his car, when he didn't know Steely Dan.

He was doing all of that for me.

Mom softens. "Honey, that man is head over heels for you. And if we all have to listen to your sniveling ex sing about you smoking up a mirror every time we turn on the radio, then at least do us all the favor of going after someone who really cares for you this time around."

She kisses me on the forehead, leaving me to unravel.

25

f you don't stop right now, I'm going to sock you," Tyler tells me, eyes on the road.

"I'm sorry," I say again, the last refrain in my chorus of apologies.

She makes a fist.

"All right, all right. It's just, maybe we should forget about this? Turn around. Pick up a pizza. Watch our old movies. You know?"

"No."

"We could read scripts people have sent you," I pitch. "I have a good eye. I think you'd do well with a coming-of-age thing. White girl submerged in a pool, caught up in her feelings. I can picture it already."

"Bub. You're seeing Joe tonight. Get over it."

She makes a hard right that sends my hand straight for the panic handle on the passenger door. She has always been a terrible driver. Time has only made it more obvious. "I should've called a Lyft," I mutter, praying for my life as we merge onto the 101.

"If you did that, you would've backed out completely. I know you."

"He thinks he's meeting Mom," I protest. "Maybe you should come with. He's going to be disappointed it's me instead."

"Yeah. And bringing your lesbian sister along on your secret surprise date won't be the biggest letdown of all time." She cuts one quick look my way. "You're going."

"Fine. But you need to stay in the parking lot for like five minutes, at least."

"Dude, you sound like you're in the seventh grade. I'm not paying twenty dollars to park downtown for five minutes."

"Fuck you. Seventh grade was a hard year. You'll understand when you direct an indie masterpiece that encapsulates it completely."

"I hate you."

"I hate you too."

Twenty-seven minutes and four and a half fights later, Tyler throws on her hazards and pulls over to drop me curbside. She slams her hands on the steering wheel and lets out a scream, so unexpected it makes me scream too.

"What the hell!" I say when she starts to laugh.

"You forgot you were nervous, didn't you?"

My scowl serves as confirmation.

"Listen, if it's really and truly a disaster, sneak into the bathroom and text me. I'll come get you. And if it's nothing at all, I'll be waiting at your house when you get home. We can order a pizza and watch our version of *Newsies*. It's been too long since I've seen Powell do any accent work." She smiles. "But I'm expecting a text from you that tells me I need to get the hell out and sleep at my own place tonight."

The idea of that seems so far out of reach I don't even dare entertain it, instead letting out my own quick scream, which does the job and shocks Tyler.

"Get out of my car and go get that handsome dummy, like they do in the movies," she says, lightly shoving me.

So I open the door and step outside. Lean down and give her one last worried glance, hoping the blatant terror on my face convinces her to take me home this very instant.

She gives me a thumbs-up instead.

It's happening. There is no going back.

"I love you," I say.

"I love you too," Tyler answers, pressing a hand to her heart. Then she peels off like an eager extra in a *Fast and Furious* racing scene, cackling the whole way, a chorus of disgruntled honks greeting her recklessness.

The restaurant sits all the way up on the rooftop of this high-rise, requiring two separate elevator rides to access it. The first one, I stare at my outfit, green scoop-neck tank tucked into high-waisted blue jeans, a pair of faux leather brown booties boosting me up an extra four inches. It's casual without being too casual. It says, *Hey, this is an easy, nonthreatening encounter. Whatever happens, I'm relaxed. I know the green may be reminiscent of a certain dress I once wore. That was accidental. Completely a coincidence.*

By the second elevator ride, I'm rubbing my wrap-gift bracelet so much it's making my fingers hot. This is the wrong outfit. This is the wrong move. I shouldn't have agreed to Mom's bait-and-switch plan. I should've forced Tyler to come. I should've done all of this differently.

Then the doors open, and I'm giving my credit card to the host to let her know I'll be paying for this meal, and she's leading me to Joe's table, and my nerves reach such a peak all I can think is Wow, *who invented string lights like these? What a good idea. So simple. Tiny lights on a string! Soft and effective!*

Then I spot him. A few tables ahead, his back to us. He's wearing a gray Henley, and his hair is a bit longer but back to its naturally dark blond, a color that really could be categorized as brown, except for in high sunlight, when the golden threads shine through.

Knowing he's really here makes it easier somehow. He's not a face on the *Swiped* billboard I drive by every morning to pick up coffee. Or a voice I recall in the dark of my bedroom. My nerves flutter up and dissipate, replaced with something different: a desperate wanting, deep in the core of me, pushing me forward.

He's scrolling through his phone when we walk up, the host announcing my presence with a loud "Here you go."

"Surprise," I whisper to Joe.

A bolt of energy shoots through his arm, making him fumble his phone.

I am so on autopilot I ignore it, not even waiting for the host to get past me before I say, "I know you'd once asked for a lunch. I'm hoping this will do."

I've mentally rehearsed and rewritten this line at least a hundred times. It needed to be short enough to get out without getting tripped up, yet meaningful enough for him to know my intentions. Which are to be absolutely anything more than we've been these last few weeks.

If he doesn't want me to sit, he doesn't say it, so I slip into the spot across from him, quick to put my hands into my purse and rummage around for nothing at all.

"I'm sorry," I blurt. Tyler told me not to start with that. *I told me not to start with that.* Seven seconds in and it's flying out of my mouth. "I shouldn't have come."

"No," Joe forces out. "It's okay." When I look up from the nothing I'm searching for in my purse, he doesn't meet my eye.

"I have to tell you right now that my mom doesn't have a potential project for you. Neither of us were sure you'd show up if she didn't give you a good reason. So we lied. I'm really sorry," I say again, knowing this time it's necessary.

"I would have come if you asked," he tells me.

My entire stomach somersaults. This conversation is capable of going in too many directions, a lot of which could end badly for me, so I opt for a soft toss next, commenting on the beauty of the night. Sixty-eight degrees, a navy sky with the moon a glowing semicircle, big and glossy and bright. There's a great, sweeping view of Los Angeles from where we are, countless building lights shiny as the stars this piece of sky doesn't show.

"Not quite Ireland, but it can still take your breath away." We both look out over my hometown.

"A lot of things here can do that," he responds.

Our server comes to take our drink order. Joe doesn't drink, I remember with a start, pushing away my hope to drown this burgeoning mistake in a river of tequila. He won't so much as glance at me. This is a disaster. But if he has to endure the surprise of my presence and the potential awkwardness of this dinner completely sober, so do I.

We both ask for water. With the server still at our table, Joe says to me, "You can get a drink."

"I don't want to."

"It's quite fine. You wouldn't be the first."

"I don't want to," I say again, more insistent.

The server slips off and Joe starts to tap a familiar rhythm into the table: a slow arpeggio on repeat. I'm about to fill the anxious quiet with another comment on the weather when he surprises me and asks, "Have you been well?"

I take a quick beat to admire him. The gentle flutter of his lashes. The way his every breath comes out in a definitive exhale, like each is a very deliberate choice. To think that I might only get to see his face up close in movies and on billboards, never again getting the privilege of running my finger across his jawline or laying my head on that shoulder? It's too much to comprehend.

"I've been okay," I say. "I miss having work to do." *And I miss you*, I think but do not speak, hoping by the end of all this that it's at least implied. "Have you . . . been well?" The phrasing doesn't roll off my tongue like it does his.

"Sure," he says, leaving out any follow-up details.

This small talk is a prison. In a desperate bid to escape it—forgoing all other easy topics like work or food or who came up with string lights—I pivot. "My mom told me something the other day. About when you auditioned for *Horizons*."

"Did she?"

"Something about the music I would listen to in my trailer." I can't bring myself to say all she shared. It's too vulnerable for this moment, our shields up as high as this building.

Joe's posture shifts. He leans his elbows on the table, closing a bit of the distance between us. "Do you remember when I told you Calvin had a small memory he couldn't share with Elise yet?" He asks as he stares at the lights lining the concrete half wall beside me.

"Of course," I overlap, far too eager. With an intentional breath and a small prayer for grace, I don't hold back. "I remember everything."

"I wasn't talking about them," he admits.

Hearing what I suspected still knocks the wind out of me. *He was talking about us.* I wish I hadn't been so scared then. I could have properly appreciated what that meant.

"The clearest memory I have of filming *A Little Luck* is the sound of your voice coming in through my window, singing along to those old American rock tunes," he tells me. "That's why I started playing them on set. I was hoping it would make you . . . I don't know. Make you not hate me. It's absolutely shit, I realize now. And it's exactly why I was such a fumbling, bumbling mess when we first started shooting. Because you showed me all the ways I'd been such a hack, and I didn't know how to fix any of it."

"Joe," I interrupt, all rules out the window, no sense of pacing. "I want to know you. Everything there is to know. Even if I don't like it. I apologize if that's too forward, but I can't sit through this whole meal without being clear. Especially when you say things like that."

He places a hand atop mine to stop me from wildly gesturing. And finally, he looks at me. All our history in this look. The old hurt that made me hate him. My cold shoulder and his unending patience, peeling back my layers day by day, proving to me he'd changed. Every gentle touch we found between bigger moments of passion. Even the gaps we haven't filled. All the stories I don't yet know, and the ones told in scraps and shadows, waiting to be fully assembled. Everything's here, laid bare between us.

"For such a *strong woman*, you sure do have a hard time picking up what I'm saying to you." He wears a fond smile, the kind that twinkles in his eyes, warm and sincere. We've come so far since that moment. One of our first tentative jokes as we stepped out of his trailer into the morning sun, inching toward forging a friendship. "I don't know many other ways to explain that I'm not going anywhere," he tells me.

The tension in my shoulders releases like cut cords. "Saying 'I'm not going anywhere' does a pretty good job of getting the point across."

"I was hoping it would."

The server drops our waters beside our linked hands. Their attention lingers on the gesture for an extra beat. All sense of my surroundings left me the second those elevator doors opened, and it's only now I realize how big a deal it is for Joe to have grabbed my hand here, out in public on a Saturday night. Surely there are people we know at this restaurant. There always are at places like this.

Joe's thumb brushes back and forth across my knuckles. He requests more time before ordering. We peruse the menu like this, hands held as we read, real conversation on pause. My mind races, desperate to make sense of all that's happening.

"Chicken looks good," Joe comments, like he's said it a dozen times. Like we've gotten the chicken at other places and found it only passable, and this one might exceed our baseline expectations. "What about for you?"

"I usually get the gnocchi here," I tell him.

He scans the menu for it and reads over the ingredients with earnest investment. "Good to know."

It's such a small thing, but I forgot how nice it can be to share something and be greeted with gentle kindness, every tiny new piece of information a welcome gift.

After we order, I'm the one to let go, knowing we have a good amount of time before the food comes and needing to use every minute to be sure that what I think is happening is really, fully happening. Trust can only stretch so far without honesty to bolster it up. "I have to ask. Why are you so okay with this? After I came to your trailer, you made it clear you never wanted to see me again. And now you're holding my hand."

"Can I ask you the same thing?"

"You have to answer first. I'm the one with a failed apology under my belt."

"Fair." He takes a moment to consider me. "Is it too simple to say that the second you walked up, I missed you more than I was ever mad at you?"

"No." I reconsider. "Maybe?"

He laughs. "All right. Give me a second. I didn't know I'd see you tonight, but I've thought a lot about what I'd say to you if I got the chance. Now I have it and I can't remember any of it." He looks away from me, intently staring at a plant on the other side of the rooftop, drifting into soft focus. It's fascinating to watch someone think this hard, so completely in their own head that they are lost to their surroundings.

When he's back, he places his attention on me, fully engaged again. "Here we go. Off-the-cuff because I still can't think right. You look glorious, by the way."

My cheeks warm. "Thank you. So do you."

"Enough of that before I get distracted again." He rolls out his neck. "Telling you that we don't know each other at all was the biggest load of shit I've ever spoken out loud in my life," he starts. "The fact that you'd come here to win me back after that means you actually know me even better than I thought. Because somehow you knew the one thing I was never sure of was if you might be embarrassed to be seen with me, or you didn't like all the ways I'd maybe hold you back by not drinking, or having a tough time with big crowds. My stage fright. You know, all the really fun things about me." He tries to smile through the vulnerability, but I see through it.

I see him.

"I hope that doesn't sound small to you," he continues. "I used to be the life of the party. Now I have a hard time staying out past ten. Sometimes I feel like Mam died and I forgot how to be anything other than a sad bastard with a decent face and a free ticket to Hollywood from my father. Even right now, saying this makes me wanna get up and prove I still know how to jig. To show you I can be fun. I didn't want to keep you from living life the way that makes you happy."

"Joe." It's my turn to reach across the table to hold him, gripping his forearm. "If I thought being around you would hold me back, I never would've shown up to your trailer beyond that first rehearsal. You're not the only one here at this table with a famous family and a lot of baggage. There's nothing about the way you are that I'm not willing to understand. And I promise you, I do not need a life of parties. I did all of that in my early twenties and I hated every minute of it. All of the fun I've had in the last year has been with you."

I pause. Take in his face. It's so amazing we are here together, outside of our work, just two people enjoying a meal on a rooftop in Los Angeles.

It's real life.

And it's wonderful.

"You show up for me in a way only my family ever has before," I continue. "You pay attention. And you keep me steady. I'd like the chance to do the same for you. You are my first best friend, after all."

We both smile at that. Then his expression shifts, a flash of sorrow coming through. "I'm really sorry about how I acted when you came to my trailer. More proof that you're a better person than me."

"That's not true. It's not a contest between us and it never will be. Okay?"

"You're right. It's not."

"Let's get to know each other. The *real* stuff," I say, a hint of self-mocking peeking through. Set life isn't all of life, but it's not fake either.

What Joe and I have?

It's very, very real.

So Joe runs me through his audition for Daya. How satisfying it was to get the entire team laughing. "It's easy to win over a room for a drama," he explains. "Be a man who cries and you're at least getting a callback. Comedy is tough. Every bastard in this town thinks they're funny. I have no idea if I actually was, or they were deeply generous, but I'll take it. It's refreshing to leave a room feeling like I did something that scared me and I survived."

"I read for that Romana De Lasso Regency romance project last week," I tell him. "And I felt that too. I've spent my whole career avoiding historical stuff. I don't even understand why, other than the thought of doing it terrifies me. In a good way. I want to try it all."

"Does that mean one day I'll get a *Seeker* spinoff starring Tess as a hard-hearted ghost who comes back seeking vengeance against Colfax?"

"Can you please explain why you ever started watching that show? All this time and I truly don't understand. I know you have better taste than this."

"It was for you," he says simply. Our easy joking rhythm slows, halted by his candor. "This will sound a lot more intense than I mean it to, but I spent a lot of the last five years thinking about you. In an admiring way. Your talent really amazes me. A big part of why I took *Horizons* was because I thought you were going to be in it with me."

"Wow." I'm truly touched by his admission. "Well, good. May you spend the next five years doing the same," I joke.

"What happens after that?" he asks.

"We renegotiate the contract, of course. Ten more years thinking about me, and a promise for at least three more movies in the *Swiped* universe from you. My terms are firm."

"Oh, I'll sign on for that right now. So long as Tess gets the closure she deserves. Even if that particular show airs only in my living room."

"That can be arranged."

"I may need to get that in writing," he says with a grin.

Our evening fades into a haze of good food and good conversation, the two of us rarely breaking eye contact. By the time we've finished our meal, it's all I can do not to switch sides and sit beside him, leg across his lap. I refrain, never one for big public displays of affection. It's too easily weaponized in our business.

The server returns with the bill paid for by me, my card tucked into the inside panel and receipt waiting for my signature.

Joe can't hide his shock. "When did you do that?"

"This isn't amateur hour. I gave them my card when I walked in," I say as I sign.

"Christ. You are something to behold." He gets up and walks to my side. "The next one is on me."

"Fair." My heart flutters at the ease with which he's assured me there will be a next one.

He sticks out an elbow for me to hold. The exact level of public contact I can handle. Enough to say this person is mine without revealing every way we move together.

Like I figured, Joe and I pass by three people I know cordially. I give all of them knowing nods. Yes. *This is exactly what you think it is.*

When the elevator opens, Joe and I are the only two entering. The doors close on us, and Joe presses me up against the side, one arm around my waist and the other behind my head.

"Hello there," he whispers as I savor his familiar weight against me.

"Hello."

And just like that, he's kissing me, soft and slow and wanting, fighting against time, the floors ticking down faster than they should. They open, and we break apart, stepping out to greet the bouncer as we walk to the next elevator arm in arm, as composed as two members of a bridal party gliding down the aisle.

Elevator number two closes on us, and I seize the opportunity to pin Joe, leg up around the side of him. "Hello again. Long time no see."

This ride is longer. But not nearly long enough. Floating us up as we soar down, there's more urgency now, though Joe's hands only have time to roam under my shirt while mine enjoy the feel of his back, all the divots and grooves I've learned but haven't yet memorized. Once the doors open, we walk out again, laughing, not arm in arm but hand in hand.

"Where are we going?" he asks me.

"Home," I say, squeezing tight.

Joe's orange Camaro is parked in my driveway, and he's kissing my ear as my hands fumble to turn my lock.

Tyler, I remember with a start. I didn't tell her we were coming.

Every inside light in my house is off, save for the small side lamp on a console table in my entryway. It illuminates a sticky note with a message sprawled across it in imposing capitals.

I TOLD YOU SO. SEE YOU TOMORROW.

—T

Joe and I slow dance our way through my living room and down the hallway, shedding layers of clothes between careful dips and gentle twirls. I open the door to my bedroom, then turn to face him, with my back pressed into the knob.

"One more thing," I say.

"Yes?"

"We're not going to get it all right. All I ever ask is that you don't give up on me. Or leave without saying why."

"Done. And I ask the same of you."

"Done."

He reaches for my hand.

"Wait, wait," I say, resisting his pull. "Another thing."

Joe's smile looks greedy. Bare feet on the hardwood. Shirt in a pool somewhere near my banana leaf chair. Backlit by the moon flooding my bedroom. "Yes?"

We have spoken a lot of beautiful dialogue to each other. Said pretty lines full of deep meaning. Summed up dynamics in succinct sayings designed to end-tag trailers. There is even a stunning phrase etched into gold, pressing against my wrist at this very moment. *It's always been you.*

I wish I could say that right now and have it be the truth. It's a line that means the world to me, and I love the way it sounds in my head whenever I think of Joe saying it. But the reality is, I didn't see this coming. No matter what my family believed. The story I imagined for myself never featured Joseph Donovan and me as the romantic leads.

But it's happening, and it's real, and it's so very worth everything it took to get us here.

"It will always be you, Joe," I tell him, watching his expression light up at a truth that suits us better, because it doesn't live in the rearview. It focuses on the future.

And then I pull my bedroom door shut behind the two of us. The latching mechanism slowly clicks into place, closing us off into a private world that is only ours to know.

Acknowledgments

Thank you first to my amazing agent, Taylor Haggerty, who wholeheartedly encouraged me to finish this book after I surprise-dropped part of it into her inbox. You are the best, T. I am so grateful to be on this ride with you. Huge virtual hugs to you and to the entire team at Root Literary for everything you all do to help bring books into the world!

To my editor, Kerry Donovan, you completely understood what I was trying to do with this story and then smartly pointed me in the direction of Even Better. I really value your thoughtfulness and your keen eye, and I am so grateful to work with you and all of the awesome people at Berkley. Mary Geren, Tara O'Connor, Jessica Mangicaro, Angelina Krahn, Vi-An Nyugen: You've all treated this book with such love and care. Words fail to describe how lucky I feel.

Mom, you always read my every word and then lift me up into the clouds with your support. You're a rare gem and I love you. Ryan Salonen, you are the most generous and enthusiastic early reader of all time. Every writer (and person) deserves a friend like you. Hollis Andrews, thank you for—as we would say—getting eyes on this for me. You gave me industry insight, thoughtful critiques, and unabashed hype. This one is for the house in Maine. Rose Morrissey, my sister closest in age to me and my queen of bowling, we have spent our whole lives bugging each other while entertaining each other, and everything I write pays tribute to that in one way or another. BS4L! Aminah Mae Safi, Emily Wibberley, and Austin Siegemund-Broka, I am beside myself that I get to call you talented, amazing people my pals! It is the crystalest of blessings, as beautiful as a sunset over the mature Joshua trees of Spararrow. To my LA Electrics, it remains a supreme honor to continue along this publishing journey with you all.

Being the youngest of five and having authored this book about big families, I'd be remiss if I didn't thank every member of my own wonderful immediate family. Love you always Mom (again); Dad; my brother, John; my sisters Liz, Raina, and Rose (again); and all my nieces and nephews: Deklin, Brielle, Caleb, Brannon, Lily, Sophie, and Emma.

To the actors I know and love who talked to me about craft, craft services, and everything in between, thank you for being so generous with your time and experiences. All mistakes and inaccuracies are my own or in service of the story. Sometimes you have to sprinkle a little movie magic onto things to make them shine.

My gymnasts, I cannot say it enough: You teach me more than I could ever teach you. I am so proud of you all for being brave, thoughtful, curious, and generous. May we continue to grow alongside one another. And to Arden, my former coworker and forever friend, chassé leaps and levers until the end of time.

Finally, to the readers who find their way to my corner of the fictional universe, I hope this story makes your heart as happy as it made mine. Thank you so much for being here.

Continue reading for a special preview
of Bridget Morrissey's

A Thousand Miles

· · · · · ·

Coming from Jove in Summer 2022!

DEE

It's very hard to break up with someone you were never really dating. Which is why a man named Garrett, who I met three weeks ago on an app, is currently crying in my bathroom.

He doesn't know I saw the tears. It would probably embarrass him if I mentioned it, so I am sitting on my couch reading listener emails while I wait for him to finish up, wondering if I should put on a movie or put him out of his misery and suggest he leave.

My extremely nonchalant request that I "take a little more time for myself" was met with the classic "that makes sense" from him—a veteran move that made me entirely too comfortable with the whole process. I skipped right past the usual assurances: what a fun three weeks we've had; how great it's been to get to know someone new after a recent rough patch. We've been having sex in my apartment and sometimes ordering takeout. I've never even tagged him in an Instagram story. I truly thought he understood what was going on with us.

We have a similar dry humor. It's how we connected in the first place. But tonight, for the first time ever, we went out to dinner together. He was so rude to the server in the name of being snarky that I thought I might walk myself straight to Lake Michigan and take up boat living. In the middle of a rainstorm, no less.

My choice to continue our breakup conversation by saying, "We clearly aren't the kind of people who should ever go out in public," did not land as I'd hoped. He let out a hollow, wounded kind of laugh that made me immediately backpedal, even though what I'd said was true. In front of an audience of fellow restaurant patrons, our connection had dissolved like cotton candy in water. All that sweetness between us vanished into nothingness. But I dared to call attention to it, and next thing I know he's telling me he has to go to the bathroom, and tears are rimming his eyes.

He doesn't even have my number saved! Just three days ago, I texted him a meme while he was taking a shower, and from my nightstand I saw my full ten-digit phone number flash up on his screen.

How could he not feel the straining awkwardness throughout our meal tonight? Is it really possible that my empty "yeahs" and colorless "wows" came off as anything other than detached?

It's all so absurd it makes me cackle. By the time he's back in my living room—tears dried and brow furrowed—I am laughing louder than the thunder that booms outside.

"What did I miss?" he asks.

Everything, Garrett. You missed everything.

"What's my last name?" I prompt.

"Um . . ."

"Do you know my job?"

"You record a podcast or something."

"How many siblings do I have?"

"I don't know."

"Your name is Garrett Matthew Robertson. You work in finance, in an office near the Hancock building. Your little sister

Hannah just graduated college. Communications degree from DePaul. Send my congrats, by the way."

"Okay, so you're a stalker. Good for you."

There it is. The darkness that always comes out at the first sign of real trouble. A bruise that blooms from whisper-soft pressure. It's amazing how quickly it happens. How little effort it requires on my part.

"I'm a *stalker?*" I ask.

Predictably, he has no follow-up.

"We've been hooking up for weeks and I follow you online," I continue. "Your full name is in your bio. You post a skyline shot almost every day. I watched part of your sister's commencement ceremony when I accidentally clicked into your livestream of the graduation."

Garrett glances forlornly at my door. He pushes back the top part of his hair—a truly aspirational sandy blond, if I'm honest—then lets it fall again down his forehead. "Look, this clearly isn't working." He says it with such finality, you'd think it was his idea. If it gets him out of my apartment, he can keep thinking that for the rest of his life.

Still, it's hard to resist a comeback. "Good observation." I give him a thumbs-up.

"Dude, why are you so fucking mean? Like what the fuck?" Suddenly, he gets teary again.

Now I recognize it for what it is: a manipulation tactic. No one gets the upper hand over a handsome man who is crying.

"I'm *mean?*" I ask, incredulous. "For asking if you know my name?"

"I don't have time for this shit."

He picks up his overnight bag and huffs to my door. He's still wearing his shoes, because no matter how often I ask, he never takes them off right when he enters. It's such an irritating little detail that I almost throw a pillow at him, but he exits too quickly for me to react, slamming my front door shut with an aggressive theatricality that my nosy neighbors will certainly register. Add it to their long list of grievances with me.

It devastates me to realize my heart is racing. That Garrett Matthew Robertson, the finance bro, has gotten any kind of reaction out of me at all. In an effort to squeeze out every last ounce of residual adrenaline, I slip off my bra and lean back into my couch, letting the green velvet cushions hug the sides of my face. Not the most orthodox of calming methods, but it gets the job done.

I can't believe I put on nice clothes for this. What a waste of a powder-blue halter jumpsuit and teardrop earrings. I could feel myself overdoing it when I was getting ready—it's been months since I'd bothered to curl my hair into long copper waves—but in spite of every piece of evidence to the contrary, there was a part of me that wanted to believe that Garrett and I had the potential to be something more than hookup buddies.

No choice but to incinerate that part of me to dust!

Three minutes later, he's knocking. He may not know my last name, but it's nice to see he remembers that my apartment door automatically locks and he can't just barge back in and yell, or whatever it is he thinks he needs to do to prove this was all a part of *his* plan, not mine.

"What do you want?" I call out.

He doesn't answer.

It infuriates me to imagine him waiting for me, ready to unleash a list of grievances he made up on his walk toward the train station.

I gave him a chance to go quietly, and he's not taking it.

Neighbors be damned. I want a fight.

With as much gusto as possible, I swing my front door open and bark out one loud, aggressive, "What?"

But it is not Garrett Matthew Robertson, the finance bro, waiting on the other side.

It is the last person in the *world* I ever thought I'd see again.

Ben Porter stands in front of me.

It takes me a second to orient myself. Surely this is an alternate reality intersecting with my current one, and Garrett accidentally got swapped for Ben, and soon the ceiling will become the floor, and I will learn that we all speak colors and smell numbers.

He has one battered duffel bag slung across his taut midsection and three dark beauty marks dotting his left cheek. Those moles are my very own Orion's belt, because that's the only constellation I ever bothered to learn, on the only face I've ever cared to memorize.

His eyes are brown and still bashful. His hair is just long enough to curl at the ends now, soft brown waves ringleted by the rain, contrasting the new sharpness in his cheeks. A stipple of scruff further accentuates the angles. No more worn-out Chucks and rumpled band shirt. No more baby face. He looks steady. And well aware of how good a drenched navy blue tee clings to his skin.

"A promise is a promise," he whispers, soaking wet and breathless, dripping puddles onto the carpeted hallway of my apartment complex.

My hands lose feeling. My mind insists on running a highlight reel of memories for me, making sure I haven't forgotten that this is a person I've slept with, and dreamt of, and written intensely embarrassing Notes-app poetry about—that I've already asked my co-host, Javi, to read on our podcast in the event of my untimely demise. Just so Ben would really feel my absence.

Now I feel his presence, and my first instinct is to close the door, lock myself in my bathroom, and stare at myself in the mirror until the pores on my nose upset me for a week straight. But for as impulsive as I can be, I am great at silencing my first instinct and waiting for a better one to emerge.

It turns out, in the event of my high school best friend arriving unannounced in the middle of a thunderstorm—after an entire decade of complete silence between us—my second instinct is to intimidate. I fold my arms across my chest, mostly because I am furious at myself for daring to answer the door while not wearing a bra. Lucky for me, the gesture lends to the steely mood I'm hoping to strike.

"What does that mean? What are you doing here?" My foot taps against the floor, as if my time could be better spent looking anywhere but at Ben Porter's face.

If he's expected a kinder greeting from me, he doesn't show it. Instead he smiles. A heartbreaking, earth-shifting, choir-of-angels-singing kind of smile.

"Hi, Dee." He pauses. "It's good to see you, too."

At once I'm flooded with the same bone-deep nostalgic longing that makes me open YouTube at three in the morning and watch all the videos we posted together back in the day. I've made all of them private so my listeners don't stumble across them and uncover the one thing I refuse to directly discuss on my show. The first time Ben was ever mentioned while recording, I made Javi bleep out his name in post. Now Ben is known on the podcast as Name Redacted, an infamous, mysterious side character in my otherwise very open-book life.

One of our YouTube videos is just ten minutes of us walking around our hometown. We spend the first half coming up with an elaborate undercover identity for our science teacher, Mr. Davidson, all while navigating the aftermath of the previous night's snowfall. The video takes a turn when Ben steps into a snow pile that's not sturdily packed, and he ends up chest-deep. Instantly, the two of us are nearly heaving we're laughing so hard. I can't grab onto him tight enough to pull him out because my arms are getting a tickle sensation. It's so cold his cheeks are flushed berry red. I set the camera down on another snow pile, and for the rest of the video, all you can see is his face and my back. And the way he's looking at me. It's like I created the constellations with my own bare hands.

Here's that very same Ben Porter. And the way he's looking at me right now—it's really not that different from the old clip of us. Even though everything is different. Down to the shade of red in my hair and the city we're in and surely every single thing about our lives.

"Can I come in?" he asks, because I have been standing here waiting for the sky to fall through the roof. "I can explain everything once I'm inside."

"I don't know if I want you to," I accidentally admit.

Ben backs up until he's against the wall across from my door, a trail of rainwater marking his path. He slides down until he's sitting, all the while never breaking eye contact. "I understand. This is a lot."

"Yeah," I say weakly. Leave it to Ben to understate a thing.

"I'll wait here. And if you still feel the same way after an hour, I'll leave."

All those well-practiced talking points I've assured myself I'd launch into immediately if I ever saw him again? I can't remember a single one. In this moment, I truly cannot recall why we haven't spoken or why it is that I'm not supposed to be nice to him. It's a marvel I even know my own name.

Second instincts be damned.

I slam my door shut.

Bridget Morrissey lives in Los Angeles, California, but hails from Oak Forest, Illinois. When she's not writing, she can be found coaching gymnastics or headlining concerts in her living room. This is her adult debut.

Ready to find
your next great read?

Let us help.

Visit prh.com/nextread